THE PHILISTINE

The following is a work of fiction. Many of the locations are real, although not necessarily as portrayed, but all characters and events are fictional and any resemblance to actual events or people, living or dead, is purely coincidental.

Prepared for the press by Elise Moser
Cover design by Debbie Geltner
Cover art by Khaled Hafez, "Flight of the Half Gods"
Author photo: Nicole Périat
Book design by WildElement.ca

Printed and bound in Canada.

Library and Archives Canada Cataloguing in Publication
Marshy, Leila, author
        The Philistine / Leila Marshy.

Issued in print and electronic formats.
ISBN 978-1-988130-70-5 (softcover).--ISBN 978-1-988130-71-2 (HTML).--
ISBN 978-1-988130-72-9 (Kindle).--ISBN 978-1-988130-73-6 (PDF)

        I. Title.
PS8626.A76755P55 2018   C813'.6   C2017-906567-X
                                                      C2017-906568-8

The publisher gratefully acknowledges the support of the Government of Canada through the Canada Council for the Arts, the Canada Book Fund, and Livres Canada Books, and of the Government of Quebec through the Société de développement des entreprises culturelles (SODEC).

Linda Leith Publishing
Montreal
www.lindaleith.com

THE PHILISTINE

A novel

LEILA MARSHY

DEDICATION

For my *binat*, always.

TABLE OF CONTENTS

1

cheeks pale like wax

He gave her a fax machine the day she turned twenty. It was cumbersome and took up almost the entire desk. "Happy birthday, *laziza!* Two decades! You are the future, you are technology. No more envelopes and stamps, no more waiting." It took some vigorous fiddling—*What this cable? How this fit, how, how?*

"Now, when I want to say hello to my daughter *poof!* the machine will whir and you will have it in your hands." Whir it did. He began his letters—*faxes!*—the same way every time: *Greetings from Egypt!* Next to his signature he wrote the time to the minute, even though the machine date- and time-stamped it along the top. His enthusiasm for the technology never waned. She kept the faxes in a folder, then a second folder, then a third. Until they stopped coming.

Every ten years, Kiddo! He had last taken her to Cairo when she was ten. At twenty she wasn't expecting a fax machine. It was already a rare trip back to Montreal for him, and he liked his visits to coincide with as much pomp and circumstance as possible: Christmas, birthdays,

1

celebrations of any sort. She took the oversize box to be a ruse, a puzzle to solve and reveal. As she peeled off the meticulous wrapping she couldn't help but wonder what he had done to make it so heavy and unwieldy. Maybe deep inside she'd find a heavy brick with a weightless plane ticket wrapped around it, a mixed metaphor he would enjoy. She wondered what she'd pack in the small carry-on she stored unused under the bed for when she returned to Egypt with him. The timing was perfect: CEGEP was over and she could easily spare a bit of travel time before looking for a summer job or starting university in the fall. Her chest filled with excitement and courage. She looked around for her mother but she had gone to the kitchen with a handful of dirty plates.

It was a massive fax machine by Okidata.

"Plus extra toner," he said brightly, raising a finger in the air.

He bent over the monstrosity and busied himself with threading the heavy roll of thermal paper through it. The machine impressed him and his Arabic utterances sounded like refrains from Om Kalsoum songs. *Ya allah, ya salam, ya qalbi.* Otherwise, Nadia hardly understood a word. Every brick she had imagined was now in her stomach.

Satisfied, he smiled broadly and pulled a cigarette from a nearby pack. Dinner eaten, gifts dispersed, time for his evening smoke. Nadia followed him out to the balcony with an ashtray. "What the problem? Neighbour complain again?" he laughed. He flung the match to the yard below and winked at her.

"You said every ten years." Her voice trembled already. She wanted to kick herself.

"What, *ya bint*?" Bint meant girl, she knew. If he had said *binti* it could have meant *my daughter*. But he didn't add the *i*.

"You said every ten years. It has been ten years. Ten" —she paused, but not for long— "years. Thanks for the fax machine, it's really great. But I kind of thought a plane ticket... Baba, don't you want to bring me to Egypt again?"

It struck her that maybe he did not remember his promises at all. She reminded herself to prepare for the worst, to stop being so gullible and stupid, to accept that she had no control over the situation, that he was a busy man. All that music she still could not understand, all those words she still spoke only haltingly, all those dishes she had no idea how to cook, all those stories that remained undeciphered on postcards. The Middle East had nothing to do with her and she had nothing to do with it. She was supposed to be in Montreal and stay in Montreal.

"*Ya-aaaaaa*," he said wearily. He inhaled deeply on the cigarette, nodded. He took the ashtray and concentrated on grinding out the smoke. She hadn't inherited his long limbs, nor his tight dark curls. She was stockier, like her mother, lower to the ground. And though she had his curls, hers were looser and not always committed to the task of curling.

"Yes, yes. I said that." He sat down, put his hands on his knees and talked into the middle distance, as was his

3

habit. "Nadia, first you must finish your studies. You are starting university, and you must finish university. There is nothing more important than education. You must complete your education. It is the difference between life and no life."

She folded her arms and looked away. He was looking for excuses, as always. "It's not right," she muttered weakly.

He looked beyond her into the house, searching for Nadia's mother. He would be wondering how much Clare was behind her pestering and restlessness; whether, yes, she had provoked this to show him up in front of his daughter. But his wife was still in the kitchen cleaning up after the meal. Of the three of them, only Clare had openly expressed disappointment in the trajectory of their lives. His long years studying and putting them in debt, his inability to find a decent job—or, worse, keep one. A baroque moral code coupled with a sliding relativity regarding his own behaviour. And finally, his insistence that taking a "proper" job in Cairo was a good idea. From the outset, there was no question that Clare would follow him to Egypt. Their lives were in Montreal, she told him. Besides, she had her own proper job, *merci beaucoup*. Mostly though, she was adamant that she was not going to raise their daughter in the Middle East. He, on the other hand, thought it was the best place in the world to raise a daughter.

"Then I will bring her with me," he declared.

Nadia had gotten out of bed, nudged her door open a

crack, listened. She was fifteen, an age when all was possible and the only thing getting in the way of adventure and fulfillment was her mother. There was a long silence, the kind Clare cultivated. Then a low hiss, barely decipherable, a bass note upon which the next half-decade played out. "You. Just. Try."

"It *is* right." The vertical line in his forehead deepened like a scar when he was angry. He scattered his hands through the air as he defended himself. "It *is* right. I send money, I support you. I have good job. I will pay for your university."

"Half." She remembered his agreement with Clare.

"The best half!"

Nadia couldn't help but smile. Encouraged, he continued. "I tried, *ya Nadia*. Come, they said. Come and learn and we will teach you what you cannot have. I was so excited. *Ya Allah*, Nadia you have no idea, I was so excited. Who knew I would have such opportunity? A scholarship! To Canada!" He knew she loved hearing the story. *Kan ya makan*, he said, allowing himself a smile. Once upon a time. He nodded as if setting the rhythm of a melody.

The fighting was getting worse every year, he began, first little skirmishes then out-and-out battles. People were losing their homes, their lives. First the Turks, then the British had stood in the way of their destiny. Now, the end was in sight, they would have a free Palestine, their land, a land for everyone. But suddenly there was a different enemy, one they didn't see coming because it was the familiar faces of their neighbours. "Such a shock," he said. "My best friends were Jewish, and now our fathers were aiming rifles at each other." Usually these clashes settled themselves over a glass of tea. "They were our neighbours! Our friends! How could we hate each other?" But these Jews had different leaders now, strangers from Europe, unfamiliar immigrants who spoke European languages and carried with them a not-so-hidden desire for revenge. "How could we know? Our enemy now was all of history. All of history!" His parents started taking the children to Alexandria for the summer. "My aunt was there and at least my parents knew me and my brother would be safe. Then we would return in September for school. Beautiful Alexandria. Oh the beaches, *ya Nadia*."

"Your brother?" His family, his history, his stories, always confused her. Now he had a brother?

"*La, la,*" he corrected, waving it off impatiently. "My friend. We were like brothers. He is... gone, I don't know." He spoke to himself in Arabic. Sometimes Nadia wondered if he lived with his stories like a dog lives with a porcupine's barbs. She could try to help but he growled and ran away.

In September 1948, they were not allowed to leave the ship as it nudged against the Haifa harbour. Stern border guards dismissed their travelling papers and sent them back to Egypt. "The Jews were met with cheers but the Arabs were swept away to drown. They found Israel, we lost Palestine. And that is how I became Egyptian and you became Canadian. But there is no life for a Palestinian in Egypt, *ya bint*, no life. Canada gave me a future until, *khallas* …" He shook his head theatrically. "A long line of disappointments, *yanni*."

Yanni, yanni. The multipurpose word here functioned like a curtain in a funeral parlour, closing off the story to further probing or open displays of grief. She had to wonder if she was included in the long line of disappointments.

Five years after the fax machine, a warm November wind was coaxing despondent trees into budding. Nadia left work early and took a small detour through Parc Laurier, while the sky was still orange and clouds were still visible. She regretted not calling Daniel before leaving; he could have met her. It was his favourite thing, to wander around and around a park, around and around talking of anything and everything, his arm around her shoulder like an old scarf. An idea had come to her that she was excited to discuss. On the metro she'd spotted an ad for an EgyptAir seat sale—a flight to Cairo could be had for almost half price. What if, she found herself thinking, what if she just bought a ticket and boarded a plane and took herself to Cairo? She could take extra days over the Christmas holidays. It was incredible, this sudden and massive feeling of possibility. Years of waiting and deferring, dissolved in an instant by the fairy dust of a seat sale. Is that how great things are accomplished, she wondered, through the serendipity of a poster in the metro? She was smiling so hard that she had to stop walking and savour the crystallization of a decision—a sensation, she was forced to admit, she wasn't used to. There was a *decision* to

7

make. It felt so adult, and at twenty-five that is what she barely was. She found a picnic table and sat down. Not far away a thin woman wrestled with a mean-looking dog that pulled violently against its leash in the direction of squirrels and pigeons. Nadia moved to the other side, putting a few planks of wood between her and the animal. Just in case. Two teenage boys squatting on skateboards passed a joint back and forth, the sweet aroma getting her attention. Rush-hour traffic inched around the perimeter of the park, containing and restricting her, leaving streaks of light as the sky abruptly went grey. The sounds of the city shifted to a new register, the key of nighttime. She was shivering and bloodless when she finally stood up and headed for home.

Bishara tried to inject some humanity, as he put it, into the "other side." A few articles, letters to the editor, speeches at local churches, mosques, and even two or three synagogues. He didn't fit most people's preconceptions of what a Palestinian looked like. He wasn't hijacking a plane, for one, nor was he Muslim. But the phone calls started. After a while, the menacing escalated to bomb, fire, and even kidnapping threats. The most ridiculous was when an irate woman got Clare on the phone and damned her with the worst thing she could think of: "Go fuck an Arab!" Clare gave as good as she got, but Nadia knew the calls were getting under her mother's skin. The arguing between her parents increased and her name was invoked as much as any outlawed organization. *You're putting our daughter in danger. No, the real danger is she lose her birthright. You don't need to be so outspoken. Why you? Why me? Because if I am silent then I agree with Golda Meir: there is no Palestinian people, there is no such thing as Palestine, a land without people for a people without land. What are you going on about?*

"Where is Goldie, Baba?"

He tried to ignore her but Nadia was pulling at his arm. There was a neighbourhood dog named Goldie but it had been lost for weeks. Did he find the dog? "Where is Goldie, Baba?"

"She means the dog," her mother said wearily.

"Shall we go look for her, *ya Nadia? Yalla.*" He took her hand and led her outside where they roamed the streets until sunset calling *Goldie! Goldie! Goldie!* Sometimes he laughed and gave it a last name: *Goldie Meir! Goldie Meir!*

Whether it was Clare's impatience or his own inability to secure a stable life from which he could risk politics, he eventually stopped taking Nadia to his speaking events, and stopped urging her to read this book or that article. His friends from the old country stopped coming around. Om Kalsoum and Warda disappeared from the record player. Sliced white bread replaced pita—finally. He even seemed to stop speaking Arabic in the house. Palestine was a ghost and her father did not want to be haunted. In the news and all around them, there was consensus: the Palestinians were an affront to the civilized world and the safe passage of the chosen people. Then one day Nadia woke up and he was gone. "He thinks he can go to Palestine," her mother scoffed. "To some parallel universe where politics is more important than his family. Who knows, maybe in forty days he'll cross the Sinai and actually get there."

Next spring would be another five-year mark, a half-decade, a half anniversary, a reminder of her half-present parent. The decades sliced her in half measures. She was almost afraid to wait for it, to head to that half-open gate and face the loneliness of being always half alone.

When she walked in the door, Daniel had dinner ready and a long story about work. He might be a thief, he said.

"Who?"

"Serge. *Je t'ai dit*. Are you listening?"

"Yes, sorry," she said into her food.

"He has friends who 'buy things' then return them."

"What about the receipts?"

"He makes those up too!" He pushed his plate away. Daniel ate quickly, methodically, and always finished first. He proceeded to tell her about cash registers and receipts, buttons with hidden functions, simmering resentments between managers, head offices that drank away the afternoons, and an ever-widening circle of friends who cultivated winks and nudges and discounts that translated into beer and pizza. Daniel was doing his masters in business and working part-time at a hardware store. Everything transactional made a kind of beautiful sense to him. He was ethical, however. No matter what, she had to always give him that much. He finished the story and bounced into another one, with a plot so twisted she stopped trying to follow it. She decided to not tell him about Cairo.

Maybe another time, another day.

Clare was not impressed by the seat sale. "Fifty per-cent off is still expensive."

"Yeah, but I can afford it, that's the main thing. I've been saving up."

"What about your job? I didn't think they closed the office over the holidays."

"They don't. I'll take my vacation early." An English lit degree might not be worth much, Nadia had to agree with her father once, but it did guarantee that she was an ace typist, which helped land her an office job shortly after graduation in a brokerage firm downtown. Sometimes she wondered if her enthusiasm for Egypt was now further fueled by the fact that she would jump at any excuse to not go to work.

"How about for when you are there? How can you afford two weeks in Egypt?"

"A hotel for a day or two, then… I thought I would probably end up staying at Baba's. In any case, maybe I'll stay three weeks."

"So you *have* contacted him? Nadia, I am confused."

The logistics took shape as she spoke: "I'll call him when I get there and then check out of the hotel after a couple of days. Of course he's going to invite me to stay at his flat. I mean…" Her voice trailed off.

"You might not like what you find, Nadia."

"What do you mean by that?"

Clare struggled with her words. "He has a life there

11

now," she finally managed.

"Yeah? And? I just want to visit that life. That's all."
Nadia didn't hear her mother's hesitancy, the sound of
old hinges on a Pandora's box. Instead, she was bursting
with memories and the excitement of revisiting them.
She wanted to tell her mother that Bishara was the only
person who called her *bint*, who knew that she loved *koshery*, who clapped when she danced to Farid Al Atrash,
who taught her enough swear words in Arabic that when
he said them with a straight face, a sly wink in her direction, only she'd know he was secretly insulting someone.
It would just be *kalam fadi* to her mother. Empty words.

"Will Daniel go with you? That's not a bad idea, you
know, bring him. I bet he's a good travelling companion."

"I haven't said anything yet."

"Hmmm," Clare said, insinuating that she saw what
was coming. Because she probably did, Nadia groaned.

Daniel's eyes widened with excitement. "How about we
go to Greece first and then take a boat to Alexandria? We'll
cross the Mediterranean and write a hundred postcards!"

Nadia put a hand on his knee, so square, so angular.
His whole body was a compendium of lines and directions. "I'm going alone, Daniel. I don't want to be distracted or have to worry about seeing the Pyramids or the
Acropolis or whatever."

Daniel, who had twice as many active parental figures
in his life after his parents' divorce, could barely imagine her worries. He and his three siblings and two half-

siblings were shuttling, visiting, talking, fighting, or otherwise engaged with each other at any given moment. In the two years she and Daniel had been seeing each other then living together, she could never keep track of who it was they were meeting up with next. He always said the same thing when she brought up her father: "I wish *my* father was in Egypt, then I wouldn't have to go to Laval."

Daniel was as buoyant as an air mattress in the middle of a summer lake. His ease with the world calmed her and helped her understand that no matter how far out she might drift, it was just a matter of steady paddling to get back to shore. He never worried how deep the lake was. Nadia, on the other hand, peered into the liquid darkness and saw trenches thousands of feet below. *Bof,* he said, dismissing her fears, drowning can happen in only two inches of water, so why worry?

"I won't distract you. I'll take tour buses while you visit with your father." He sat up straight and pretended to tighten a non-existent tie. "It's time he meets his daughter's *chum*," he grinned.

"Daniel, I am going alone. *Toute seule.* I need to see my father *puis c'est tout.*" Alone, that's all. Just alone. "*Dats it dats all.*" The bastardized English was Quebecois slang now, and she said it as such.

But he was nuzzling her neck with his nose, his deepening breathing a signal that, for him at least, talking was over. Now, there were other priorities to attend to, other opportunities. He was an attentive lover—that's what his ex-girlfriend had assured Nadia once during an awkward moment at a bar, as if *attentive* were a mechanical feature or something to check off a to-do list. It was true, he did all the right things and made her feel all the right ways. There was no reproaching him, so she never did.

As the departure date approached, Clare gave Nadia an envelope of travellers' cheques. "It's not a lot. Just enough to stay at a proper hotel, the Nile Hilton. We stayed there when you were ten, remember? I want you to have enough so you can stay there the entire time."

"But I'll probably just stay with Baba."

"Take it."

Nadia remembered the Nile Hilton. Marble tiles in a lobby as large as a basketball court, big chairs she hid in one afternoon, making her parents frantic with worry. The fat Egyptian woman who found her and, in her parents' stead, slapped her as punishment. Set between the Egyptian Museum and the Mogamma building, the Nile Hilton overlooked the Nile on one side and Tahrir Square on the other, the centre of the sprawling city. Built by Nasser in the 1960s—and looking it—the hotel had been the site of countless summits, clandestine meetings, and expat business deals. With its American bakery, Italian coffee, and French food, it was an oasis for the monied and the sophisticated. Mostly, it figured on the postcards that Bishara had sent his daughter.

"That was the one hotel I was going to avoid," Nadia laughed.

Her mother shook her head. "It's a good safe place for

a foreigner to stay. Promise me you'll go there?"

"Okay, Mama."

Clare smiled. Nadia knew she loved it when she called her Mama. "Nadia, you can come home any time you want. You know that, right? Just change your ticket and I'll get you at the airport."

"Three weeks is not a long time, I'll be fine. And it's okay, Daniel is on airport duty."

"God knows, your father could find you a job at BP, and then what?"

Nadia had watched her mother had give up trying to understand her husband or even make excuses for him. Clare understood his pride had been at stake once upon a time, that the rainbow at the end of his immigrant journey had never materialized and that he'd suffered because of it. But whatever failings he appeared to have in the Canadian job market were irrelevant in Egypt. There, he was only an asset: he was trilingual, having learnt French in Montreal, and possessed a Canadian engineering degree, a Canadian passport, Canadian experience. It was almost as good as hiring a foreigner. So when an old friend shared his connections with British Petroleum in Cairo—*paying foreigner salary!*—Bishara jumped on it. I'll be back every month, he reassured them. Then, I'll be back for the summer and at Christmas. Nadia was halfway through CEGEP when he skipped a year entirely, followed by just a short visit the next year. That was already three years ago. She had spent her entire adolescence planning for a holiday in Egypt. She had graduated from high school, then CEGEP, then university; she had gone through boy-friends and breakups; she had moved in with Daniel; she'd had jobs and vacations and adventures. All of it, every last single thing, without her father's input or blessing or even criticism. Throughout it all, Clare was furious.

"You don't even care," Nadia had said once, accusing her mother of not making an effort to hold a place at home for her father.

Clare stiffened, exhaled loudly. Nadia braced herself for an outburst or a lecture. Unlike Bishara's loose and forgetful relationship with his own emotions, Clare's Scottish roots lent her control and precision, but also an inability to forgive. Everything mattered all the time. It was exhausting.

"I am angry," she said slowly and with great measure and finality. "And I have every right to be angry." She was going to hold on to that with an almost spiritual conviction. She was religious after all.

Nadia couldn't afford to be angry, or even hurt. It took all her energy just to wait.

2

a tail for animals magic and not

Three days before the end of 1987, Nadia settled into an Air Canada flight first to New York then, after a short layover, France. She crossed the terminal in Paris and boarded another plane for Cairo, falling asleep over the Mediterranean. The pilot broke through the engine noise with a mellifluous accent as the plane began its descent below the cloud line, waking her up. "Passengers, we will be circling Giza. Watch for the Pyramids on your left." The wing dipped and, murmuring with delight, the right-side passengers got up to lean over the left-side passengers. Cameras clicked and whirred. A large man leaned heavily over her armrest. "Hey look, look, Honey," he said to his wife behind him. Nadia didn't believe in jumping just because someone said jump, nor staring down at vague triangular shapes in a desert countless kilometres below. She looked in the other direction, at the clouds they had torn through. Only foreigners cared about the Pyramids, she knew. What Egyptians wanted was to see the blue sky above those clouds. All you ever saw from the ground was grey.

Cairo tackled her like an angry dog, knocked the wind out of her lungs. From the first step on the tarmac to the drive to the hotel to the collapse on her bed, she moved as if through an oven, no corner cooler than the next. She marvelled at how less than a day of travel had propelled her to another world, another climate, another time zone, another language, another self. There was something to be said for six-week ocean voyages, she thought, where by the time you landed your skin had sloughed off to reveal another layer, one ready for the business of change.

This was the Cairo she remembered, and yet it wasn't. Without the protective shell of her parents, she was disoriented. People moved more slowly than she remembered, cars sputtered faster. The animals that jumped in and out of view were haggard and dirty and slightly menacing. The dense heat deposited a mirage at the end of every street, where robed figures moved in and out of focus as if in ritual.

Her room, nine storeys up, looked north, with a view of the Nile on the left and a slice of the city on her right. A dirty haze hovered over everything, darker and heavier at the horizon like mythic mountains, but of pollution. It was barely noon and the dense traffic was already serpentine, slithering up and down the Corniche. Everywhere else, a sea of people walked, cycled, drove, even crawled. Hungry, she ordered room service. Two plates, one of spaghetti, the other of tahini. The way she'd done when she was ten, a combination that always offended her mother and made her father laugh. She was excited to call

18

him, to listen to his shock as she told him she was only a taxi ride away. But the combination of jet lag and hunger and just plain over-excitement kept her from picking up the phone right away. She lay down on the stiff bed.

A brisk knock at the door startled her awake, followed by a cleaning lady. Nadia quickly ran to the bathroom, making it in time to heave into the toilet. The woman handed her a bottle of water.

"*Malesh, malesh,*" she smiled softly. "Poor American. *Malesh.*"

"*Canadiyya,*" she said needlessly. *Malesh* was almost as good as *yanni* or even *yalla*. Arabic allowed for extremes and ranges of ambiguity that English could only dream of, full of elastic words that could stretch wide enough to reveal a back door perfect for escape or alibis. *Malesh*, her father would say, you can do better. *Malesh*, sorry. *Malesh*, it's okay! *Malesh*, calm down. *Malesh*, I know you're disappointed but there is nothing we can ever do about it.

She was grateful for the water, and flopped back to the bed as soon as the woman clicked the door behind her. When she woke up again her forehead was hot to the touch. She stayed in bed another day and rose on the third. Timing is everything, she thought.

"I've been worried about you!"

Nadia moved the handset away from her ear. "It's okay, Mom, I was just settling in."

The international telephone *centrale* was a nook off the hotel's lobby, a long row of cubicles with black telephones. Nadia had given Clare's number to a woman behind a counter, then went to one of the chairs and waited by a phone for it to ring.

"I've been a little sick, travel-sick. Nothing to worry about."

"Sick?"

Nadia cringed, sure her mother's voice could be heard throughout the *centrale*.

"Do you need to see a doctor? You have Blue Cross, don't forget. You can see a doctor any time," she said. Then, in the same breath, as if forcing herself to ask, tacked on: "How is your father?"

"I haven't called him yet. I'm doing it soon."

"Okay, okay, take your time. Let me know how it goes."

The phone call to Daniel went much the same way. He had given her a parting gift of a notebook with postcard-style pages that she could tear off and mail.

"You can write me every day," he said. "Okay, every second day. Okay, okay, weekly. Three postcards at least!"

She was forced to admit that she had barely explored the hotel, let alone the city.

"That's okay," he said good-naturedly. "You have three weeks. Some people get to the top of Mount Everest and back in that time."

He did that, made her feel both relieved and anxious. As far as he was concerned, she was on an orienteering adventure, map, compass, and sharpened pencil in hand. He had bought her a *Lonely Planet* book and had gone through it, highlighting in yellow everything she should see or visit. There was no such thing as aimlessness in his world. Inside the back cover he wrote the dimensions for a carpet he wanted her to bring back. So they talked carpets and leather bags and Pyramid key chains and ottomans and spices and papyrus paintings.

"Don't you think so?" Daniel's voice cut into her thoughts.

"Think what?"

"Come on, Nadia. It would be fun if we met in Athens. Just for a few days at the end of your trip, maybe a week."

"Daniel, you're stressing me out. Can we not talk about Greece? Can I just get through this trip? I have enough to think about right now."

"Of course, of course. *Désolé*, sorry. But if you change your mind I am just a phone call away."

Afterwards, she found a comfortable chair in the lobby and sat there for the rest of the afternoon. A roving waiter offered her a drink from a wide silver platter, a glass of very cold, bright red *karkaday*. When he noticed that her glass was low, he offered another. He seemed to honour her aimlessness. She wasn't going to change her mind about Greece. And she wasn't going to visit every highlighted landmark in the book—she didn't even want to see the Pyramids now that he had highlighted *and* circled them *and* left a note *and* brought them up in their first call. She hadn't quite articulated it to herself until now, but maybe it was a good idea to take a little break from him. She had lost her carapace of purpose since her arrival, but maybe that was part of travel. It was time to cut away the ballast of bravado and set herself adrift.

Nadia had anticipated neither the heat nor the utter dauntingness of calling her father. She ordered breakfast in her room. Had she known what "continental" meant, she might have chosen something else on the menu. She called down again and asked for a shwarma, a mango salad, and a glass of mint tea. After eating she closed her eyes for a long time. When she opened them, she was in Cairo.

She let it ring. Hung up, dialled again. Let it ring. Of course, she was almost relieved, the number was at home and he was at work. She found an Egyptian soap opera on TV and watched it, barely understood a word. She realized with no small pleasure that it was the same soap that had been running when she was ten. She'd have to ask her father about it, maybe he watched it too. For lunch she ordered *koshery* and a feta salad. By the time supper rolled around she was craving a hamburger and french fries, and called down. Afterwards, she took a shower, tidied her room, called Bishara's number again.

"*Aiwa?*" It picked up after one ring. "*Aiwa? Hallo. Hallo.*"

"Baba…"

22

The line went quiet. She thought it had cut out or he had hung up.

"Nadia?"

"Baba. I'm in Egypt. *Ana fi il qahira*," she said, wiggling her head. "I'm in Cairo." It came out like a spilled bucket. "And guess where? The Nile Hilton. I just got here—well, a couple of days ago. I was tired for the first day, a little sick. I called you already but you must have been at work. I wasn't even sure if I had the right number! It's hot! We always came in summer so I just assumed that winter would be cool, you know. Like, not so hot. Well, okay, it's cold at night, but still. Can hardly call that cold, can you. So, yeah. I'm here." She took a deep breath.

"*Stana, stana,*" he said, wait, wait. "Where here? In Cairo?" Cavernous spaces were opening up between his words, like an earthquake in full motion.

She hopped around the room on her toes, twisting and untwisting the phone cord behind her. "Yes!"

"With your mother?"

"No, just me! Aren't you going to *ahlan wa sahlan*? I bought a plane ticket and just came. *Magique, kidda!*" She didn't know the Arabic word for magic, French would do. In any case, Arabic was laced with French words: *jupe*, *gateaux*, even *merci*. She wanted to shout them all out her window all the way to Nasser City. "Can you believe it? And you know what? It's been way more than ten years. But you don't have to bring me, I can bring myself. I came on my own!" She was making herself dizzy with excitement and the effort of excitement and, finally, the release of excitement.

"*Ya Nadia, tabaan*, of course. *Ahlan wa sahlan ya bint!* Welcome! Where are you?"

"At the Nile Hilton."

"The Nile Hilton, *ya salam*. And for how long you are here?"

"Three weeks. Minus a half-week already. I took some time off work because the Christmas vacation is not long, as you know. I guess that means I won't have much of a summer holiday. But who cares, I hate my job anyways, maybe I'll quit it haha. I work in an office, can you believe it? It's alright, I speak French all day long, which is great. But it's just temporary; it really has nothing to do with my major. I brought my graduation pictures with me. The ceremony was a little over the top." There was too much to tell him. It was hard to breathe. She wanted everything, she wanted too much. He wasn't saying anything. "So, can I see you?"

He forced a chuckle, but only after a beat of silence. "You are at the Nile Hilton?"

"Yes."

"Okay, Nadia, okay. Okay." Maybe he was dizzy too, she thought. "I meet you for lunch. *Meshi?* Okay. Let me see. Tomorrow is, hmmm, no. We can meet the day after tomorrow. At two? I will come to the hotel. They have good restaurant."

He said tomorrow, not today, not this minute, not right now I can't wait to see you.

"Good girl," he added pleasantly to the silence. "Yalla bye-bye."

The phone was heavy, a dial phone from an earlier era, with a handset hard enough to bash a hole in the wall. She didn't hang up for a while.

She grabbed her bag and rushed out. She needed to put distance between herself and her room, herself and the telephone, herself and her disappointment.

Stepping out into Tahrir Square she was immediately engulfed by the writhing city. Unlike how she remembered them, the great masses of people seemed lumpy, bedraggled, even boneless, like old throw covers on even older chesterfields. Women moved like pieces on a board game, forward, backward, diagonal, with no affectation or extraneous movement, wearing trench coats and scarves or tottering in heels and tight skirts. She wanted one of them to look at her, to ask her how she felt and if she knew where she was going, maybe take her hand, *yalla*, come with me. But the men, perpetually leaning forward in odd s-shaped postures, round potbellies on even the slimmest of them, stared her down with a hardness that took her breath away. They spoke to her in a constant stream of hisses and exhortations. *Hello? American? Where you go? What time is it?* Everything else was in Arabic, a dirty, ominous, unfriendly Arabic. It was another layer of sound under the clanking din of the city, this one more rodent-like, like the invisible rats scurrying between the walls of her first apartment.

Crazy Cairo, her father used to say, it sings when it should be silent, laughs when it should be serious. To the self-possessed Palestinians, Egypt was a country they tolerated the way parents tolerate a rambunctious youngster. She remembered holding Clare's hand and being proud of the attention her mother received as they strolled the city one afternoon while her father slept. They'd had lunch at a café, bought sweets at a shop, tried on shoes. But by the time they got back to her aunt's apartment, Clare was raging. Nadia had thought it was about the dogs that roamed freely. *Animals,* Clare kept saying, *they're animals.* Nadia had wanted to pet one. Was that the problem? She slunk lower in the couch while her parents quarrelled. *That's enough,* her father had finally said. *This is not your country. You do not understand. It is nothing. They mean no harm.*

"Oh really," Clare said, raising her voice again. "I think that's for me to decide. Goddamn pigs."

Nadia hadn't seen any pigs. Maybe her mother was getting her animals mixed up? "But Mama, but Mama, they were dogs."

Bishara winked at her, he would take care of it.

But now she could see the animals now. She could see them and hear them and every now and then feel them. The city was an overcrowded sty of pigs. The sidewalks were sliced in two between the men who ignored her and the men who wanted to eat her for lunch. After a few blocks, the only thing she could do was trail as close as possible behind one woman after another and try to disappear in their slipstreams. An insectile buzzing followed her, the hissing, straying words of men who wanted to latch on to her like larvae. She kept her arms forward to protect her chest and in position to slap away the twitching hands. She was staring at the flimsy plastic shoes of a woman in front of her when she bumped into the back of a tall man. She prepared to defend or excuse herself, but neither was necessary.

"Well, pardon me," he said in an English accent. He was her age, maybe older, maybe a lot older, wearing a bright orange T-shirt and a pair of white linen pants.

"Oh! I'm sorry," she said.

"Entirely my fault. After you?" He bowed slightly and swept a hand between them.

"Excuse me?"

"The vernissage? It's here if you were looking." Behind him a door opened onto a staircase. The sign above said *Galerie Mashrabiya*. "Cairo's only independent gallery. Where the wine is French, the money is American, and the art is—well, did I say the wine was French?" With his arm still outstretched, and a broad and inviting smile, the offer intrigued her if for no other reason than it might provide relief from the sidewalks. Behind him, a small group of people chatted and slowly made their way up the steps, another group finished their cigarettes and, mounting the steps, lit up more. And another streamed out of taxis. The momentum was difficult to resist.

"Why not?" she said, mostly to herself. She mounted the steps behind him, brave, reckless and curious. The narrow staircase turned slightly at the top and led into a large room that opened into an even larger room. Paintings covered the walls, each separated from the next by a niche into which a sculpture or carving had been placed. Music rumbled from a far corner and when a group of people shuffled to the next painting, a trio of tabla and oud players could be seen behind them. The gallery sparkled with sparkling people speaking loudly in English, French, and Arabic, eating off plates and napkins, drinking, smoking, and flicking their ashes to the scuffed wooden floor. She felt wide-eyed with a sense of displacement and even emptiness, but no one looked at her strangely or wondered where the interloper had come from.

"Name's Wills." He was still at her side and held out his hand. She told him her name, her home country, and gave a vague story about why she was in Egypt: visiting family. It was true, though it somehow didn't feel it.

He wore a gentle, affable expression, his eyes only moderately scanning the room as she spoke. "Ah ha," he said. "The wine table." Then he was gone. "Red? White?" he asked over his shoulder.

"White," she called after, but doubted he heard. She laughed to herself. This is what she remembered of Cairo. Not the Pyramids or the rapacious street life or the noise that assaulted and hurt, but the oases of warmth that thrived in the oddest places at the oddest of times. It reminded her of dinner parties, nighttime conversations on balconies, backgammon tiles slapped down amid laughter and teasing, card games where no one won and no one lost. Her father called everyone friend or brother or sister or *sitti*—grandmother. Millions of strangers, but not one of them a stranger. Millions of discordant notes, but one chord. A sense of belonging to history, to family, to self. Could it be possible that she knew what she wanted, that she knew why she was in Cairo, why she had to come back, and even, to her shock, why she might never leave? Something thundered through her body, shuddered down her spine, dried up her mouth, compressed her lungs until she had to remind herself to breathe. Breathe. A large canvas loomed in front of her and she leaned in to look, as much out of passing curiosity as a need to focus and calm herself. The painting was imposing, almost dominating the room, but there was something familiar about it. Lines she had seen somewhere else, forms and colours borrowed and pasted and shrewdly mixed together.

There you are. Wills handed her a glass of wine then just as quickly disappeared. Relieved to have something to do with at least one of her hands, she sipped while staring at the colours, the thin lines left by the brush, the plain wooden frame, the wall behind it.

Another voice materialized out of the din. It was deep and rich, funnelling soft consonants, tumbling with little shell-like t's and floating r's, all of it directed at her. Nadia understood only one word: *Moscow*. Embarrassed, she was nonetheless thrilled to be taken for an Egyptian. She turned around. "I'm so sorry, I don't speak Arabic."

A woman raised her eyebrows and refocused her gaze. Her regard was bemused and, Nadia shifted slightly with discomfort, almost intimate. She was more or less Nadia's age, slightly taller, slightly darker, significantly more at ease, with a roundness that was pure Egyptian where

Nadia was sharp with the Levant, not to mention Canada. The woman's thick hair was held back with a gold cloth bandeau, the rest of it falling around her shoulders like heavy sails. Looking into her face Nadia understood for the first time how Egypt was an African country, that its river had roots south of the Sahara, not north of the Mediterranean. Clapping her hands together, the woman's eyes lit up. "I'm sorry, I thought you were Egyptian. But you must be..."

"I'm Canadian," Nadia said reluctantly, but also immensely relieved that this person spoke English and the conversation could continue. "Actually, my father is Egyptian. Well, Palestinian really." She was used to the disarming Arab habit of parsing the other: Who is your father? What country are you from? And please, Miss, *are you married?* She was prepared to disappoint.

"Are you what happens when Palestinians-not-Egyptians go to Canada? Well, then. Welcome to Egypt!" She laid a warm hand on Nadia's arm. It was nothing, a polite gesture in a hot country, but it was touch and when she pulled her hand away the spot was indented and tingling. The heat she left behind spread outward and rushed up to Nadia's chest. It reminded her that the sun had just descended, that she was alone in Cairo, that she was looking for her father, that she didn't speak Arabic, that she was angry that she didn't speak Arabic, that one of the greatest disappointments in her life was that she didn't speak Arabic, that it was entirely unfair to have an Arab father, a missing Arab father, a Palestinian father for what it's worth, and to not even speak the language; that she only knew food words and swear words and some words from songs but not one whole sentence that could serve her at this moment, talking to this strangely alluring woman. What was she doing throwing herself across the Atlantic? Was she a complete idiot? He barely even wanted to see her, she knew that, it was obvious. Nadia's stomach lurched; she fought against it. Her cheeks flushed, her neck burned, her forehead oozed droplets. The woman was indeed strangely alluring. She sought the wall; it was cool.

"I was just saying that Wael Nosry studied in Russia and you can see that in this painting. Don't you think? Everyone who comes back from abroad has at least one painting that looks like somebody else," she laughed. She leaned in, paused, her breath a mix of cardamom and mint, a combination that instantly plunged her into another time. Her Aunt Josephine used to smell like that, or maybe just the *bowab*, the Egyptian version of concierge plus janitor plus doorman all rolled into one shoeless man who lived in the lobby and kept out both intruders and bad spirits.

"Maybe you need to sit down," she said. She took Nadia's hand and pulled her through layers of people and clouds of cigarette smoke. Her hands—large, strong, gentle—pushed Nadia down on a bench at the back of the room.

"You stay here. Yes?" A hand touched Nadia's forehead and felt for heat. "My name is Manal."

31

Nadia fought back nausea, forced herself to look straight ahead. Like in a car. She always vomited in the back seat when they went on camping trips. Her father loved their "Canadian holidays," though her mother would have just as soon stayed at a hotel. Even a crappy motel, she said, just as long as she'd never again have to wash the smaller pots in the bigger pots. Either way, they were lucky if they made a trip without having to stop the car so Nadia could hurl by the side of the highway. She learnt to stare at the lines on the road ahead of them. Now, the lines turned into Manal, who moved steadily through the gallery. She touched everyone, not just Nadia, threw her head back in laughter, touched more arms and leaned in closely for secrets and stories. When she pulled a red dot from a sheet of stickers and placed it next to a painting, Nadia realized she worked there.

"Cola?" Manal was next to her, a small bottle in her hands. "Or ginger? Canada Dry!" She smirked at the aptly named soft drink.

Manal looked over often, sometimes winked, sometimes touched her heart, sometimes lifted her eyebrows, laughed. She put one dot after another next to the paintings. At one point a wisp of breath blew against Nadia's ear. "You must be bringing me good luck," she whispered. Then she was gone again.

"Oi, there you are!" Wills stood swaying before her, his legs spread apart as if the gallery were a boat in a storm. "We're going to Maadi, want to come with?"

"Sorry, what?"

"I always forget what it's called, but it's a dance club and they serve beer and, if you're nice, whiskey shots. Come on, we're taking two taxis, you'll fit."

"Oh, I don't know—"

"Tena, Tena, come here." A smaller woman in the crowd turned around and joined Wills, wrapping her arms around his waist and planting a little kiss on his chest. Their height discrepancy was almost comical. "Tena, this is Nadia, she's from Canada."

Tena held out her hand, shook Nadia's forcefully. "I'm from Sarajevo," she said. "Yugoslavia. Are you coming with us? I think everyone's already outside. Come on."

"Oh. I don't know. I'm not really feeling all that well." She looked back and forth between Wills and Tena, neither of whom seemed to be convinced by her answer. Between them, in the empty space, she caught Manal's eyes. Her definitely watching eyes. "I'm going to stay here. Thanks for the invitation," she said.

"*Mafish mushkilla*, no problem," Wills said. "We come to all the vernissages. See you at the next one? Ta-ta."

By 11 pm the hum of the room settled to a murmur. Manal sat down next to her and caught her breath. She was quiet for a few minutes, once or twice looking at Nadia and smiling. A tall, blond woman strode up to them and squeezed behind the desk.

"That's Brigitte," Manal whispered. "She owns the gallery."

Brigitte ré-emerged with an unframed painting,

an abstract in primary colours, and held it up for a serious-looking foreigner. Wrapping his hand around hers, the gentleman took it and peered at it at arm's length in a fair semblance of discernment. Brigitte took the opportunity to cast a sidelong glance at Manal, who hopped up with a receipt book. In the background, among the dwindling crowd, a young man was observing the transaction with hungry attention.

"She can sell cats to the mice," Manal said when she sat back down. "The German comes to every vernissage and always buys. I am sure he doesn't even like art, he just takes the cheapest painting."

Brigitte tore the receipt out of the book and exchanged it for a small wad of cash. "Manal," she said, "*amène-moi deux verres, s'il te plaît.*" She strung her arm through the gentleman's and led him to the front of the gallery. Manal followed with two glasses and a bottle. She returned a minute later and quietly poured some wine into a glass for Nadia.

A voice echoed back up the stairs. "*Tu fermes les portes, Manal?*"

"*Oui!*"

The young man stepped forward and leaned into Manal. "How much?"

"The price it was listed at," she frowned.

He hissed under his breath. "I asked you to raise it."

"You know I can't do that."

But he continued. He'd had a plan, as Manal would tell Nadia later. Print up two price cards, one higher than the other, and when the time came to sell, swap the cards. It was a preposterous and stupid idea, Manal said, not to mention it would jeopardize Brigitte's relationships with her clientele. He matched Manal step for step as she tidied up, his words bouncing louder and louder in the empty-ing space.

Manal stopped at the door. "That's enough, Imad. You have to go. If this happens again I will have to tell Brigitte."

He shrugged her off. "Ha! And then we will see whose side she is on."

She swore as he bounded down the stairs two steps at a time. She put the last of the empty bottles in a box. "Did you tell me your name?"

"Nadia."

Manal's long eyelashes cast charcoal shadows on her cheeks. She threw an empty can across the room, expertly making the bin. "*Yalla*, let's go."

"I'm staying at the Nile Hilton," Nadia said once they reached the sidewalk. "Not that I know where it is any-more."

"I walk you there. I take the bus at the *centrale*, just in front."

"Are you here on a little holiday?" Manal asked, snak-ing her arm through Nadia's like it was the most natural thing in the world. It helped offset the stings of both *little* and *holiday*.

"Actually, I came here to look for my father."

"Where is he? Did we forget him at the gallery?"

Nadia laughed. "He lives here. It's just that I hadn't heard from him in a while. Well, a year to be exact. I thought I would come to Cairo and find him. See him."

"How strange," Manal said. "You came to Cairo to look for your father. That is very mysterious. Cairo is a big city. Do you know where to look?"

"Yes. We're having lunch the day after tomorrow."

"Mystery solved!"

They walked in silence along Champollion Street towards Midan Tahrir—Manal having already instructed her to use the Arabic term, Midan, instead of Square. "Square? What is square here? It's all round!" The dark electric buzz of the streets was invigorating. In Manal's company, the city shifted into something smoother, almost sweet. The flashing neon, music from the passing cafés, cars just rumbling instead of honking, parents and children strolling in the cooled air. They crossed countless lanes of traffic by nudging out onto the road and making their way one passing car at a time. When they got to the other side, Nadia doubled over with relief. "That was amazing!"

"We can do it again. *Yalla* let's go!"

"No, no. Believe it or not, I need to survive this trip," she said.

The hotel was only steps away. Nadia wanted to show her gratitude, maybe prolong the casual intimacy they seemed to be sharing. She didn't know what to make of it, but she didn't want to lose it. "Do you want to have a drink? Lemonade or tea? They have a really nice café."

Manal looked at her watch.

"Come on, it's still early."

It was an enormous relief to finally feel *here* here. Nadia wanted to hang out, to drink, play pool, call Daniel, wander, dance, cross the city on her bike, climb Mount Royal in the dark. Montreal was where she learned to be feral and alive at night, and she was craving the same thing in Cairo. Standing in front of this young woman from a gallery, a girl her age, an Egyptian, someone who spoke Arabic, in the late cool night of a new year, it felt possible.

"*Asir limone*," Nadia said, tempting Manal with a cool drink of lemonade. Behind them, the hotel's terrace brimmed with adventurous foreigners and comfortable Egyptians—or the other way around.

"I've never been to the Nile Hilton."

"Firsts are the best!" Nadia took a step but Manal didn't follow.

"Thank you for the invitation, *ya Nadia*, but I really must go home. My mother will be expecting me. It is late, *yanni*. I am sorry. *Malesh*."

"Oh, of course, I'm sorry." She was mortified that she might have gone too far and made assumptions and connections that did not exist. "I understand. I'm so sorry, it's not my place to...to...pressure or anything. Of course you have to go, it's late." She felt crass and shallow. "This is Cairo, not Montreal," she added, mostly to herself. "I'm stupid."

"*Malesh*." Manal brushed everything aside. "But you come visit me at the gallery again. Yes? Promise?

I am serious. You must come again." She touched Nadia's arm, rested her hand there for a moment longer than she expected. "Please."

"Yes," Nadia said, unable to break eye contact. "I will."

"Promise?"

"*Aiwa*."

Manal melted into the crowds milling at the bus *centrale*. Nadia remained on the wide marble steps watching her blue sweater and black hair vanish into the neon night.

Nadia didn't like heights, but something about being seven stories above one of the oldest cities in the world eclipsed her fear. Cairo was smooth and benign from this height. Warm oil, it flowed back and forth like someone tilting a terracotta bowl this way and that. Somewhere out there, in a district called Nasser City, was her father. Working, speaking Arabic, wearing his *galabiyya* and *shib shibs* on the weekends, eating *koshery*, playing dominos in a *qahwa*, smoking shisha, listening to Om Kalsoum. She tried to imagine him looking up into the grey skies and thinking about her, missing her, wondering if he should buy her a plane ticket, that she was old enough now, how proud he was, how proud she made him feel. How many times had she done this to herself, conjured up an image of him missing her and gone through the emotions one by one, feeling them on his behalf? Wasn't it all a little exhausting, she wondered, not to mention pathetic? She was indeed exhausted. She slid into bed, and on the way to sleep, slid through thoughts of Manal, her voice, her laughter, her touch.

The waiter placed her at a round Parisian-style table at the back of the terrace. It was filling up with lunchtime tourists and business diners. Too many people in shorts and sleeveless tops. She shuddered at the gall required to wander about in short shorts in a city like Cairo. Thick-brained or thick-skinned, she didn't know which. Nadia, on the other hand, had a highly developed sense of *I do not want to offend*. If it was required that she cover her face, as extreme as that was, she would probably do so. There didn't seem to be any covered faces in Cairo, however, and not many hijabs. She just had to make sure her clothes were relatively shapeless and embroidered with gold or silver thread. Do that and all manner of sins would be forgiven.

She caught sight of him as soon as he broke through the layers of people milling between the hotel and the rest of downtown. The long legs, the forward hunch in the shoulders, the body crimping in the way she now recognized as more generally Arab and less specifically Bishara. He wore a pale blue safari suit, an outfit that had cost him some chuckles in Montreal but that looked entirely at home in Tahrir Square. Like almost every man around him, he dangled a keychain, jingling and swaying it for rhythmic and aural effect. She noticed how he was the exact opposite of feral and athletic. No wonder he would never play ball with her, she finally understood: he was completely uncoordinated. She remembered the plastic baseball glove he bought, putting it on the wrong hand. *I know, I know, of course!* She lobbed him soft underhands that he failed to catch every time. She wouldn't begrudge her twelve-year-old self her indignant mortification, but how unfair she had been, she thought now. How unfair to have judged his accent, his uncalibrated emotiveness, his attempts at tact. He tried to be Canadian, she could see that now. The wobbly skates, the too-fast tobogganing, hot dogs on a stick, unfriendly neighbours. But now, striding through Cairo like he owned it—no, like it happily owned him—she could see the difference between being and belonging.

He didn't see her. He checked his watch multiple times, lit up a cigarette, took a table close to the entrance, ordered and drank a coffee. Strangely, she didn't want to impose herself—she was the one out of place now. She wondered if she could slip out the back and disappear either into the hotel or the street. She hesitated, poised between options, then chose.

"Baba."

He stood up, grabbed his chair to keep it from falling over. "Nadia!" He lifted her off the ground with a slightly painful hug. "Sit, sit! What will you have? Are you hungry? Are you tired? When did you get here? Cigarette? Coffee? The best lunch, we will have the best lunch!" He fussed with his hands, shifted again and again in his chair, took out his cigarette packet, removed a cigarette, put it back in. "A drink! What would you like to have? *Yalla garçon!*"

Nadia basked in the attention. She wanted to hear how

pretty she was, how much older she looked, how much he missed her, how proud he was that she had come to Cairo on her own: *bi wahida!* She needed him to be cool, cool water in this relentlessly arid country.

"Welcome to Egypt," he beamed, over and over.

The waiter arrived and they ordered lunch. She gave him a broad rundown of her adventure so far, including the gallery and Manal.

"Four days in Cairo alone! *Yalla, Nadia, mabrouk.* You are now more Egyptian than I am!"

"Well, you're not even Egyptian…"

"For intensive purposes," he said. She laughed at the familiar error. *For all intents and purposes*, Clare would chide until he convinced her he was doing it on purpose. "I am Canadian here. Canadian businessman!"

"How is your job anyways?"

"My job?"

"Yes, you know," she said. "British Petroleum. Funny you come back to Egypt so you could work for the British."

"Funny?" He tilted his head. "Because of the qualms!"

He might as well have been speaking Arabic. "Huh?"

He attempted a British accent. "*Oh dear! Oh dear!* Nadia, I thought Canadians were bad, but the British are even worse." He pursed his lips, wiggled his head, resumed the accent. "They are so *proper*. So very precise and proper. They have *qualms*." He relished the word. "Qualms, no qualms. Qualms!"

Yes, Nadia thought, you wouldn't like that very much. He never had any qualms about opening a bag of cookies while they grocery-shopped so he and Nadia could share the bag, then discreetly stuff it back on the shelf without paying. He had no qualms about returning from almost every trip with a Gideon Bible or two hidden in his bag, adding it to a dusty pile in the closet. He had no qualms about teasing their next-door neighbour about his stuttering. "He like the attention," he insisted. He'd had no qualms about leaving Montreal.

Nadia wondered if he was nervous. He was always an effusive talker, and could dominate most conversations, but he was being even more one-sided than she remembered. He checked his watch as the cheque came, then motioned to the waiter to stay while he peeled bills off a clip. "I would walk you to your hotel but we are already here," he laughed.

"You're going back to work?"

"Yes," he said, looking at his watch again. "Late!"

"Sorry about that."

"No problem, no problem. You are my daughter," he said solemnly. But he was already striding out of the terrace and down the steps ahead of her.

"I'm here for three weeks," she said. He stopped. She wondered for a second if he had not factored in a second visit.

"Can we have lunch again?" she asked quickly. "Tomorrow? Or the next day? Eating at the hotel is expensive. I can come by your work, or your apartment."

"No! Not necessary. Of course, yes, lunch again. Tomorrow. Yes, of course. No, wait." He pulled a little notebook out of the breast pocket, flipped through it. He mumbled to himself in Arabic, a habit Nadia was familiar with. She had always eagerly parsed his words as if threshing for gold, and would be ecstatic when she'd understand a word, adding it to her vocabulary. Not this time. They stood in the paths of seemingly hundreds of people, who simply detoured around them and created new paths.

"Okay," he said. "We can meet the day after tomorrow. Good, *mish kidda*? Good, is it not?" But she knew what *mish kidda* meant and bristled at the translation. He gave her a peck on one cheek then the other, Montreal style. Was it also Egyptian style? She didn't know. "Don't order room service," he said over his shoulder as he walked away, a finger waggling in the air. "Explore the city! Many restaurants!"

After he dissolved into the crowd Nadia looked down at her feet and almost expected to see a tide washing back and forth, burying her legs deeper and deeper in the sand.

The hotel bookstore consisted mainly of guidebooks and murder mysteries, neither of which Nadia had patience for. When she asked if they didn't have anything else the clerk leaned forward and whispered, "Ayoosee."

"Sorry?"

"AUC. The bookstore at the American University of Cairo," he elaborated. He took Nadia to the entrance of the store, pointed past the lobby. "Turn right," he said. "It is in Garden City, after Midan Tahrir, not far. You will see it. Best bookstore for you. Best."

Garden City was as intriguing as *best bookstore*. She followed his directions and almost immediately a street veered off into a quieter neighbourhood. It was lined with trees whose broad canopy created a microclimate that, if not actually cooler, created the impression of coolness. The European architecture reminded her of Montreal, small buildings laden with balconies and decorative ironwork. Every few corners a soldier stood sentry in front of a tiny striped kiosk, a dusty uniform to go with a bored smile, the rifle an afterthought. Behind them, embassies stated their presence with flags and plaques, smaller countries in smaller villas, larger countries behind stone walls and gates. She wondered if the Canadian embassy was nearby and regretted not carrying the *Lonely Planet* with her. She was getting hot in any case, and walked towards the next sentry booth, intending to ask where the university was. Two soldiers were sitting on a low stone wall on the other side of the booth—the second soldier must have crossed the road to sit in the shade. They were leaning against each other, arms around each other's shoulders. One of them pointed back where she had come from. "*Yimeen*," he said. Ah, turn right. Their easy and generous affection startled, even though she knew well enough that physical intimacy between men in the Middle East was not an indication of homosexuality, not in the slightest. But it still tickled her to see it, especially between rifle-packing soldiers. It took all the menace out of them.

Bordering the edge of Garden City, the American University in Cairo stretched behind an ochre limestone wall lined with late-model Mercedes and BMWs. Another microclimate, Nadia thought. She passed through a gate into a central courtyard crowded with cackling students who swung car keys and gold jewelry and lounged over each other's limbs. They conversed in American-accented Arabic and Arabic-accented English, a creole designed for maximum show and minimum effort. *Yalla, hatti the keys, yalla now. Izayak ya bastard, feen, your books? Iscouti, would you shut up? Anybody seen el kitab?*

The bookstore was quieter. As she flipped through the books on the shelves her hands trembled slightly—could be the angle, the heat, the fatigue, the surfeit of every single thing in her life. She didn't remember Cairo being so exhausting and demanding. There was a section of books by Arab authors translated into English. She chose two books by Egyptians she had never heard of: Naguib Mahfouz and Nawal Saadawi. On the way out, a corkboard caught her eye. Notices and announcements were slapped on many weeks thick: flats for rent, roommates wanted, leases to be taken over, books for sale, companions for trips needed, tickets to be exchanged. At the far end were messages in search of friends. *Mona Almaadi, if you read this I will be in Jordan. Leave a message at the Cliff Hotel! If you are Robert Connors, please contact your sister in Boston. All inquiries after January for John Bergman of London can be made at the Ramses Hotel.* People lived here. Foreigners. It was a revelation.

Nadia lay on her bed and read, slept, ordered room service, read some more, then slept until another day had passed.

45

The alarm jolted her into action two hours before their rendezvous. She peered into the mirror after showering. Wan, she thought, though she wasn't entirely sure what wan mean. But wan she looked. She should have gotten her hair cut before leaving Canada, or at least made use of the salon in the lobby. Clare had the habit of always drawing attention to her hair, pulling at it, commenting on its chaos, making a point of telling her when she thought it looked good *this time*. Cairo's dry and dirty air was perfect if she wanted an unkempt, frizzy, and fluffy head of hair—to hell with Clare. She covered her mouth as if she had said it out loud.

An underlined and highlighted section of the *Lonely Planet* described Felfela's as being "fun" with a "bizarre jungle theme." She was hoping that it was more staid and intimate than that, but the first impression from the taxi dashed her hopes as a group of tourists thronged loudly in front of an air-conditioned bus. It was relatively dark inside the restaurant, and she had to wait half a minute for her eyes to adjust before exploring beyond the entrance.

"Nadia!"

Bishara pulled her to his table, put her bag on the floor between them, poured her a glass of water. The jolt of seeing him again burnt away the thin layer of nonchalance she had been affecting for two full days. He went through the menu and explained what was good, what she must order, what was only *yanni*.

"Do you come here a lot?"

"Me? No, no. Not since a long time. Typical Egyptian

food," he laughed. "The whole country knows the menu. But Nadia, you don't remember? You came to Felfela's before."

"Did I?" She smiled, touched by his unearthing of a shared memory. "Didn't I fall asleep under a table somewhere? Maybe it was here."

"Maybe," he nodded, already distracted.

The waiter began bringing their food, plate after plate of dips and salads, meats and soups, and bread. Lots and lots of bread. They ate with gusto, laughing at each other, pushing plates across the table. "Did you try this?" Bishara licked his fingers noisily each time he switched from one dish to another, a gesture that in Canada made Nadia grimace with disgust but here revealed itself to be an appropriate response to the abundance of food and the mechanics of eating. She licked her fingers too.

"*B'ism allah*," he said with finality as the last of their dishes was cleared. "Do you remember what that means, *ya bint*?"

"In the name of God. Well, Allah."

"*Bizupt*." Exactly.

He picked his teeth as the waiter placed a tray of mint tea on their table along with two small bowls. "*Om Ali*, the queen of desserts," her father told her. As she ate the filo dough crushed in cream, pistachio nuts, cardamom and rosewater, a small panic remained undigested in her full belly. The possibility that this lunch could go the way of the one previous was looming large. Content to exist in the moment, he hadn't asked her about herself nor had he proposed anything beyond another meeting in the vague future. Her cheeks burned, putting her in mind of her mother's cheeks, which would also burn red even when nothing else gave her away. Bishara tilted his head and knotted his eyebrows. "You look just like... well, somebody."

"My grandmother? My aunt?" Nadia offered him a profile of remembrance and familiarity. She wanted to look like someone from his side of the family. Ahhh, he used to say to her, my girl is like her, my girl is like her. Sometimes it was his Aunt Josephine, sometimes his Cousin Arwa. Josephine had taken them in when they were stranded in Egypt. He had never seen Arwa or her family again. Last he heard, she was married and in Kuwait, where a large population of Palestinians lived in some comfort. "Oh, you know," he said, sounding distracted again. "Sometimes you remind me of Josephine, maybe Arwa too. She was very sweet."

"Which one?"

"What?"

"Which one was sweet?"

"What are you asking? They were both sweet. My family. My family who I see no more."

"What about Josephine? Isn't she in Alexandria?"

He shook his head dismissively, stared at something behind her shoulder. "I have a boyfriend," she said suddenly. "He lives with me, his name is Daniel, he is francophone. And I got my BA. Did you know that? Do you remember what I studied? I've been working since then, not an interesting job, in fact I hate my job, it's only temporary until I find something in my field, something better and that I like. It's kind of ironic I work in a customs office, don't you think? Stamping the papers for things that come in the country. Yeah, maybe not that ironic. Just stupid and boring. There are no jobs for people who can recite John Donne or Ibsen. Who knew? I should have taken an Arabic class. Mostly, I shouldn't have *needed* to take an Arabic class. Ha ha funny not funny. A thousand words will not leave so deep an impression as one deed. Ibsen. So here I am, the deed is done. You stopped writing so I came here to find you. Daniel wanted to come too. Maybe I should have said yes. Mum thought I was crazy to come. What do you think?"

At the mention of her mother, Bishara shifted in his seat, took out a cigarette, offered her one, lit his.

"Can you not smoke while we eat? You used to say that was disgusting."

He put it out in the ashtray. "*Malesh, ya Nadia.*"

She was just a bundle of inchoate words now, some of them going this way, others going that. She followed wherever they went. "Malesh yourself. Why did you stop writing me, Baba? How could you do that? Are you staying in Cairo forever? I thought family was so important to you. I thought you cared about us. I am your family. Have you forgotten?" She stopped when she heard her mother's voice, that familiar indignant tone, the resentment, the pushing and pushing at him to acknowledge her pain. *Don't you know what you're doing? Don't you know it hurt me?* She never quite understood what her father had done, what the terrible transgressions were, but she always knew just how indignant and offended Clare was. Nadia looked away, unwilling to see her mother's reflection in his face.

"*Nadia*. I am here because I need to work. Do you need money?"

"It's not about money," she sighed. Her thoughts moved far slower than her feelings and the only thing that could sync things up was swearing. Fuck, shit, even the Quebec *câlisse*, were splices in a tape recording that allowed her to realign her brain. Fuck, shit, fuck, shit, *câlisse*, *tabarnak*, shit piss fuck cunt. There was nothing else going on inside. He would just have to wait.

He sipped a hot coffee with the slow gestures of a patient man, gave his attention to the waiters who ran in and out of the kitchen doors as if pushed. His willingness to wait or listen was never conditional. He would wait for the anger to lose its impact, the broken dish to be swept up, the departing feet to return. But maybe it was just distance and detachment, the inverse of caring. Maybe he literally couldn't care less. He drank his coffee, read his newspaper, went on with his life, while the women around him had their various meltdowns.

"I never forget anything," he said, continuing some thought Nadia had already lost track of. His eyes glistened as he looked at her, the coffee cup upside down in its saucer. "I never forget, *ya bint*. Your favourite subject: English. Your sport: swimming. Class you fail in grade 11:

50

chemistry. You miss party, what, your *prom*, because you were sick. The letter when you rewrote "Flanders Field" for the Palestinians. I still have it. I show you one day. Let me think, let me think. Your bike was stolen."

"Twice. Two bikes. I told you, it's impossible to keep a bike in Montreal."

"And the third bike?"

"I still have it."

"*Il hamd'il allah*. Good sign."

A small quiet settled on them. He had opened the door, laid down a prayer rug. They finished their dessert.

"Nadia, you come with me? I have something to show you. And to tell you. Are you busy now, this afternoon?"

"No."

"Good. *Yalla*, we go."

"Nasser City," he said to the driver. The route was longer than she thought possible while still remaining in the city. Over a bridge (or was it two?), up a flyover highway then down again, past sign after sign in Arabic that she couldn't read and English translations that she couldn't understand. They turned off a busy road onto streets that were increasingly quiet. Large apartment buildings, one after another, baking in the hot sun. Then they stopped at one of them, indistinguishable from any other.

"*Yalla*."

They went up in an elevator then down a hallway. Every time she looked to him for answers, or began a question, he nudged it away with his chin. *Tchsshht*.

He took out his keys and opened a door. The

apartment was white and boxy, modern in a way that made it all but lifeless. From the large living room window Nadia could see the desert stretching out with nothing to stop it, at once forbidding and horrible. She looked for her father but he had disappeared. She wondered for a brief second if she should be afraid or worried.

He returned from the dark hallway with a woman beside him. He was speaking to her. They were arguing. Her voice was high, almost a squeak, in odd contrast with her serious expression. She left the room then returned again, this time with a child in her arms, a toddler holding a stuffed whale against her sleepy face.

"What is going on?" Nadia whispered.

She needn't have asked; she knew in an instant.

"This is your sister."

"Wait a minute wait a minute wait a minute wait a minute. You knew? Am I hearing correctly? You KNEW?" Nadia didn't care whose heads were turning to catch her part of the conversation. It wouldn't be any worse than the drunken German who taught everyone the meaning of *scheiden* one afternoon, or the American couple who made daily hysterical calls to their children's nanny, all the time fighting each other for the phone. "How is that possible? How did you let me come here without telling me?"

"Nadia, listen to me," Clare said. "I wasn't a hundred percent sure. We never talked about it. Your father and I have had an understanding for a few years now that, well, he would go his way and I would go mine. It just made sense, Sweetie. I had my suspicions about other things. Well, more than suspicions."

"Suspicions? Other things? I can't believe what I'm hearing. Why didn't you just get a divorce?"

"It's going to happen, it just hasn't yet."

"Oh my god. So first he abandons the family in general and now you in particular. What are you waiting for? The kid is already two years old."

"Come on, Nadia, you're not ten. Anyways these things are complicated and one thing your father and I have in common is we both hate paperwork. I'm so sorry you had to find out like this. I thought he might find a better way to tell you about the... his situation. Then again, subtle communication is not exactly your father's strong suit."

"And it's yours? That's very funny. You both basically handed me off like a hot potato."

They paused, allowed the conversation to recover, stretch its legs, settle in a different position.

"So what happened?"

Nadia tried to tell her mother but it was like conjuring a dream too long after waking. There was the child then the child was in her arms. They sat on the couch, a long chesterfield, the longest one she'd ever seen (it took up the whole wall), white and gold, off-white with gold stripes. It was low and comfortable. *Yes, yes, Nadia.* They sat on it, three in a row, the kid in her mother's lap, awake now, laughing, the centre of attention because everyone was afraid of looking at everyone else. Bishara kept saying to her, *This is your sister, this is your sister.*

"We had *karkaday*, that's an hibiscus drink. It was delicious."

"Yes, I know what *karkaday* is," Clare said.

There had been a bowl on the table with many kinds of nuts and seeds. From the window you could see into the monstrous inhospitable desert. It can eat you alive, she told her mother, I'm sure of it. Nadia could remember two names, Noor and Nora, but she couldn't remember which was the baby and which was the mother. They stayed in the living room, on the couch, drinking *karkaday* and eating seeds and nuts. Two fans kept them cool.

"Nadia, Nadia, Nadia."

"What?"

"It must be late there, why don't you go to bed?"

With her mother's permission, the fatigue finally landed. Her head ached, her neck ached, her eyes ached, her skin was layered with grime, her hair was a mess, and she had brought the wrong clothes, just jeans and T-shirts. She hated walking around, the men hissed and stared, the women looked away; the animals were filthy. And the children, barefoot, brown-toothed beggar children, they lived under flyovers, between buildings, on the grassy medians on the highways. She gave them money and whatever pens or pencils she had in her bag, until they ran after her like puppies, tails wagging their rumps so fast it threw them off balance.

"I don't know what to do anymore."

"Just change your ticket and come home early," her mother said soothingly. "I'll pay the difference."

Nadia groaned. It was enough that she had let down her guard with her mother, she didn't need to follow through. "No. I'll stay. I came here for a reason and there's no reason to leave early."

After they hung up, she sank into one of the lobby's large leather chairs and slowly drifted to sleep, the bright lights overhead transforming into a dazzling sunrise somewhere else on the planet.

"*Min fadlik, min fadlik.*" A cough. Someone was imploring: please, please. "*Law samahti.* Miss." A hand on her shoulder, a warm hand, large. It should stay there, Nadia thought, rustling. She needed a hand on her shoulder.

"Miss."

A beautiful man in a fez stood over her and apologetically asked her to please move from the lobby.

3

pennies from the jinn is not wealth

They had plans to meet again. Another lunch, a supper, a restaurant, his apartment, brunch at the Nile Hilton, *qa-hwa* in the shadow of the Pyramids, a dinner cruise on the Nile. He cancelled them, one after another. Nadia's agenda had a different rendezvous scribbled out for every day of the past week. And now it was almost time to leave the country.

Sometimes she thought of the snow and cold she had left behind, a little surprised that she hadn't missed it at all. Not the beauty of it, the evenings skating or the afternoons cross-country skiing, or even the Sunday *grasses matinées* when they watched a snowstorm from their bed until noon, then finished off the day with a croissant and espresso in their favourite Little Italy café. Luxurious mornings that Daniel specialized in. A coffee, a newspaper, a convivial chat with the old waiter, and he was at his happiest. She missed him sometimes—at times like this, thinking of the ease and comfort of their lives together. A trajectory was spread out before them as clear as a runway: he would finish school, they would get married, have kids with hyphenated last names, spend Sundays with his parents, Christmases going back and forth, and summers camping. He would be deliriously happy. She could imagine being happy. She found a postcard for him, the Sphinx at night. *I wonder what he's thinking*, she wrote.

Then she wondered what Manal was thinking. She didn't know what to make of the space inside her that had been carved out the day she went to the gallery. Was it Manal herself, or just the opportunity of making a friend and the possibilities available to her if she ever decided to stay in Cairo? She tried not to dwell on it too much; she tried to be in the moment, not like a tourist but like a traveller. Yet, that spot on her arm was still warm.

Restless, she took walks downtown, a different direction each time, got lost and hungry and disoriented, then returned to the hotel in a taxi. After a few days she realized she had acquired taxi vocabulary: turn right, turn left, not now, here please, is that enough, not so fast, *insha'allah*. In spite of the cool nights, the days were unrelentingly hot—people in bulky sweaters and thick scarves in temperatures that would prompt Canadians to strip down to nothing. Who knew that 25° Celsius could mean so many different things to so many different people?

Suddenly, the sidewalk was blocked by a pile of garbage that leaned against a building and spilled out onto the street. There was movement at its peak: a goat had climbed to the top and was leaning over to nibble on the laundry that had been hung up to dry on a second-floor balcony. A woman ran out onto the balcony, screaming and weilding a broom, and knocked the animal clear off the pile and onto the road. As if on cue, a boy ran into the melee and collected the goat. He shook his fist at the woman, who shook hers right back and brandished what remained of her nylons. By then a small jury had gathered, half taking the boy's side, the other half the woman's, all of them at some point touching each other, holding onto shoulders, reaching out with hands. *Malesh, malesh*, they said to one another, to the woman, to the boy. At the end, the boy was made to give the woman something, some *piastres*, pennies really, something symbolic, which the woman accepted with equanimity. By then she had descended to the sidewalk with the rest, her housecoat and *shib shibs* testament to a life rudely interrupted. She thanked the boy for his just gift, nodded indulgently, then gave the money back. The surrounding group, now friends for life, nodded and smiled, one or two even clapped. Then, one by one, a smile and a handshake here and there, they left the scene until the street was empty again; even the goat had gone.

Nadia was exhausted and hailed the next taxi she saw. *Midan Tahrir, min fadlak, Nile Hilton*, she said. The driver took one small narrow road after another, shadows elongating with the setting sun. She leaned back in the seat and felt herself falling asleep, even as the honking increased as they neared the city centre. She opened her eyes when they went over a small bump, then suddenly sat up straight. *Stop!* she cried in English, unable to process any other language. She gave him ten pounds and hurried out of the cab. *Galerie Mashrabiya*.

In spite of the sudden gesture, a shyness gripped her at the door: what if Manal were busy or not even there; what if she didn't even remember you; what if she found out you knew absolutely nothing about art and were just a tourist after all; what if her words had been *kalam fadi*, empty and dry and meaningless? Why would she expect anything else? She climbed the stairs feeling sweaty and covered in dust, each step more reluctant than the last. To her relief, people were milling about, some of them for-eigners. She could blend in for a quick minute then leave. Stay long enough to tell herself she didn't just spend her days in a hotel room.

"Canadian girl!"

Manal shuffled towards her with a broad smile on her face, arms extended like a net. Then she was close, pull-ing at Nadia, kissing both cheeks. "*Ahlan, ahlan*," she said, holding on to her hands. "How nice of you to come." She gestured around the gallery. "And we have a new show. The vernissage was last week. There is something new for you to look at."

"I don't want to disturb you if you're busy."

"*Eh da?* I am happy you have come. It's…" She hesi-tated. "It's nice to see somebody twice, *yanni*. So many tourists come only once."

"I'm not really a…" Nadia stopped. What could she possibly say, how could she elevate or change her sta-tus in Manal's eyes? Furthermore, why did she want to? Her head was a knot of thoughts, yet in the tangle was a pulsating softness that alarmed her and kept her feeling she was just about to keel over.

Clearly unencumbered by such drama, Manal took her around the room. At the end of the tour she paused at the little bench in the window. "Remember this bench? It is yours now."

Then it was dark. Though it was barely 7 pm, Cairo days were almost as short as they were in Montreal right now. Manal padded quietly, straightened paintings, picked up tiny bits of garbage.

"*Ya Manal.*"

A young man in white shirt and black pants, a broken frame in his hand, emerged from the black-curtained doorway to the back room. He acknowledged Nadia with a friendly nod. "*Ahlan,*" he said, approaching her with an outstretched hand. Manal came over and introduced them. Tewfiq was her assistant at the gallery.

"Tewfiq has been here since one year, but he has recently graduated from sweeping to framing. *Mish kidda, ya Tewfiq?*"

He smiled eagerly and with deference. Manal followed him behind the curtain. They were there for a half-hour, during which time Nadia, enjoying the relief of absent expectations, did nothing. When Manal finally popped out she pointed to the clock. "*Yalla,*" she said, "we finish tomorrow."

Nadia found herself closing up the gallery with them and walking to the bus centrale. Tewfiq's bus was already there and he ran to get it. His shoes, at least a size too big, flapped loudly.

Nadia looked around. "Where's your bus?"

"Maybe I take *taxi service* and share with strangers," Manal offered. "Or maybe I come to Nile Hilton and we have *limonade*."

Nadia's heart bloomed, surprising her with its intensity. "Are you sure?"

"Nadia, what is this question?" But once inside the lobby, instead of heading for the terrace, Manal pulled at her arm and led her straight through and out the other side. "Have you walked along the Nile Corniche?"

"Last time I did, I was ten."

"Too long! And yet I suspect nothing has changed."

Manal took her arm and stepped into the traffic, steered them through four lanes of boxy Ladas, Fiats, and Peugeots bouncing around like pebbles. On the other side, a wide walkway ran the length of the concrete bank of the river. In stark contrast to the traffic, time slowed down by the side of the water. Boys huddled in groups, couples strolled arm in arm, and fishermen crouched in their tiny boats, by now only cigarettes and the blue lights of kerosene lamps visible in the dark. Manal sat down on a bench as sorrowful music floated by from a drifting barge. She patted the seat beside her and harmonized, moving her hand as if it floated in the air.

"She's never coming back."

Nadia looked around. "Who?"

Manal tsked in the Egyptian shorthand for *No*. "The song. She will marry someone else. Her father won't let her.

61

Old story, *nafs el hekaya al-adeema*. Your father will let you marry who you like? You may be Canadian, but he is not."

"I doubt he would care either way."

"The lost father," Manal nodded, remembering. "Did you find him, *ya Nadia*?"

"Yes. No. Yes and no."

Manal pulled a bag of *liblib*, roasted seeds that could have been pumpkin or watermelon, from her pocket, cracked them deftly in her mouth and spit the shells out towards the water. "So he is a spy after all."

Nadia laughed. "He is not a spy."

"Did you have a nice visit? Did he take you to all the tourist spots?"

Nadia wrestled with the seeds but only succeeded in pulverizing them into tasteless shards. She got up and spat over the railing, muttering an apology over her shoulder. Manal joined her at the water's edge. A restaurant boat was moored a hundred metres away, red paper lamps strung like Christmas lights overhead.

"He wanted to see me but underneath that he didn't want to see me. Happy to see me, then happy to see me go. I guess I wanted more. I don't know, I feel like such a baby." She stopped. She should not be telling her life story to a stranger, a woman who likely knew nothing about fractured families and stupid quests. "I'm sorry. Why would you even care or know what I mean? God, I am being very boring."

"It's okay Nadia, *malesh*. You came to Egypt for your family and you are disappointed. I understand."

Manal turned so her back was to the water and propped her elbows up on the iron railing. The street lamps and passing cars took turns swiping along her face, changing its colour and contours from one second to the next. She seemed transfixed by the music, her hands moving rhythmically with the song, back and forth, up and down, like a conductor. Nadia had an urge to step in closer, to enter whatever private circle Manal was defining with her fingers, to feel the imperceptible breeze of her hands against her own, to hear the music through her skin.

"Nadia?"

"Yes?"

"I think you need to be in Egypt for yourself, not for your father."

"What?"

"Did you see the Pyramids? No. Did you see the Old City? *La*. Did you go to Luxor? *La*. Alexandria? Sinai? Cairo Tower? Did you see the mosque of Ibn Tulun? Did you go to *Khan el Khalile*?"

"Wait, is that the market? Yes, I think we went there. Well, near there." But she had no idea.

"Of course, *yanni*," Manal said dismissively. "Did he buy you a papyrus? *Ya rob*. That is too typical." She shook her head. "Listen to me. I see your Egyptian heart. Okay, your Palestinian heart. You have not yet been in Egypt. You cannot leave here without ever being here."

"I can come back."

"Really? When?" Her face was open, teasing, beckoning, even daring. "And where will I be?"

Nadia squinted at her. "What do you mean where will I be?"

But Manal broke eye contact. A fish had got away, a spell was broken. She pointed with her chin farther down the Corniche to where a red and white neon light dangled by one hook over a kiosk and flashed above the heads of a group of men pressing against the window. "Hungry?"

Not waiting for an answer, she pushed off the railing, returning a minute later with two *shwarmas* and two bottles of Coke. The thin slices of meat tasted like they had been marinating in a succulent mix of spices and oil for years, aged like wine. They ate in silence, as if Manal's words had pulled up something that then had to be let go, a deep-water fish that would suffocate at the surface if they weren't careful. Nadia reproached herself. What did she know of Egypt, of intimacy or friendliness or even honesty? Her father, with his smiles and grand gestures, had no interest in claiming her. And now Manal, with her sidelong looks, lingering touches, her whispers and murmurs and even promises—it left her confused, almost as dizzy as she had been that night at the gallery. She didn't know if Manal's presence was making the world spin faster, or stop spinning altogether. Either way, it shattered her equilibrium and made her want to reach out again for walls, for railings, for a human being.

"Won't your mother be worried?" she finally asked, needing to make conversation but also cognizant of having tested Manal's boundaries once before.

"She's sleeping. And my uncle is in Port Said on business."

"Where do you live?"

"Over there, Miss Detective." She pointed east. "*Misr al Gadida*. Also known as Heliopolis."

Nadia shivered involuntarily and pulled her shoulders up. She wished for a scarf around her neck. An arm around her shoulder. Daniel crossed her mind. Not Daniel's arm.

"I painted something like this once."

"Like what?"

"Men eating *shwarma* at night." Manal held up her sandwich, turned it around and stared at it. "So much appetite. Look at them, quiet and hungry. Where is their family? Where are their wives? Are they coming from work? What price do they pay to be here eating *shwarma* alone, late at night, famished?"

"I'd love to see it."

"Brigitte hated it. She said 'Les étrangers don't need to see this. If you want to paint folklore go to Luxor.'"

"Ouch."

"Did you notice anything about the art at the gallery, Nadia? Did you notice that the Moscow-trained artists paint Soviet-looking peasants? Or that the French-trained artists put a pond in every painting? Or the ones that just stay here—do you know what they paint? Do you?"

"No."

"They paint abstract! Do you know why?" Her arms opened wide, then closed again. "They have nothing to say. No one has anything to say." She exhaled for a long time. "We live in a puppet show where to speak is to be silenced. There is no difference."

The murmurings of the sandwich-eating men reached them where they sat, driftwood words scraping the shore with no consequences. Manal fiddled with the paper around her food.

Then her voice changed, became quieter, softer, a little fearful. "I have a question to ask you, Nadia, Canadian girl. A favour. You can say no."

She said nothing for a long time. Nadia waited, almost unbearably curious.

"I would like to paint you." Manal pushed the rest of her sandwich into her mouth. "Naked." She spoke quickly as she chewed. "I finished school two years ago and there is no opportunity to paint live models. And nude ones? They never let us do that. It's not illegal, of course, we will not be arrested, don't worry, but I would never be allowed. Maybe if I went to AUC, but not at an Egyptian school. Cairo University is not exactly international institution. I need to be taken seriously, more seriously. All the applications they want a portfolio, and I have one, but it is unfinished it is amateur. Maybe I need much more serious art I need …"

"Naked?"

She was surprised by her own embarrassment. She imagined Manal behind a canvas, her eyes peering over the edge, boring into her own, dropping to her body, outlining the edges of her cold limbs with melting charcoal. She managed to keep staring at the water and fought back a pressing grin.

"But I'm leaving in two days, Manal," she finally said with genuine distress, remembering, regretting.

"That is enough time," Manal said, shaking her head vigorously. "Can you come tomorrow? *Bukra*? I don't work, the gallery is closed, it is Friday. Maybe it is my only chance. My only chance, *ya Nadia*. I know it is a lot to ask. But you seem, *yanni* I don't know, you seem open. From the first minute. I can imagine things. I don't know, it's silly."

"A chance for a show?" Nadia cringed at the thought of naked paintings of herself hanging at the Mashrabiya.

"No, a scholarship." Manal stood up. "I have to get out of here. Now. Let's go." Then she spoke a long steady stream of Arabic which, Nadia realized by the end of it, were curses.

Nadia woke slowly the next morning, an incessant honking rising from the street below till she could ignore it no longer. The telephone rang, but by the time she picked it up it was too late. The red light on one of its buttons began flashing immediately. As she suspected, when she called down to reception she was told that her father had left her a message. He wanted to meet her for lunch, she was to call him. The receptionist's high voice was annoying, a caricature of a female voice, like so many women in Egypt. Except for Manal. Her low voice was a consolation in a country determined to infantilize its females. She wanted to hear that voice again, perhaps be reminded that Egypt, Palestine, even her entire trip, was bigger than her father. She had been doing herself a disservice, being so dependent on his approval and attention. She doubted that her father, twenty-five years ago a new student in Canada, had moped about and pined for his family. Why should she? She didn't call him back.

An hour later Nadia met Manal at the closed gallery. She had followed instructions and brought a towel.

"I will paint you in perfumes and powders."

Manal unrolled a frayed canvas sleeve and laid out an array of small bottles and vials, each looking a hundred years old and glistening with ground metal and stone: a dozen variations on the colour brown, just as many more blues and greens and reds, all of it makeup powders she had been collecting from the markets.

"*Kohl*."

The word had two syllables in her mouth, the breathy *h* stayed in her throat with promise of more. She poured it into the palm of her left hand and added drops of amber, a heady scent released from another vial.

"*Anbar*."

With her thumb, she drew the outline of Nadia's body on the large strip of paper tacked on the wall.

"*Al Azraq*."

She shook glistening blue powder from another vial onto her palm. Her voice was deep and steady, her eyes never meeting Nadia's.

"*Sifrun*."

She rubbed copper-coloured powder over the blue, deepening and darkening the flesh. Manal's face was stained where she touched herself and the perfumes spilt more than once over her clothes. She was oblivious to everything but the smearing of the paper.

Mineral dust filled the air, landed on the floor. Manal wiped her hands with an oiled rag every time she changed colour. She stood in profile, her shoulders and arms held up, one hand painting and smudging, the other outstretched as a palette, her skirt hiked up, her feet bare. Nadia was mesmerized by the long muscles that shadow-danced in and around her shirt, up her arm, down her legs. There was an equine firmness to the line of the jaw and the long profile of her nose as she turned her head back and forth from paper to Nadia to paper again. She breathed deeply, expanding her chest like an athlete. Thick lengths of flesh and bone sharing the arm in a rippling choreography that ended at the fingers.

"Stop moving," Manal ordered.

This moment does not belong to me, Nadia thought, and it was an immense relief. She was learning something new, a feeling of submission to the will of another. The ecstasy and divinity of submission. Translated literally, the word Islam meant submission, but to the will of God. Nadia didn't know much about Islam and hadn't really cared to explore—until now. She could see that there was a beauty and an expansiveness in submission, in giving over to something. It felt almost heretical to think in such a way. Her mother would not be impressed.

Manal took many steps back and stood still for the first time in hours. "This is how I will always remember you."

"Can I keep it?"

"No. It stays in Egypt."

They said their goodbyes at the bus *centrale*, halfway between the gallery and the hotel. Manal would not smile. But at the last minute she leaned her body on Nadia's arm and whispered something into her ear. "What was that? I didn't understand," Nadia said.

"It wasn't words."

She touched Nadia's arm, the same spot, kept her fingers there. Then ran for her bus.

The taxi driver put her luggage in the trunk, then took a different route to the airport than when she had arrived. They straddled the Nile this time, going north to the outer highway and turning east towards the desert. More than enough time, he assured her. "Pretty this way! Pretty to say goodbye to *Misr*." The sun rose slowly over the city's crowded rooftops and clotheslines. *Misr*. She wondered how *Misr* and Egypt came to be known for the same country. But now she was leaving, and now she would never know.

The lineup at the EgyptAir counter was short, and she had her boarding pass in hand in a matter of minutes. It was still early so she decided she'd better do some souvenir shopping, at least get something for Daniel. She found a coffee-table book, *Mosques of Upper Egypt*. He wouldn't care much for the subject matter but it fit other criteria: it was large, heavy, and looked expensive. She paid for it with zero enthusiasm, stuffed it in her bag with even less. She was angry. Angry at her father, angry that nothing had come of this trip, angry that she was going back with nothing resolved between them. Angry that she'd have to explain it all to Daniel, then explain it all again to her mother. See, I could have come with you, Daniel would say. I told you not to bother, her mother would say. Buried under that indignation was a helpless shock that she might never see Manal again.

She stood still as people and luggage carts flowed around her. The way forward seemed as blocked as if an earthquake had left an abyss between where she was and where she was supposed to be going. Up on the flight board her number blinked 9:05 9:05 9:05 9:05. Then the numbers disappeared, leaving an empty blackness. A second later they were replaced and flashed something else: Delayed Delayed Delayed. A shudder went through her, the tightness in her head suddenly released, and an otherworldly urge burst forth. With a jump she ran back to the EgyptAir counter.

"Is it possible to change my ticket?" she asked breathlessly.

It was the same man as before. He looked at his watch and smiled. "You are fine, the plane did not leave."

"No, I know. But can I switch it to another date? Can I leave another day?"

"Which day?"

71

"Oh." She dropped her heels back down to the ground. "I don't know."

He flipped through schedules in his binder, cross-referenced with another binder. "The next flight to Paris is in eight hours. What is your connection?" He studied the boarding pass. "New York. Okay, let me see. We have a flight in three days that is very good timing for the New York flight. And you have another connection, I see. Montreal. Let me look."

Nadia began bouncing again, afraid she would lose her nerve. "I don't want to go back," she blurted. "Ever."

He nodded indifferently. "No problem, *Mademoiselle*. Would you like an open ticket? It must be used within a year. It has a cost however."

"Oh my god, yes."

"Yes," he repeated.

He tore up her ticket and boarding pass and proceeded to create another one, filling in page after page of detail. Finally, long minutes later, he folded it in three, placed it precisely in the envelope, and handed it to her.

"Welcome to Egypt," he said. "Again. Enjoy your stay. If you stay longer than three months you will need a visa."

"A visa?"

"Yes," he said, but waved away her concern. "Easy, very easy. No problem for you."

She instructed the taxi driver to take the Ring Road. He protested—it was longer—but she leaned back into the seat and watched the city pass by in reverse. She felt different—settled and brave. The confusion and cacophony of Cairo rumbled and opened up for her, parted like the Red Sea. She wanted to jump up and down, scream, dance. The driver slid in a dusty cassette and music played. "Louder, *min fadlak,*" she said. Louder. Please.

4

the jaguar who outwitted three men

Nadia wondered who would call her first. Though she was obliged to make international calls at the hotel's centrale, in her room she was able to receive them. Daniel would be at Dorval airport by now, she knew, much earlier than necessary, checking arrivals against the flight number written on the palm of his hand. He'd speak to an agent, first politely then adamantly: were they sure there wasn't another connecting flight from Egypt via New York? He'd call her mother from the airport, ask her if she'd had any news. Clare would assume that Nadia had simply missed her flight—Egyptian time and all that, Clare knew all about it, she'd say, after all she had married one. She'd dig out Bishara's old number. It's what parents did. How would her father react when Clare reached him? Would he feel called out, hunted and found, caught, seen? Or just annoyed and burdened and confused? Would his first instinct be to deny everything? She's *your* daughter, we only had lunch once or twice, okay three times, how could you let her come like that, why did you not tell me, you should have warned me.

Nadia stopped. The full impact of her decision hit her. Daniel, Clare, Bishara, none of them would understand. She ran down to the telephone centrale and placed a call. As expected, as she desperately hoped, she got his machine. *Daniel*, she spoke quickly—wanting to give the impression of urgency and decisiveness, worried that even from five thousand miles away he might cut in and spoil her plans—*I missed my flight. Well, not missed. I am coming home later, I rebooked another flight. I don't have a date yet. It's kind of crazy, I think it's crazy. You'll think it's crazy. But there is nothing to worry about. Please call Clare for me. I'll talk to you in a couple of days. All is well. I have loads of souvenirs for you.* Then she hung up.

Back up in her room she picked up the phone to call her father and was assaulted by the full-throated growl of the Egyptian dial tone. She hung up, did not try again. She had stayed but wasn't ready to do the one thing that followed from it: see her father. There was even an urge to punish him with her absence. She would be here and not here, in his country but not available, a phone call away but not reachable. His daughter, still unfamiliar. But he had to know that and he wouldn't know that unless she called.

She tried again. After many rings Noor answered. Making her English as simple as possible, Nadia told her that she was in Cairo, that she hadn't left, that she was back at the hotel and had decided to stay a little while longer. But also that she was busy and had much to do. That she'd get in touch with him later, much later. Days, hard to say. Hard to say, she said again, repeating words and phrases like he did.

The emptiness of the new room mocked her. It was slightly smaller than the one she'd had before and lower down, on the third floor this time. This time, there was a sliver of the Nile to the right, but directly in front there it was, beyond the roundabout, beyond the hundred-foot neon Coca-Cola sign in Arabic, beyond the soldiers, the donkeys, the black taxis, the tourist buses, the convulsing traffic, the mirages that made make-believe out of the horizon. There it was, *Sharaa* Champollion.

Would her feet carry her there on their own, she wondered. Or were they still holding on to memories from when she was ten? Would they take her to the gallery or veer off and find the ice cream that tasted like roses, or the noisy cinema where she and her mother sat out a scorching afternoon, the floor slippery with pumpkin-seed shells and spit? Or maybe she'd end up at the train station where they had watched a small flock of chickens board one of the cars in the back. She had kept vigil on the doors that separated her car from the ones following, willing the disciplined chickens to please enter. They had been travelling to Alexandria, its beaches a respite from the thermal hell that is August in Cairo. That dark apartment, walking distance from the sea, whose curtains and shutters remained closed to the prying sun. Josephine's apartment.

Nadia hesitated before exiting the hotel lobby. How odd that Josephine, the only member of her father's family still in Egypt, hadn't figured into her trip. If she was old then, she'd be elderly now, fifteen years later. But this was the land of four-thousand-year-old Pyramids and two-thousand-year-old feuds and five-hundred-year-old alleyways and hundred-year-old *bowabs*. She must call Josephine one of these days, she thought, as her feet led her onto Champollion, then up the steps of the Galerie Mashrabiya.

Manal, Tewfiq, and Brigitte were hunched over the tall counter table. They raised their eyebrows in matching arcs when she entered. Only Tewfiq moved towards her. "*Ahlan*," he said warmly, and other things she didn't understand. He brought her a stool to join them, then a bottle of Coke from the fridge. Happy with himself, he nodded to Brigitte to continue. Manal asked a thousand questions with her eyes.

"*Bon*." Brigitte turned over a sheet of paper. "Ahmed El Haq has sent us an incomplete application. And Eman Badawy, this is her third year applying. For the third time her work is of no interest to me."

She put the application in a pile but Manal blocked it with her hand. "I think her drawings show great improvement. Look at these pictures. The portraits are very bold," she said, holding up a slide.

"They are depressing."

"Therefore bold."

Brigitte inhaled pensively, but then nodded, clucked her tongue, drummed her fingers on the table, kept nodding. "Good point," she finally said. Tewfiq wrote the name down on a list.

It took them another hour to make their way through the applications. Tewfiq brought Nadia a second Coke. By then she was jittery with caffeine, sugar, and nerves. When they closed the binder, Brigitte made a few phone calls, smoked another cigarette, then left. Tewfiq offered Nadia another bottle.

"*La, shukran,*" she said, declining, putting her hand on her heart.

Manal raised her hands and twirled them in an interrogative gesture. "*Eh da, ya Nadia?*"

"I changed my flight."

"You missed the airplane?"

"No, I *changed* it. I'm staying. I don't know how long, but for now I am staying." She shifted awkwardly in the creeping awareness that this news might have only passing interest for Manal. "I just wanted to tell you. But it's okay, I see you're busy." She turned to go but didn't move. She was out of decisions.

Tewfiq, having understood enough, stood up and clapped. "Welcome to Egypt," he said. "Welcome to Egypt!"

"Really," Manal said, more flatly than Nadia could bear. "What will you do? For how long you are here?"

"I don't know. First, I have to find another hotel. The Nile Hilton is too pricey to stay there any longer. I guess I'll stay in Cairo as long as it takes." Then she added, realizing *it* could be anything: "Whatever *it* is."

Manal frowned and nodded. Tewfiq said something Nadia did not understand, but his tone was gentle and warm, entirely accepting. If for no other reason, Nadia wanted to learn Arabic so she could understand Tewfiq. But for now she was crushed by Manal's unwelcoming demeanor. She felt silly and humiliated, a lost child in a strange city. She needed something from Manal, needed it desperately, but her inability to name it was sapping whatever little energy she had. "I think I am keeping you from work. I'll just go."

"We are choosing artists," Manal said. "The gallery has a very popular group show in the spring and we were looking at the submissions. It is the most popular art show in the country, *yanni*. At least."

"At least," Tewfiq echoed.

"Everyone comes. Artists, Egyptians, expats, students, foreigners, even tourists." She paused. Was that a dig? Nadia wondered. "You can help us. If you like, *yanni*."

"Oh?"

"Sure, sure. We can't pay you. But you can come and help us. If you like. Something to do while in Egypt." Manal seemed at a loss, but there was a smile at the corner of her mouth. "*Yanni*."

"I really don't want to intrude," Nadia said. But she did. She wanted to intrude and make herself comfortable till everything about this gallery, this moment, this woman was familiar.

Manal stood up and went into the back room, returning with a large, thick manila envelope. "In fact, I have a job just for you. It is my application to study art in Paris. You could help me. *C'est compliqué*." She spread its contents over the table: flyers, forms and instructions for a scholarship at the Institut d'études supérieures des arts in Paris. Nadia's French, while excellent spoken, was only middling written and read. It was a language that would eat you up for breakfast if you didn't master the conjugation and its rigorous orthography. But she didn't tell Manal that.

"This is going to be the year," Manal said, leaning in closer. She lowered her voice to a murmur but her eyes flashed and danced as if in a ballroom. "I will paint more, I will be in this show, and I will get this scholarship. I can feel it. The sands are shifting. Do you know how I know all this?"

"How?"

"Because I have met you and you did not leave."

The room darkened, Tewfiq vanished, the cacophony of background honking disappeared. A body only inches away vibrated and ululated and melted into the air, coating her with its salt. "How strange we met," Manal said, holding her gaze.

"Yes," Nadia said, working with all her strength to slow down her breathing. "How very strange."

At the end of the afternoon, Manal took her arm. "Where do you want to go? It is your first day in Cairo."

"I was just going to go back to the hotel. I don't know. It's been a long day."

"No problem. I shall bring you."

They walked with the same cadence, left foot, right

foot, left, right. Nadia didn't know if it was because they were unconsciously mirroring each other, the way walkers sometimes do, or if it was something that happened when strolling arm in arm, shoulder to shoulder, hip to hip with someone who had the ability to electrify your insides. Manal was athletic and decisive in her movements, possessing a body suited to running and jumping and throwing balls from one end of a field to the next. Beside her, Nadia felt both safe and matched. It was an exquisite combination.

"Have you ever played sports?" Nadia asked.

"Of course, haven't you? Name a sport, I played it. In school, of course."

"I didn't know there were sports for women in Egypt."

"It was a girl's school. Unfortunately, it is not a girl's world. Now I just paint. I have a very strong right arm," she smiled.

They stopped at the steps of the Nile Hilton, its windswept 1950s turquoise blue architecture making Nadia feel that they were instantly glamorous and out of time. They should have scarves tied under their chins and cigarette holders in their hands as they drove a Mustang convertible somewhere on the Mediterranean coast.

"I've never been inside the Nile Hilton," Manal said. "Never in the rooms."

"You want to see? Come on."

Manal's eyes were bright with curiosity as she looked in the closet, peered in the bathroom, and bounced up and down on the edge of the bed. Finished with that, she opened the mini-bar and took out a small bottle of wine. They stood at the window together and passed the bottle back and forth, sipping and, in Manal's case, grimacing.

"*Ya salam*, look at that Nile over there. It is ugly, is it not? Don't misunderstand me, Nadia, it is beautiful, I know it is beautiful. We are proud of our river. But look at it, *il meskina*, the poor thing. It has nothing to do, it doesn't even move. It is a dead river. Do you know it used to flood, really flood? All the way to the desert, *yanni*." She took another sip, sucked in her lips. "Until the Aswan Dam, of course. Now, we have the magic of electricity, *il hamd'il allah*, but no life in our magic river. Which is more important, *ya Nadia*? Electricity for our televisions or a river to keep us alive? Which?" She drank again. "There is a real Cairo hidden somewhere, Nadia. But you have to know how to look. Everything else is *maquillage*." She turned the bottle upside down. "I am not used to such fancy hotel rooms and I am not used to such bad wine. Actually, I am not used to wine at all. I should go home." But she sat down at the foot of the bed and patted it for Nadia to join her. "Ouf, my head! Is it the heights or the …"—she read the back of the bottle—"...*appellation d'origine contrôlée?*"

She spoke French perfectly, her accent softening the language and giving it space to breathe. Nadia instantly preferred it to the hard and rapid joual of Montreal.

"Nadia, I am very glad you are in Cairo. I need a friend, if you must know. Do you need a friend?"

Nadia chuckled. "Yes, I could use a friend. I think that would be nice."

"Good. We are friends."

She shook Nadia's hand but then didn't let go. She curled her fingers through Nadia's, left them there. "You have an artist's hands. Are you an artist? Or a worker's hands. They are hands for *doing*. I like that. It is very refreshing. You don't wear nail polish."

"No."

"I thought all foreigners wore nail polish. And your wrist, look. It is strong. You don't wear a watch. I thought all foreigners..."

Nadia laughed but her mouth was dry. She stared at their hands, brave hands, hands doing things she could barely believe. "I used to have one but it stopped working. Maybe I'll get one in Cairo."

"Yes, yes, a watch to tell the time in Cairo. That is a contradiction."

Manal's profile made Nadia ache. The long, straight line of her nose led to the fullest and most inviting mouth she had ever seen. But it was the smile that extinguished Nadia's breath. Perfect teeth behind a crooked, slightly lopsided grin. The contrast between serious Manal and smiling Manal was so great that each expression fully eclipsed the other when it appeared. Like the magic trick her father used to play on her as he raised and lowered his hand, hiding his face and changing his features from happy to sad and surprised. Nadia shivered with a laser-like awareness that informed her as to the business of every hair on her arm, every millimetre of space between them that was occupied not by fabric but by longing. Their eyes ensnared each other, held each other down, chiselled each other till only softness remained.

"*Est-ce que je peux t'embrasser?*"

Nadia knew instantly why she spoke French. Another language was needed, another lexicon that wouldn't, for the moment at least, know what it was doing and yank them back from the *falaise,* from plunging over the cliff.

"*Oui.*"

Then Manal's lips were on hers, lightly, like a corner of fabric that had been flapping in the wind but now was finally settled. A hand gripped her arm and she inhaled sharply. Then again when the other hand found her back, then again as it roamed her body, its progression leaving imperceptible indentations, tracks to follow in the dark. They lowered themselves slowly onto the bed keeping the same positions, feet still on the ground. Except for their mouths now, nothing else dared move. Manal broke the kiss first, got up to lean on her elbow. Her fingers traced the outline of Nadia's jaw, her lips, then up the ridge of her nose, parting at her eyebrows. "Hmmm," she murmured, discovering. "I…I…*Ana…Anaa…*" She drew out the word until it was less of a word and more of an intonation. "I like you, Nadia." The declaration soothed them both, oil on parched skin. "I am glad you are staying in Cairo." She leaned over and kissed her forehead.

She stood up. "I must go. I am sorry."

Her departure left the room chilled and lifeless. Nadia could barely move. She contented herself with the traffic lights streaking along the walls and ceiling. Though it intruded, the city was far away, unreal, unfathomable. Her breath came in tiny bursts. Letters, not words. The phone in her room rang late in the night, jolting her awake.

"Nadia, is it true?" Manal's voice was soft, tentative.

"Is what true?"

"Did I kidnap you and make you mine?"

As if bravery had found purchase, Nadia woke the next morning determined to see her father. She called his apartment and let it ring. Noor told her that he was at work. Silence suspended in the air between them like a dragonfly until, carried away by a sudden breeze, someone hung up first. She called again in the evening.

"I do not understand, Nadia. I thought you return to Canada already. Sunday? No? I was so surprise that you call."

"I changed my ticket to open. I just have a stupid job, no one cares if I don't go back. So I have nothing keeping me in Montreal." Not even Daniel. Then she added, because he didn't: "Welcome to Egypt."

"Yes, yes. *Ahlan, ahlan wa sahlan.* But how strange. You are in Cairo now. Again. Still. Still! It is very surprising."

"There is a lot that is surprising, believe me." She waited for him to say something about that—*what is surprising you, ya Nadia? What has turned your life in directions you barely knew existed? What?* "Hey, I was wondering," she said. "Is Tante Josephine still in Alexandria?"

"Josephine? Yes, yes. She is in *Iskandraya*, the old apartment. She is still there."

"Do you visit her?"

"Me? No, not really. Not since *zaman*—a long time. I am busy, much work, and…" He stopped abruptly.

"And you have a new kid and a new family and life is very busy."

"Yes, Nadia. I have child."

"I was thinking that maybe I would visit her. I'd like to go to Alexandria while I'm here. Maybe you'd want to come?"

"Visit Josephine? Nadia, I must tell you. She does not know. She is very conservative."

She imagined her restless and anxious father wandering through the apartment as far as the cord would take him, then back again, pacing, one hand pulling at his hair like loose threads.

"She doesn't know anything? How interesting."

"Not interesting," he said. "Bad."

"Yes, bad," she chuckled.

"So, Nadia."

"So, Baba," she said. She had to smile. It was how they had always deflated arguments. So, Nadia. So, Baba. Suddenly: a bridge.

"You come for supper soon?"

"Yes, I'd love to. Good."

He laughed. "Good."

5

return! before the birds arise

The next time Nadia walked up the gallery steps everything had changed. The heavy door on the street opened
the same slow way it always did. There were still fourteen
narrow steps. *Wahid, itneen, talata, arba, khamsa, sitta, sabaa,
tamani, tisaa, ashara, hidashr, itnashr, talatashr, arbatashr.* The
same echo as she reached the top. The same large white
room filled with art, leading to the smaller room, then another slightly smaller. But this time all of it was different,
all of it led to her, the woman she had kissed.

Manal looked up. Their smiles were flinty and secretive, mostly shy. A few people were combing the gallery
walls, taking in the paintings, making the odd inquiry.
Nadia, hesitating, wandered. Every painting, every vantage point offered a different angle from which to view
Manal. When it didn't, she moved somewhere else. A
woman waited at the desk for Manal to look up from papers and answer a question. They spoke in Arabic. Nadia
could count to fourteen but could not make out more
than just a few words. As she conversed, Manal shifted
her focus and captured Nadia with her eyes. Unable to

move, Nadia lowered herself onto the window bench, its wooden lattice dappling the floor in front of her with light and shadow.

"*Mashrabiya*." Manal, suddenly beside her and radiating heat, was whispering in her ear. "These are old windows, it gives the gallery its name. The *mashrabiya* were designed so women could look out but no one could see them." Manal watched intently as Nadia's fingers slowly traced the warm curving wood, following intricate patterns and holes that repeated and repeated like a mantra.

Outside, the night was warmer than it had been in the gallery, where a half-dozen fans had kept them cool. They crossed the boulevards, waded through the bus crowds, took no notice of either the Egyptian Museum or the Mogamma, the massive Soviet-style concrete government building that flanked the Midan. They walked in a silence so sweet it made them thirsty. In the hotel lobby Manal whispered "*Limon*" in Nadia's ear and, grinning, led her on a detour to the terrace café where she ordered two *asir limones*. The cold glasses condensed in their hands as they rode up to the third floor. Sipping quietly, they barely took notice of the people getting in and out of the elevator.

Manal took the key from Nadia and opened the door. She took the glass from Nadia's hand and put it on the bedside table. She took the bag from Nadia's shoulder and let it fall to the floor. They reached for each other like new vines on the first hot day of summer. For a brief moment Nadia remembered how the triplexes in Montreal, crisscrossed all winter long with dead and bony branches, would be blanketed in green tendrils almost overnight, signalling the city's return to summer. An entire season was passing over and through her body.

"Nadia." Manal's mouth was at her ear, her arms running the length of her arms, her breasts at her breasts. "Did you ever do this before? You know, with a woman…"

"No."

"I have."

Manal met her lips again, took them, pushed her body into Nadia's, held her wrists tightly. "Do you want to stop?" There was a fierceness in her voice that frightened Nadia, who had been underestimating everything, everything, everything. Manal had seen her, Manal wanted her, Manal knew what she wanted. The thrill and mystery and momentum almost made her lose her mind.

"*Abadan, ya Manal*. Never. I do not want to stop."

Manal got up at some point and called her mother. A cart clickety-clacked its way down the hallway.

"What did you tell her?" Nadia asked when she crawled back into bed.

"That I was staying at the Nile Hilton with my new Canadian friend because it is so late. She was excited for me," Manal laughed. "She reminded me of something."

"What's that?"

"That my parents stayed here on their honeymoon. She didn't remember which floor." Manal lay on her back and raised one arm as if it were a mast. It swayed gently, the moonlight playing on her skin. "They weren't supposed to marry. My mother is from a quiet family and my father was too political for them. Even then. Do you know the Suez Canal?"

"Yes, I think so. It's in the Sinai, right?"

"General Gamal Abdul Nasser took the Suez back from the British in, a long time ago, 1956 *mumkin*. The British, of course, were not happy..."

"They had qualms," Nadia interrupted.

"I don't know. They invaded Egypt, and Israel and France invaded us too. Can you believe it? To take *our* canal. My father was very involved, not in the army but he fought in his own way. My mother's family just wanted peace and quiet. But peace, *ya Nadia*, rarely comes with quiet."

"Hmmm." Nadia was mesmerized by Manal's arm, its sinewy hardness, the thick cushiony skin, the soft dark hairs that formed a contour even in the darkness. She reached up and caressed it, then pulled it down, laid it across her body. She didn't want peace, or quiet either. "So you've done this before," she whispered.

"Surprised?"

"Yes."

"What do you think happens in a country of marriage and only marriage? So many petting affairs, *yanni*."

"So many what?"

"Married ladies, married men, lots of evening rendezvous," she laughed. She mimicked a wife talking with her husband. "*Yalla bye-bye* Mohammed, I will do the dishes

90

when I get back.—Where are you going, Fatma?—*Yanni*, Iman is still having problems with her laundry machine, do not worry Mohammad, I will help her.—Again?—*Malesh, ya Mohammed*, the clothes are dirty. See you tomorrow." With a screech she flopped back on the bed laughing.

The phone woke them early the next morning. Nadia mouthed *Your mother?* But it could also be *her* mother, or even Daniel. She picked it up and was relieved to hear Bishara's voice. He was sounding looser and more upbeat than when they last spoke. He and Noor would like to invite her for supper tomorrow night, he told her. Manal jumped up to make coffee in the little machine on the counter, Nadia's long T-shirt barely covering her bottom.

"Tomorrow?" She made a face at Manal. "I—I might be busy." Manal shook her head: *No, no, it's okay, go.* "Um, can I bring a friend, Baba?"

Manal's eyes opened wide.

"Ahh ha," Bishara laughed. "I see! Yes, yes, Nadia. Bring your friend, he is welcome."

Nadia rolled her eyes. "Not a he," she said, but he was talking over her. "What can I bring?"

"What do you mean? Is okay, your friend is invited."

"No, I mean, like wine or bread or something." She knew right away she had gotten it wrong, like singing flat in a melody of sharps. It was a Montreal custom, a Montreal song. He had thought Canadians uncouth and completely devoid of proper manners. Bring food when you are invited for dinner at someone else's house? He invoked the saints and the prophets.

"Do you want to insult Noor by bringing bread? *Yalla* see you later. Bye-bye."

"So I will meet your father," Manal said after they hung up. "Wine or bread?"

"Never mind," Nadia rolled her eyes. "Listen, you don't have to come. It was an awkward conversation. I understand if you are busy. He lives way out in Nasser City, it's complicated..."

"*Iscouti,*" she said. Shut up. "I am happy to come."

"Well, alright then."

Manal insisted that Nadia come to the gallery, shaking her head, twisting her hands, and opening her eyes wide: What else do you have to do, her entire body was saying, except spend the day with me?

With the vernissage for *Shebab ya Shebab* approaching, there was an excitement at the gallery that Nadia found irresistible. Brigitte trusted Manal completely and so was rarely there. For the most part, she came in an hour a day, made a phone call, smoked a cigarette, gave instructions, frowned a few times, then left.

Final decisions were being made about placement, and who the next person on the waiting list was now that Mediha Saad and Georges Khoury had dropped out. They had a poster to design and print, invitations to mail, journalists to contact. They even had a long list of international art schools that were to be sent a flyer and poster for the show accompanied by cover letters in English and French.

"That's smart," Nadia mused. "Putting yourselves on the map like that. Brigitte has the long view of her artists, I see."

Tewfiq shook his head. "Manal's idea," he said.

Manal chuckled, pulled her aside. "I have a secret to tell you," she said. "I will be in this show."

"Isn't that only natural? You work here and you're an artist."

No, no, no, Manal corrected her. "It is not so natural. Brigitte is always, how you say, resistant. Apparently, I am here to help the artists, not *be* an artist. It is a conflict of interesting. Brigitte has to appear, *yanni*, irreproachable."

"She has no problem being that."

"She is an expert. She is very good so I have to be better."

"More irreproachable? Please, no."

"No, better at being a good great amazing talented Egyptian artist." She waved a handful of brushes in the air. "I am *shebab* too."

"What does it mean, *shebab*? What does the name of the show mean?"

"*Shebab* is youth. *Shebab ya Shebab* is like saying, let's see: O youth, come to life, take over the world, do it quickly before the rivers run dry and my heart stops forever." She put the brushes back in the jar. "Nadia," she said, now solemnly. "I need to say something."

"I'm listening."

"I mean, I need to say something in my art. It needs to be…meaningful. Do you know? Not just perfect colour, not just brush this way or brush that way, not just composition. It has to speak. More than speak, it has to shout." She came out from behind the desk. "I want to go underneath," she said in a softer voice.

"Underneath?"

"Underneath everything, you know. Underneath your blouse."

"*Manal*."

Tewfiq, stapling a frame together at the back counter, raised his head then quickly lowered it.

Abandoning the seduction, she sat down. Nadia was slightly disappointed. "I'm serious," she continued. "All our life we are taught to pay attention to the wrong things. Think like this, behave like that, be careful what you say, be careful what people say about you. It's like, *yanni*, it's like, okay, it's like this: Imagine a Pyramid. How big it is, how impressive! But imagine if you never knew there was a passageway inside. Imagine, especially, imagine if you never knew it was built for death. For burial! You think it is high like the sun, that it reaches the sun. But it is really all about death. It blocks out the sun. *Fahimti*? Do you understand me? It blocks out the sun. That is the curse of the Pyramids."

Manal was the Pyramid, Nadia understood, rising and smooth and majestic, full of life, death, secret passages.

She struggled to pay attention to the words. She wanted that hand back on her chest, fiddling with the buttons of her shirt, a lopsided smile teasing and teasing and teasing. But Manal slapped her arm. "You are not even paying attention."

Tewfiq continued to labour with the frame. Nadia could see that he wasn't quite sure what to do next but dared not look up again.

"This is my year, Nadia. You are here, that is the first step. The second is to get my art in a show. And the third..." She paused. "The third is to leave this country of death and burial."

Tewfiq met Nadia's eyes. She wondered how much of this he could understand. Maybe the words themselves were not that important. There were other languages to decipher, and Tewfiq was giving the impression that he was fluent in the unspoken. He shrugged his shoulders, smiled softly.

"And you will help me," Manal continued. Then she slapped her knees and stood up, looked around for a moment as if reorienting herself, and joined Tewfiq and the frame. He showed her the piece that wasn't fitting.

They waited for him to leave. It was glorious being in the gallery alone. It echoed. Nadia stood in the middle of the main room, threw open her arms, and sang. *Habaytek bi sayf, habaytek bi shitti.*

"I've sung this song all my life and don't even know what it means."

"I loved you in summer," Manal said. "I loved you in winter. I waited for you in summer, I waited for you in winter. Your eyes are the summer, your eyes are the winter. Our meeting, my love, is beyond summer and winter."

She stepped into the middle of the room and began the song from the beginning, eyes closed, her voice steady and sonorous.

They left directly from the gallery. Nadia had wanted to go back to the hotel and change, even shower. A transition was needed before moving from her new, tentative, thrilling world to her other, still tentative, still thrilling, still new world. In any case, doing more than two things a day in Cairo seemed to require superhuman resolve. But Manal didn't want to waste time, insisting that the traffic would be worse if they didn't leave now. How can the roads be more congested, convoluted or cacophonic than they already are? Nadia wondered. It was as if Cairo traffic had been staged by a surrealist multidisciplinary performance artist.

"No really," she explained, as Manal was having trouble seeing the absurdity of the situation. "You don't just have a road with cars. First of all, half the cars are from the 1950s and held together with rope. Then you have goats wandering in front and behind the cars, donkeys urinating like fountains at every corner, a water buffalo hovering just on the edge like it's going to run you over, an entire family perched on one scooter, three men carrying a month's worth of bread on their heads, and everybody else crossing eight-lane highways on foot, dribbling between the traffic as if they were basketballs. I can't believe there aren't more accidents here."

Manal translated Nadia's rant for their cab driver. He snorted and proceeded to weave in and out of the cars around him, missing each one by an inch. Manal sat back and laughed. "See? Safe."

They rang the doorbell. It opened slowly, cautiously. Noor greeted them, the child balanced on one hip. "Say hello, Nora," she said quickly, masking her own nervousness.

She stepped aside and, after lengthy handshaking and cheek-kissing, invited them to sit in the living room. They fanned out along the low couch. Manal and Noor sat on either side of Nadia and made small conversation about— if she understood correctly—the view of the desert and the convenience of elevators. Without Bishara, they were in a state of suspended animation.

To everyone's visible relief, he approached from the long hallway, the *shib shib shib* shuffle of his slippers disconcertingly familiar. He could have been coming to tell Nadia it was bedtime, to ask her what she was reading, to entreat her to dance with him to Farid Al Atrash in the living room, to call her to taste his *mujadara*, the lentil dish he grew up eating and which he made, he swore, better than anyone. *Let me tell you about my village*, he would say, coming down the hallway. *Let me tell you about Ramallah.*

He'd sit her down and draw little maps of wavy lines for the streets and alleyways of his boyhood. As he drew he'd narrate. *This house, ya salam, this house was trouble. Abu Azim would never return our footeballs! Never, ya Nadia. Yikhrib betak, we'd say, curse him that Allah would destroy his house. Young boys do not know the connection they have to God. Did you know that? Children do not know they are God. And when they discover it, it is too late. So it was like that. God destroyed his house. We are all guilty. Khallas. Did you do your homework?*

Nadia's back was stiff with cemented emotion. For far too long she had missed her father, resented him, wondered about his life away from them, and concocted stories to fill in the gaps. Without him, she could not be Arab, she had no claim on Palestine, she spoke only English and French, was subject to her mother's less imaginative interpretations of behaviour, decorum, and sense of belonging. Had he really left them just for a job? Or was this the plan all along? She had wanted to believe he sacrificed his own comfort for their benefit. *I do this for you, I do this for family.* She believed him. More than that, an imperceptible burden was placed upon her: the weight of not wanting. She didn't want to spend his money or make him work a day more just to provide for her. It was because of her—his family—that he was in exile. She blamed herself. Perhaps she should have watched Clare a little more closely, how she had reacted the day he told them about a job for British Petroleum in Cairo. Oil, she scoffed. Then you might as well go to Saudi Arabia, get paid twice as much, no, ten times as much. Come with me, he said. Yes, yes!

Nadia wanted to go. She had wanted to leave so badly it hurt. Her mother would not have it. *Yikhrib betak*, Clare, she said to herself now. *Yikhrib betak*. Her house had been destroyed.

He kissed her three times on the cheeks and sat down next to Noor. He took the child and bounced her on his knee. She wondered if he had played with her like that. If Clare had let him. He laughed some more, Manal joined him, then Noor. Nora stared at Nadia and whimpered.

"Can I hold her?" Nadia had told herself she wouldn't do this, that this baby had nothing to do with her. But as the child was put in her arms she suddenly felt a surge of emotion. She had to choke back a sob and mask it with a little cooing noise. She held the child up in front of her, hid the one tear that was breaching an eyelid. The girl played with Nadia's cheeks, making her smile then making her laugh.

Bishara was smiling at them, but stiffly, Nadia thought. He seemed different, even since she'd seen him last. The bloom was off, maybe. There was a heaviness to his shoulders, his eyelids, his mouth. Whatever exoskeleton he'd been making use of on their last visits, he was without it today. Or maybe she was seeing him with adult eyes. After all, she had to admit, he was a multi-faceted person, with parts and pieces that were greater than their sum. Something like that. For all she knew, he could just be tired and very relaxed. The point was, she didn't really know him. The way he was interacting with Manal, for example. They spoke to each other without pretense or pressure. Was it the language? Was he accessing some part of himself that was not touchable in English? He professed to be fascinated by the gallery, he had never thought of modern Egyptian art before, he said, continually switching back to English for Nadia's benefit. If he had to think of Egyptian art he could only reference the crude drawings on papyrus paper that you could buy on any street corner. He found the idea of a French woman shepherding contemporary Egyptian art intriguing. He wanted to know about Manal's art, her vision for herself, her ambitions. How is it possible to make art relevant so it speaks to people, he asked, genuinely concerned that it might not. But it was a rhetorical question. He understood the challenge, he understood how hard it must be. He understood that even if it was not possible today, one day it would be. One day, he reassured Manal.

Nadia couldn't remember him asking so many questions about her school, or work, her apartment, or even Daniel once he learned about him. Was it the language?

Noor emerged from the kitchen for the third or fourth time, a tray of dishes in her hands again. She laid the plates on the low table between them. *Itfadalu*, Bishara said, sliding down to sit on the floor and welcoming them to do the same. The table was teeming with *fûl*, an Egyptian fava bean dish, *koshery*, stuffed vine leaves, chicken baked in onions and sumac, aromatic rice, and a bowl of tahini. Unlike the Palestinians, for whom *hummus bi tahini* was pureed chickpeas with tahini paste, the Egyptians, everyone's poor but talented cousin, omitted the chickpeas altogether, leaving only the spiced sesame paste. It was exquisite.

In spite of twinges of resentment, Nadia was grateful for Manal's presence; her unencumbered status allowed her to bear the burden of the room. She was charming and no one, least of all Nadia, could take their eyes off her. She never ran out of something to say: the beauty of the apartment, the beauty of the baby, the deliciousness of the food, the price of vegetables today, the efficacy of ceiling fans, the latest Egyptian movie, the melodrama of Samira Said's latest pop hit, *Abadan*. She sang a couple of verses in that entirely unabashed way that Egyptians have of entertaining each other, devoid of vanity or even the self-consciousness of performance. They clapped when she was done. Bishara searched for a song to follow hers.

"Sing us a Palestinian song," Manal said.

He seemed to think for a minute, then gave up. He looked to Noor for help but she was absorbed with the child, who was now fussing.

"A song of loss and despair," Manal added. "Surely there must be hundreds!"

Bishara brought his hands together and closed his eyes. Nadia knew what was coming next. He began. A familiar sound; she hadn't heard it in years. A hum first, throaty and tuneful, his head swaying slightly with the melody, his hands following like leaves floating back up to the tree. This was his song, the song he'd sing her, the song she fell asleep to. She didn't know the words or even what it meant. "It's our song," he'd say. "Shhhh, *yalla*, sleep."

101

She felt her chest burst with pride, even ownership.

She opened her eyes when Manal joined in. "You know this song?" Manal nodded and Noor joined in. "Hey! How do you all know this song?"

"*Mawtani, mawtani,*" Manal sang. "It's the Palestinian anthem. Everyone knows it. It's your song, *ya Nadia.*"

Not anymore, she thought. Noor got up to dance, reaching for Nora's hand so she would join her. She put a hand on her hip and another behind her head, the child mimicked her perfectly. Manal clapped, Bishara too. They formed a circle, clapping, dancing, singing, laughing. For the second time that night, Nadia wanted to cry.

Later, as they ate, Manal peppered Bishara with questions, which he answered enthusiastically, enjoying the opportunity to tell old stories in a slightly new way. Only slightly, Nadia fumed quietly. But the *basboosa*, swollen with still-warm cheese, its honey dripping from her fingers to her lap, was distracting her.

"Nadia," Bishara said, cutting through a lull in the conversation that she hadn't even noticed. "I must tell you something."

She searched for her napkin, found it on the floor, wiped her fingers and the sides of her mouth. She never liked being sticky; she was like her father in that. Together they would wipe their hands clean after ice cream or a messy meal, jumping up to run their fingers under the tap. Clare always assumed they were rejecting her food or were somehow conspiring against her. She brandished her own smears like a badge and judged them for their squeamishness. But Bishara never cared how personally she took it, and neither did Nadia. Clare had a way of making up problems and conjuring enemies. Nadia wondered if she had been drawn to Daniel precisely because he wouldn't recognize his enemies if they spit in his face. Not so different from her father, she could see now. Both of them temperamentally unsuited for conflict.

Bishara glanced at Noor, nodded his head, put his hands together. Nadia found herself worrying.

"Nadia. There have been some changes recently. This is why I was so busy and, I apologize, not really available. I do not work for British Petroleum now."

"Did you lose your job?" It wouldn't be the first. She was embarrassed that he was telling her this in front of Manal. Her father, can't keep a job.

She watched as a shadow of frustration or even embarrassment passed over his face. "No, I did not lose my job. I have taken another job." He looked again at Noor. "I have taken a position at the Palestine Hospital."

"The what?"

"I have left BP and have position with the PRCS. The Palestine Red Crescent Society, like Red Cross. The hospital is in Heliopolis."

"Okay, man of mystery, are you a doctor now?" She looked to share the joke with Manal, but saw that she was puzzled by the disparaging tone. She had used Clare's voice; even she heard it.

"No," he said. "I am administrator. Noor is psychologist and now we can work together." He reached across the cushion and took Noor's hand.

"Wait a minute, wait a minute," Nadia said. "What?"

He reached over and tried to touch her hand, but she recoiled quickly, too quickly. She could see that it stung. She was hurt, *she* was stung, even though she couldn't figure out precisely why. People are allowed to change jobs, make decisions for themselves. What was she not getting, what was she getting wrong, what was she blowing out of proportion? She felt Clare's voice and Clare's arguments nudging up against her insides, rising, rising. It was all she could manage: she gave them free rein.

"No," she said, "you do not get togetherness. You do not get to do family, to do a great future, and you especially do not get to flaunt it in front of me and expect me to applaud you for it. So you left your job at BP—which was so important that you had to leave Canada *and me* for it—and now you're what, an administrator at a hospital? A hospital? The person who couldn't stand to look my scrapes or even put a Band-Aid on them? Do you really just go where the wind blows you? Do you? Always taking the path of least resistance." That was Clare, that was entirely Clare. Nadia could barely breathe.

He spoke slowly, deliberately, to the table. "It is not least resistance. It is *resistance*," he said. "I am sorry, Nadia. I disappointed you. I disappoint you. But you are an adult now. You have to choose your own path. This is mine, it has always been mine even though detours. I must serve my people."

"Right, detours. Have I been a detour? I guess I'm not

your people?" But she was deflating as she spoke, her anger already burning up and turning to ash. She sat on her shaking hands. Beside her, Manal moved and rustled.

Bishara reached across the table a second time. He did not relent until she let him take her hand. "*Ya bint il helwa, rohi, hayati*. You are my daughter, my soul, my life. This will never change. Seasons and roads and time, everything changes and we must move with it. But some things are rock. You are rock to me. Rock. Precious rock." He was running out of words as he worked hard to maintain composure.

But words are cheap, she kept thinking. *Kalam fadi*. So much upheaval, disappointment, waiting. For what? "You're still married to my mother," she said. She wanted to look at Noor but a sliver of humility prevented her from doing so.

He withdrew his hands. Manal touched her arm but she shook it off. Her father and Noor looked at each other. The child cried and Noor, with visible relief, took off down the hall.

"Nadia…" Manal's voice wrapped around her.

"Do not be angry," Bishara said. "I would like you to be part of this. You can, you can be part of this, of my fa—my life here. Please."

"Are you kidding me? You've barely seen me since I'm fifteen. All these stupid visits, all these empty promises. I was supposed to come back to Egypt five years ago. Every ten years. Remember that? And now you have a kid and a—a—*Jesus Christ*, Baba." She still couldn't look at

Noor. "If I hadn't come here, if I hadn't stupidly decided to come here like this, would you even care? Would you? When would you have sent me another fax? When?"

She didn't wait for an answer but caught Manal's eyes. "I think it's time to go. I don't see what else there is to say here." *This* is why she came to Egypt, now it was obvious. To hurt him.

"Nadia, *malesh. Malesh ya bint*. Don't go. There is so much to tell you. Now you are in Cairo, I want to tell you."

It was too late. Manal made apologies for them both and joined Nadia at the door. He called after her but the elevator had already arrived and the doors closed on his pained expression.

"I'm leaving, I'm leaving," she said as they rode down to the lobby and hailed a taxi from the street. "I'm leaving."

"Yes, yes. We are leaving."

"No, you do not understand. I am leaving Egypt."

"*Nadia*."

"I'm out of here. Leaving. This whole idea was just ridiculous."

They didn't speak in the taxi. At the hotel, she threw a five-pound note on Manal's lap and ran up the front steps and into a waiting elevator. The doors shut and as they did a sob shuddered up from below, perhaps the basement, perhaps her belly. She had been desperate for Manal's hand to reach in and push open the doors, to save her from herself and her smouldering stupidity. But the light blinked once then stopped at the third floor.

She understood nothing and was able to process even less. She always did that, dissolve in a conflict, lose her bearings, her words, the lines on the road. Eventually her car would careen into a ditch and hang upside down with its wheels spinning in the air. Bishara would wait it out, say something gentle, wait for her to calm down and recover. But Clare was always in tears, telling the world how much this was killing her, that all her life all she ever wanted was peace and quiet. You know nothing of peace, Bishara would say, peace takes work, too much work for a nice woman like you. Peace is not the same as peace and quiet. One comes after war, the other pretends there is no war.

She opened a bag of *Chipsy* she had bought earlier, couldn't even remember when. She decided to do what Daniel had taught her: go through every thought and feeling till she found the one that was the thorn. Then what? Then you pull it out. Then what? Throw it away and forget about it. Thorn: her father was always leaving. Or maybe not quite leaving, just not entirely there to begin with. A quality of presence that was unpredictable, subject to moods and schedules. He was from somewhere else, somewhere she was not. Somewhere far and simpler and full of better people—especially, people with manners. Somewhere that had culture, that had food, that had a language. "English is a language. French is a language," she argued. He waved it away. What kind of poetry can you make with English or French? And then, to contradict himself completely: *Arabic is like computer!*

Clare, meanwhile, had been increasingly less under-standing of her husband's distractions, which is what she called his political leanings. It might have been exciting and exotic at the beginning, but it wore as thin as his sal-ary. She couldn't care less about a "two-thousand-year-old grudge."

"*Haram!*" He almost drove off the road. They must have been on their way to Ottawa, visiting her uncle Rob. Yes, she still had the McDonald's french fries on her lap. "It is not two thousand years old. It is only from 1948. Or maybe before, when immigration began. Jews were always in Palestine, but they were Palestinians first, Jews second. We all were Palestinians first, the Muslims, the Christians, the Jews, the Druze, the Bedouin."

Clare reached back to Nadia. "Hungry, Sweetie? We're almost there. Oh! There's a yellow car. What else starts with Y?"

Nadia didn't care about the yellow car, it had already driven past them. She hated when her mother made at-tempts at playing but got the rules and the rhythm wrong. "Am I Palestinian, Baba?"

He looked at her in the rearview mirror. "Of course! You are my Palestinian honey girl! *Bint il asal.*"

Clare didn't much care for Arabic words when she didn't understand them. "You are Canadian, Nadia." She stared at Bishara. He said nothing for the rest of the drive.

Nadia drifted off to sleep fully clothed. There was a

knock at the door, then a second one, startling her awake. The figure of Manal shimmered through the peephole. She turned the handle but before she could finish the job Manal pushed through, went to the window, came back, planted herself in front of her.

"I went all the way home," she said in a voice trembling with anger. "And I came all the way back. To tell you one thing."

Anger was long drained out of Nadia. "Okay."

"To tell you one thing."

"Okay."

"You are not leaving. You are not leaving this country. Not now, not yet. You are not leaving like a coward and a baby. This is not how one lives a life. Are you so rich you can come and go like this? Are you so young? Are you so perfectly formed, are you Allah, that you can be so critical and dismissive? Are you the centre of the universe?"

"Whoa. What? This is not your business, Manal. I'm really sorry. He is my father. It was my family in Canada that *he* used up, spit out, walked all over."

"It is indeed my business. The minute you… you…" She hesitated, lowered her voice. "The minute you touched me it became my business."

The full impact of Manal's declaration hit Nadia, woke her up completely. Something was at stake, Manal was telling her. She was fighting for her. The contrast between what she was doing and what her father had never done made her want to cry out, first in anguish, then with joy. It was a minute before she could say anything.

"Manal. I came to Egypt to find my father, to find out what he was up to—and okay, I suppose I found out. But now here you are, in my hotel room, telling me to stay. Honestly, I don't understand the half of it." She went to the window and pulled open the heavy curtain a crack, letting in the blinking lights of downtown. "Anyways, it's not like I can even afford this. I am running out of money and reasons."

"That's all? That's everything? This is because of money or no money? You have nothing more to discover?"

"I'm sorry, Manal, but you just don't see. It's not fair. What he did, the way he tells me. Like he doesn't care. Did you get the impression he cares?"

Manal's voice went hard again. "I will tell you something about fair, *ya Nadia*. If you are not fair with life, it will not be fair with you. It is a—an arrangement. An agreement, a relationship. *Fair*."

"I'm being fair." But she could hear the whining in her voice. *I'm tired*, she wanted to say to this beautiful woman in her hotel room, this woman who was more beautiful every time she saw her—more striking, more lush, more unflinching. *I'm tired and stupid and have no more energy, not even to impress you. Please forgive me. Please kiss me. Please.*

Manal paused at the door to hoist her bag up on her shoulder. "You are not. You are being greedy. You want everything and you want it exactly how you see it in your imagination. It is not fair, it is childish." It shut behind her with a fine and perfect click.

6

how the monkey found its tree

Static erupted between them, a lightning storm in the arid, arid air. "Daniel? Daniel? I can't hear you."

The next morning her thoughts had returned to Daniel almost with a slap. He had no idea how far away from him she had already travelled. Somehow a phone call was necessary, if only to buy herself some time. Even, strangely, to maintain the distance. She didn't want him to come looking for her.

"*Ooh la la,*" he said in a Parisian accent. "*C'est incroyable!* Nadia, he has two lives. He has two wives!"

"It's not funny. What do I do now?"

"Now you can come home. Now you know everything. What else is there to do? Wait, have you seen the Pyramids yet? Go see them, then come home."

"Yeah…"

"I never thought he was so, I don't know, so Middle Eastern." Then he exaggerated the pronunciation, stretched it out with a long *a*, American-style, full of disdain and, worse, the assumption that it was shared. "So *A*-rab."

"What do you mean by that?"

"He leaves his family, he abandons his daughter, he finds another wife, has another kid. *Pas mal* tribal, *non?*"

"*No.* You think that's an Arab thing to do?"

"Are you sure there's not a third wife to be found?"

"He's not going to have two wives at the same time. He's not being 'so Arab.' He's just being a man, a person. And not all marriages last, as you should know. Anyways how do I know you haven't got a second girlfriend? I've been away a while now. Maybe you've had time to find someone on the side."

Would he see what she was doing? Would he see that even from thousands of miles away she couldn't stop the truth from reaching through the phone lines and tripping them both up?

But he just chuckled. "*Voyons*. Nadia. You have an imagination. I was just joking. I get it, he's Palestinian and wants to *be* Palestinian. You're Palestinian, too. *La philistine!* It's funny though. Philistine and philistine. Why do you think philistine is such a bad word?"

"What the heck are you talking about?"

"You know, when we say someone is a philistine we mean they have no culture, no art. You know? Maybe there is a *rapport* between Palestine and philistine? The *filistines,* as you say. It's the same word!"

The note of discovery in his voice made her angry. "I don't know. Maybe it's like when I say a Quebecer is a frog. Is it like that? A fucking *maudit* frog?"

"Whoa, *minute. Qu'est-ce qui se passe, Nadia?*"

"Nothing, forget it." Then, reluctantly: "I'm sorry Daniel."

"Ça va. It's okay." He always helped her hold back, hold in, retain and maintain. It drew her to him once upon a time, as if he were the backbone she'd been missing, an evolutionary next step. Now, his measured tones felt calculating and distant, weighted with judgment and a hint of smugness. *Chérie*, she could hear him say, make yourself a cup of tea, you'll calm down. But she didn't want his advice or his tea. She didn't want him anymore. She wanted someone who could beat a drum even harder than she was able. Someone who would dance with her, embrace the chaos and the anger, heat an entire furnace with it, then help her forge something new and much less brittle. Much, much, much less brittle.

"I think I should come to Egypt. I should come. We can take a holiday, see the Pyramids, go to Luxor, see the Valley of the Kings. Wouldn't that be amazing? From there we take a cruise ship to Aswan and see the dam. I've been reading about it, Nadia. It must be magnificent." He told her everything about the Aswan Dam, its height, the years of building, how it flooded almost all of Nubia, how the Soviets took over after the British left, how silt and nutrients, how engineers, how Abu Simbel, how irrigation, how long how high how deep how square feet how wattage how.

"No."

"Come on, Nadia. When else would I get a chance to go to Egypt? And the Valley of the Kings!"

"We can come back some day if you really want. Just let me finish this. Do not come."

"*Bon, d'accord.*" But it felt like a temporary placeholder for another attempt. He ended the call after a minute or two, saying what she had no idea. She had no patience for him today. None.

She was angry at Daniel and angry at Clare every time she thought of her, and behind that, angry at her father and, wrapped around that, masking it maybe, inflecting it and colouring it and almost obscuring the sum total of everything, angry at Manal. But underneath it: in consummate pain until she saw her again.

Champollion Street was a ten-minute walk from the hotel. She couldn't get there fast enough. In her single-mindedness she felt immune from the stares, the quiet hisses and whispers, roaming hands, suicidal cars, dogs, dogs, dogs. Turning a corner, the familiarity made her stomach flutter and her head reel. Heart pounding, she climbed the stairs, an involuntary smile sprouting with each step. Manal crossed the floor as if on silent slippers, took her in her arms, kissed both cheeks, kissed them again, and held her hand as they walked back to the window seat. She gave her a Coke.

"*Feen Tewfiq?*" Nadia only wanted to speak Arabic. She wished she could sing it, rhyme it, paint it.

"I am here," he called in English, popping out from the back room.

The three of them smiled at each other, looking from

114

one to the other. Something happened just then, in that precise moment. A fire like a lit fuse ran around them, energized the room, charged the air. They became friends.

All morning Nadia wanted to apologize, explain the complexity of her situation, excuse her rudeness and her lack of faith and trust. But Manal put a finger to her lips. Words, of any sort, would only spoil things. The day was languid. Empty but for enchanting looks, fleeting hands, hidden gestures, barely audible sighs, the sound of breathing. It was like a tuning fork had set the tone for *quiet* and the afternoon followed. The delicate music of stillness, the harmony of waiting, the rhythm of watching, and the discordant pleasure of knowing that the cacophony of the world outside the walls of the gallery was being held at bay by their longings. It broke when Manal exhaled a sharp word, came out from behind the curtain and, rolling her eyes, stared at Nadia.

"What?"

She joined her on the bench. "He didn't used to do this," Manal said, keeping her voice low.

"Do what?"

She flicked her hand impatiently towards the back room. "Pray. I need to gesso some canvases but now he is praying. What do I do, step over him?"

Nadia recalled the muezzin that had just finished calling from somewhere a few streets over, a recorded call to prayer echoing in and around the *wist il balad*—downtown—with varying intensity. She had never paid that much attention to it except as a quaint background noise, like a loon on the other side of a lake in the Laurentians. Even Bishara loved the sound, felt a part of it, though he was not Muslim. He could still admire a tuneful call, he said. She remembered him justifying that to Clare once, attempting to offset her scorn. "The way you can love a Psalm or a prayer," he explained. "'The Lord Is My Shepherd.' Is beautiful, no?" But Clare screwed up her face. She couldn't imagine saying anything nice about any religion at any time.

"That's nice that he prays," Nadia said.

Manal frowned at her, muttered something under her breath in Arabic.

"What's the matter?"

Manal twisted on the bench, turning so her back was to the curtain. "I don't like it. There is something a little too, how can I describe it, secretive about it."

"Secretive?" What was so secretive about a man praying out in the open?

Manal gestured that the conversation was over. They could hear Tewfiq rolling up his mat. When it was time to close up and leave, Tewfiq waited at the stairs but Manal sent him off, telling him that he'd miss his bus if he waited for them to find their purses.

"I don't even have a purse," Nadia said after he left.

"*Shhht.*"

"What is going on? I don't see the problem if Tewfiq prays in the gallery. Everyone prays around here, I don't understand. I thought everyone was cool with it. You're Muslim."

"*Tsssk*." She jutted up her chin. "I have an idea and I didn't want to discuss it in front of Tewfiq. I have been thinking. If you stay in Egypt longer, you have to leave the hotel. *Mish kidda?*"

"*Kidda.*"

Manal folded both hands across her belly and raised an eyebrow. "So you live at my flat."

"What?" She'd thought they were going to talk about Tewfiq. "Wait, wait a minute. I haven't even met your mother. Did you ask her? Where do you live, anyways? I don't know, Manal, is this weird? This is a little weird. I mean, what we're doing is, I really…"

The words were difficult to come by, there were no words, Nadia didn't want there to be mere words. She didn't want to define the indefinable or suffocate the uncontainable or grin in too unseemly a fashion. She lowered her voice. "Do you have a spare bedroom or something?"

"There is another bed, yes."

"Manal, this is…awkward."

"Nadia. You have to make a choice, and the choice is that you stay in Cairo for now. And the way to make that choice is to live with me and my mother and my uncle."

"Your *uncle?*"

"Yes, he comes with the choice," she said, rolling her eyes. "But no matter, he is never home. He is nothing. Come for supper tonight and make your choice. *Khallas.*"

Nadia wanted to correct Manal: it's a decision, not a choice. She had to make a decision. But maybe to decide was to choose. What was she choosing, exactly?

The first thing she noticed was that Manal's apartment was cool. Ceramic tile cool, cement-block walls cool, windows-shuttered-to-the-sun cool, fans on the ceilings, fans in the corners, darkness, cool. Unlike Canadian construction, Egyptian homes were built to repel heat, not contain it. They had been quiet in the taxi. Manal's fingers found Nadia's and settled inside them. They went north from the city centre, up to Ramses Road, then 6th of October Road, then Salah Salem. Nadia stopped following Manal's tour guide announcements when they began twisting and turning through the smaller streets. Finally: "*Wasaltna bi salam,*" Manal said, a little prayer of thanks for the safe arrival. "Here we are." The French had been there before them, leaving behind iron latticework, alluring balconies, debonair turrets and Napoleonic gargoyles.

"I like your apartment building," Nadia said.

"Wait till you see the view." The view was from four storeys up. Nadia looked around for an elevator but Manal had already begun the ascent.

"No way. You do this every day?"

"Twice a day!" Her voice echoed down the marble-clad stairwell. "It keeps you young, old lady. *Yalla.*"

Panting, Nadia inhaled the living room—inert musky odours, coffee and cumin—before her eyes adjusted and took in old velvet and dark mahogany, a worn rug underfoot, china figurines, black and white photos in gilded frames, and a series of small landscapes so pastoral they could almost be Canadian. Manal motioned to Nadia to follow her down the hallway. The next room was the kitchen, small and painted a drab hospital green. A bare light bulb glowed from the ceiling, casting shadows over the business of slicing and chopping. A woman, hunched underneath it, turned around.

"Mama, Nadia is the Canadian friend I told you about."

With her smile, Manal's mother transformed from a statue of salt to a radiant human being. Nadia rippled with surprise at the shift. She was wearing the sort of turban that had been popular in 1950s movies, a time when the Aga Khan courted Hollywood starlets and movie magazines tittered about harems and handsome sheiks. The line of her nose and strength of her jaw hinted at past beauty, certainly a strength of character. But now the green beneath her olive complexion had come to the surface and the sharpness of bones was obscured by folds of skin. She took Nadia's hands in hers, then cupped her cheeks, kissed everything loudly.

"*Ahlan, ahlan.* Hungry?" Manal nodded for both of them. "Good, good. Good, good. Sit. I make. Sit. *Smulla, smulla.*" Eat, she gestured toward the chairs and the table. "Canada!" she added with a flourish.

"Eat now?" Nadia whispered to Manal.

"Now," she nodded.

In a few short minutes Manal's mother had piled the table high with food: a large bowl laden with chicken drenched in sumac and onions, dishes of tahini and

119

eggplant, and a pot of okra stewed in lamb bones. In the middle of the table, as rewards, she set two dessert bowls. Nadia leaned forward, inhaled deeply, and was unable to restrain an appreciative groan.

"My mother cooks like a queen," Manal said.

"Does she ever. Every day? Okay, I made my choice."

Nadia thanked her for the spread and, hands folded and disciplined underneath the table, waited for her to sit with them. But a third place wasn't set and she had already left the kitchen, the sound of her slippered feet fading in the distance. From the hallway a door creaked open and shut in the quiet apartment.

"She's not going to eat with us?"

Manal was already chewing on a chicken leg. "Don't worry. She's happy we're here. It's okay. Don't look like that. Next time, okay? We eat together next time."

After they were done, Nadia brought their plates to the sink and ran the water.

"Are you crazy? She'll kill you," Manal said. "Leave them."

"I'm not going to let your mother cook for us and do all the cleaning up. Come on, you can dry."

"If you want to be alive tomorrow, you will not do the dishes," Manal said. But the only thing that worked to budge her was: "Next time. I promise you. You will do the dishes next time. Okay?"

She led Nadia down the rest of the hallway. At the end, past Manal's mother's bedroom, past the bathroom, past some closets and shelves, past a chair and a telephone on a small round table, there was one last door. Manal paused and, grinning, opened it with a flourish. It was much bigger than Nadia expected, both wide and long, with a wall of windows running the length of it and, outside, a balcony equally generous. At the far end were two twin beds, one of them hidden under clothes and linens. To the right of the door was a corner where Manal had set up her artwork and supplies, a large paper tacked to the wall ready for *l'attaque*. In between, it was almost entirely filled with furniture, boxes, storage bins, shelves, books. Manal bounced on one of the beds. "We can move things. And of course clean up. Fix it how you like."

"But we didn't even discuss this with your mother. Don't you think I should talk to her? Also, I know this is kind of awkward, but I want to pay you something. Rent or something."

"Pay me? *Eib aleiki!* Shame on you. What are you talking about?"

"If I live here, and I mean *if*, then I should pay you. That's only fair."

"Nadia, *ya agnabiya*, I now know for sure that you have no idea the meaning of the word fair." She began clearing the clothes off the second bed. "My mother is happy to have you. It is settled."

"What about your uncle?"

"He won't even notice." She threw a pile of linens at her. "Help me fold."

"What does *agnabiya* mean?"

"Foreign lady."

They folded housecoats, nightgowns, T-shirts, socks, towels, all of it stuck together by the tensile strength of polyester and electricity. The basket of crackling laundry, full of intimate items daring Nadia to touch them, was making her blush.

"How long have you lived here, Manal? Is this where you grew up?"

"We moved here when I was fifteen. My father died and his younger brother took us in. We were lucky. I suppose."

"Sorry to hear about your father."

"My father supported General Nasser. But when Nasser died there was no more room for revolutionaries in the new capitalism. Sadat had him arrested. Many times. Always for a short period, a month, two months, like that, *yanni*. It destroyed his reputation and his business. No one wanted to associate with him." She shot a look towards the door. "Even Uncle Nasser. Especially Uncle Nasser. They named the wrong son Nasser." She paused to throw a pair of nylons towards a pile against the wall. "He had a heart attack. Even the ones who don't have heart attacks still have heart attacks, *ya Nadia*. It is an explosion in the hearts of all who love you."

"I'm so sorry, Manal."

"We lost our apartment, our money, everything. Malek went to Dubai, sent us money, but it still wasn't enough. I was too young to work. It wasn't a life. After a year, we came to live here, with Uncle Nasser."

"Malek?"

"My older brother. He is an engineer. He is married now. My nieces are beautiful, but I don't see them. It's like I have family but I don't have family. Maybe you don't understand."

"Maybe I do," Nadia said.

"It's a strange thing to be in Egypt and have no family. Believe me, very strange. Malek says the solution is to get married." Manal looked away. "I will not get married. I will go to Paris."

Nadia caught a glimpse of Manal's geography. Beyond the shimmering heat and the limestone bricks and the slow pulsing river that spread the city apart like a vivisected animal, there was an unseen architecture that was sometimes visible, most times not. A framework of obligations, diminished expectations, and only the illusion of opportunities. The world was not beckoning Manal with open arms.

"If you don't go to Paris then you come to Montreal," Nadia said, believing that one could still cheat destiny if one were young enough and brave enough and in love enough.

Manal threw the last of the clothes back into the basket for another day. "How do artists live, *ya Nadia*? Do you know? It's funny, I work at the gallery but I don't even know. Do they paint every day? Do they paint everywhere? On canvas and on napkins? Do they only have conversations about primary colours and perspective? What a life. What a life," she said wistfully.

"You *are* an artist already, Manal. You paint, you draw,

you spend your days in a gallery."

"I am the art secretary. I am not the artist."

"That's just a detail. The rest is up to you."

"Ha! Easy to say, easy to say."

"I'm serious. *Be* an artist and everything else will follow. All you have to do is, I don't know…" She was stumped.

"And everything else will follow," Manal repeated. "Everything like what? Like acceptance? Like approval? Like not having to do what everyone says morning to night? Like not having to get married and have babies and make meals and make conversation and cook every day and say *aiwa* and *la* and *min fadlak* and *insha'allah* as if those were the only words anyone wants to hear from you? Or maybe just go to sleep all day and just avoid it. You do understand, don't you? Tell me you understand. Tell me you know that this chance is the only thing I have, and already it is a far-fetched. It is a long shot, what do you say?"

"Yes, long shot."

A car honk punctuated their conversation, giving it rhythm and urgency. "Look how you came here, *ya Nadia*. An idea, a feeling, a plane ticket, an airport, a hotel, an adventure. Sometimes I wonder what foreigners are thinking when they come here 'on holiday.' An Egyptian only travels to find work and then more work. And if they find work and never come home again and die of loneliness they are still lucky. Oh yes, one or two get scholarships. *Ana*, me, I have no chances. Nothing. I have no opportunities. I have no adventures. I have work and more work and maybe a scholarship. And if there is no scholarship, then what?"

"I'm not on holiday, Manal."

Manal threw something, a pillow, and hit Nadia full in the face. "If there is no scholarship then I get married."

Manal went to the kitchen and forbade her to follow. Nadia listened to dishes and the kettle and stirring and clanking and silence, then the kettle again, the fridge, water, more silence. She was getting sleepy but dared not make any assumptions or take any decisions. It was Manal's permission she needed; even more, her blessing. No, it was her forgiveness.

And then she was there, standing over her as if she had drifted to sleep under the bare light bulb, which, she realized to her embarrassment, she had. "Sorry," she said, sitting up quickly and shading her eyes from the light.

"Are you tired?"

"Don't you work tomorrow?"

"Yes." Manal sat on the bed across from her. "Will you come with me?"

"To the gallery? Are you sure? This is all a little, I don't know, intense."

"Yes, I am sure."

Manal mercifully turned off the light then switched beds and sat beside her, tucked a lock of Nadia's curls behind an ear. "Don't worry," she said.

"I'm sorry, Manal. It's true, I don't understand your situation. I wish I understood more."

"You will. You are still a tourist on holiday."

Nadia slapped her arm and was relieved when Manal laughed. Then they flew at each other like dark birds in a dark room.

The next afternoon, on the pretext of wanting to buy some sweets, Nadia left the gallery and headed towards the Canadian Embassy. It was within walking distance in Garden City, not far from the Nile Hilton, the American University of Cairo, the bus centrale—a topographic triangle of her emotional landscape. As she walked she tried to figure out if it was a scalene triangle, or obtuse, or right, or acute. High school math had to be good for something, and it was: she paid less attention to the chaotic and still-threatening distractions of the street.

She was glad she'd remembered to tuck her passport in her bag, and presented it at the reception gate. Inside, she was met by an Egyptian woman whose name tag read *Maha*, who immediately looked at her watch. "We are only open till two. The documentation centre closes in half an hour."

Nadia spoke quickly. "My friend is Egyptian and wants to know about universities and scholarships in Canada. Do you have flyers or booklets? Oh, and art schools across the country."

Maha opened drawers, dug out boxes, reached up on shelves, and gathered up flyers and applications for a dozen Canadian universities and as many scholarships.

"Do you also have international scholarships by any

chance?"

But Maha gave her a withering glance. "If you want the addresses of other embassies I can give you that, they have their own libraries." At two she ushered Nadia out of the room and locked the door behind them.

Bag in hand, Nadia took a detour back to the gallery and turned right into the still-intimidating streets beyond the square. She had to twist to the side every few steps to make way for large-bellied men and massive, imposing women in noisy *shib shibs*. Countless pairs of eyes fell on her with bald interest, assessing distance, communicating judgment. As she made her way it struck her that she was walking differently, holding herself differently. She didn't own her body or her posture anymore; they did, strangers did, with their eyes, their glances of conditional respect, and their quiet clucks of censure. They did. She caught herself raising her eyebrows in disapproval at the too-blond foreign women or the too-stupid foreign men. *Yes,* she wanted to agree with the collective, *America bad Egypt beautiful American women sharmouta Western culture haram.* Yes, yes, yes. It was a fine line and she felt compelled to cross it, to shift her alliances and engage in private betrayals. You couldn't belong everywhere at once, you had to choose. That was the cruelty of a country like Egypt, she thought, it forced you to choose—between less and none, between always wanting and never getting, between never being happy and always being miserable. The poverty in Cairo was knee-deep. Even wealth was no protection when the streets sloshed in sewage, dead animal carcasses stunk up doorways, and barefoot children lived under bridges. Manal had refused to buy ice cream one day, saying it was an affront to snack on the streets when half the people you passed had not eaten since the day before. Nadia's decidedly middle-class upbringing had shielded her from anything resembling the struggle for survival. But wasn't that the true genius of being middle class, she wondered? The ability to live life unawares. Leave survival and grappling with life's questions to the poor and the very wealthy. Just a fairly decent house and a fairly decent job and a fairly decent car was all you needed to be shielded from death, ethics, guilt, yourself. How freeing that was.

At the intersection, as the lights changed to no effect, a black-suited policeman in white gloves gave directions to deaf vehicles and blind pedestrians, she sensed a man move in behind her almost like a car, his mouth opening and shutting his greasy parts together. A tongue softly swung on its hinge, making a whir only she could hear. She turned around this time, for once too angry at herself to let it pass. "*Aiwa?*" she asked, shaking her head into a question mark.

"Pretty girl," he said, radiator eyes steaming in the heat.

"*Toz fik ya ibn il homar min gher gazma!*" She threw together her father's choicest curses, something like fuck you son of a donkey with no shoes. It worked and, eyes wide with hurt and indignation, he held up his hands and backed away. She stepped off the curb with a relief as sweet as if she had drawn blood.

She turned right and headed towards a dusty store she knew to be there. The one past the block of shoe stores, before the cinema, across the street from the Italian bookstore. Karim's Paper had what she wanted: a box of twenty-four chalk pastels from China. She opened the box and fingered the sticks, chalk dust instantly covering her hands and clothes. The blue was a pale, smoky, almost creamy hue, the one that frustrated Manal the most with its stubborn refusal to deepen.

7

an eye the colour of silk

For two days in February, artists brought their paintings and sculptures to the gallery. They hovered around the desk as Manal and Tewfiq took in their work, labelled it, had them fill out forms, amended the layout plan, erased it, and amended it again. For the most part Nadia stayed in the back and busied herself with the bag of university and scholarship applications. Tewfiq was sweeping at the end of the second day when the door below banged open, followed by a rumble of feet. A panting man stood at the top of the stairs. Behind him three other breathless men nudged him forward and made room for themselves.

"*Ya Brigitte*," he called loudly. "*Feen Brigitte?*" He was tall, on the edge of lanky, as if he had only recently grown into his limbs and his height. But his large eyes, flared nostrils, and long face gave him an alluring and limpid beauty. He knew it, Nadia could tell, using his eyes to capture, his handsome face to impress, and his restless body to seduce.

Manal got up. "She left."

"Did she say anything about me? Where did she go?"

"I have no idea, Imad, and no, she did not talk about you all day long."

Like most Egyptian men, Imad travelled *en gang*. His friends, arms loping over each other, jangling key chains punctuating the jostling, were all jokes and downturned eyes one minute, greedy stares the next. They had brought up three paintings, each mummified in yellowed cotton sheets. As one, they lit up their cigarettes, protecting the flames against an imaginary wind. Tewfiq manoeuvered around them and took the canvases to the back one at a time. They let their eyes brush haughtily over his dusty faux-leather shoes, his white shirt frayed at every seam, his deferential smile, his downcast eyes. They stood taller.

Imad leaned over the desk and pointed at the binder. "Just make sure you have me down for three paintings."

Manal closed it. "One per artist."

"Brigitte said I can hang three," he said with a smirk.

"That is impossible. You know the rules, not that you ever follow them."

He gestured towards Nadia and said something she didn't understand.

"She's Canadian," Manal said flatly, protectively.

"*Canadiyya*! Welcome to Egypt!" He strode over, grabbed her hand. "I hear it is even colder than Russia. Is that true?"

"Probably." Nadia smiled, but then caught the reticence on Manal and Tewfiq's faces and tried to be equally unforgiving. "I wouldn't know," she said.

But Imad wasn't put off. His interest was piqued by

the papers spread out in front of her.

"Hey, I know that scholarship. Are you applying? But it's for Egyptians, no? Are you Egyptian? How delightful!"

"It's for Manal," Nadia said, much too quickly.

"None of your business," Manal growled at him.

"*You* are applying?" He opened his eyes as wide as they could go and tilted his head. Like a stupid dog, Nadia thought. No, a crueller animal, one capable of teasing its prey. A sphinx, whatever that was. "Have you shown your work yet, Manal? Did Brigitte say she would support you? She only supports one artist for the scholarship, you must know that. Only one artist." He twirled his keychain between them. "Are we in competition now? Maybe you think working at Galerie Mashrabiya is an advantage?"

His friends banged against each other like hollow pipes hanging from trees, pretending to make music. "Should I change my strategy?" Imad asked them but directed the question to Manal.

"You can leave now," Manal said. "One painting."

"One *artist*," Imad said, backing away and wagging his finger in the air. "One artist!"

He paused at the top of the steps and exhorted her to accompany them, to have some *gateaux* at Groppi's or *basbousa* in a café on Talat Harb where he knew the owner. There was no question of her agreeing but he pleaded long enough to embarrass her, to insinuate to his friends that she *was* the type to join them, that there was no father

132

or brother to strike the fear of Allah in him, that one day, one day, he would invite her and she would say yes. It was inevitable, said the slight nod of the head and curl of his lips. And if it wasn't, he didn't give a shit anyway.

Tewfiq found Imad's dark eyes and walked slowly towards him until, finally, he retreated. *Yalla*, he said to his boys. They rolled down the steps two and three at a time like rocks off a landslide.

Manal's face remained red for a long time. She sat down at the desk, opened one or another of the ledger books, proceeded to tick off or annotate whatever was in her pen's path. Tewfiq, behind her, winked at Nadia then loudly whispered into Manal's ear.

"I don't believe it," she snorted, sitting up straight. "Are you sure? *Ya Nadia*, did you hear? Tewfiq says he is her lover."

"Who is whose lover?"

"Tewfiq thinks Imad Hassan is Brigitte's lover. This year."

"But isn't Brigitte married?"

"Of course she's married."

"What do you mean *this year*?"

"Every year she has a different lover. *Mish kidda , Tewfiq*? And it's always the next big star. The one who gets the best spot in the group show, then who gets his own show. Who gets..." Manal trailed off, swore. "Never mind." She got up and put some magazines back on the shelf, banged and shoved them into their slots. "The one who goes to Paris."

"Wow, that doesn't sound fair," Nadia said.

"Fair!" Manal threw up her hands and laughed.

No one spoke after that. Tewfiq darted around the gallery cleaning up, arranging, filing, busy always busy, careful to disturb no one with a look or a word. Manal straightened paintings against the walls. Nadia finished the application to the Paris scholarship, even writing a first draft of the personal statement. She wanted to show it to Manal, but was rebuffed. "Just tell them to pick me. I don't care what you write," Manal said. "I don't care."

On their way out Nadia touched Tewfiq's arm. "What is a sphinx," she asked in passable Arabic.

"The Sphinx? It is by the Pyramids."

"I mean what kind of animal is it?"

"Not animal," he said in English. "Not animal. A combination. A…" He found an Arabic word, one that Nadia had never heard before.

"A beast," Manal said over her shoulder. "It is a beast."

Imad returned several times during the week. He came to wait for Brigitte and they'd leave together. While he waited, he asked to consult with lists that had not changed since the last time he'd been by. He stared at the walls, held up his hands to make camera compositions, and loudly voiced several contradictory ideas about where his paintings should hang.

"*This* is the spot," he called out. "*Ya Manal*. Here,

come see. Now I am sure of it."

When she didn't come running, when Tewfiq didn't raise his head, when Nadia looked away the instant their eyes met, Imad finally paused. The blank wall stared back, gave no quarter. Nadia, not looking back, heard his feet shift, heard him turn around, lean, move into the leaning, then cross the room in front of her. He was heading for the back, behind the curtain, where Manal was. In a move she didn't plan, Nadia got up and inserted herself between him and the counter. She looked quickly around for Tewfiq and summoned him silently in her head. If he had left, they had not seen him leave. He could have gone to get sandwiches; he could have gone to get nails or tape or more paper. He could be on the stairs or at the post office.

"That was a good spot, Imad." Her words were place-holders and buffer zones. She gestured to the far wall where he had stopped and stared at one point, as he had at all the walls.

He squinted at her. "You are an artist?"

"No."

"You know about spots? About good spots? You work here? You are here every day. I come, and there is, what is your name, Nadia. There is the Canadian girl Nadia on the bench. Nadia at the table. Nadia in the middle of the room. Is the gallery a tourist destination now? Is it in the brochures? *Ya Manal*, is it in the brochures?" He spun around as if he knew Manal would be right behind him. Instead, Tewfiq was. He was almost unrecognizable, a crisp white *galabiyya* over his clothes and an impeccable

135

white crochet *taqiyah* on his head. For the first time Nadia noticed the beginnings of a beard. His hands met in front like locks on a gate.

"Manal is busy," he said flatly.

"*Eh da,*" Imad demanded. *Eh da*—what, what is it, what the heck, what the hell, what the fuck. There was a verbal back and forth. Tewfiq remained implacable while Imad seemed to heat up like kindling on a fire.

Suddenly the street door slammed and a second later Brigitte was in the room. She surveyed the tilting paintings and the paused arrangement of people in the room, including Manal's head peeking out from behind the curtain.

"*Eh da?*"

Imad sputtered, then followed her around as he recalibrated his energies from Manal to Brigitte. He pointed at the walls, pointed at the list, pointed at the heavens. He said the word *scholarship*, in English. He looked at Nadia as he said it. Just one word in a longer sentence, the purpose of which was to display his proximity to Brigitte and his rapacious intent. Then he said *letter*, also in English. Repeated it in French: *lettre*. Worse: *lettre de soutien*. "*Ah, ah,*" Brigitte said, the Egyptian equivalent of uh-huh, with no small impatience.

He waited at the top of the steps for Brigitte to get her bag. Nadia had to look away. The thought of rushing across the floor to push him down was too vivid.

That evening they sat on the balcony off the bedroom,

dipping *aish baladi*, flatbread, into Om Malek's cumin-filled baba ghanouj. There was a wailing from the street below and they both looked down. An old woman and a boy, probably eight, but smaller and thinner than he should be, were walking slowly in front of the apartment buildings. They were grubby and barefoot. Manal translated: *Charity! Alms! Mercy on my son and me. Dear God, dear God, bless your hearts.*

"I haven't seen her in a long time. I was thinking she was sick," Manal said. She went into the bedroom, rummaged through her things, and ran out of the apartment. A minute later Nadia watched as she wrapped the boy's hand around some money and gave the woman a bag of clothes, muttering words of blessing. The woman thanked her but did not move on. Even from four storeys up the sound of water tinkling on concrete was unmistakable. The blind woman had spread her legs, hitched up her dress, and was urinating. A puddle formed on the ground and splashed onto their feet. Manal stepped back, horrified. The boy paid no attention. The woman rubbed her crotch through the dress then continued on her way.

The door slammed when Manal returned to the flat. Nadia could hear her stomping down the hall. Another door slammed. When she emerged from the bathroom ten minutes later her eyes were red and puffy. She refused to discuss it.

She painted furiously for the rest of the week, and the next and the next. Dirty streets and dirty feet, breasts and vultures, automatic weapons and mountains of food, so much black that colour was violence, territories of white that were invaded by charcoal scrapings and dripping ink. The art was fierce and shocking.

"You don't paint like anyone else."

"And you know so many artists now? Are you expert, like Imad said? Sorry, Nadia. But you have to stop moving." Manal put down her pencil. "Really, I am sorry. I know. Come here. No wait, don't move!" She crossed the room and sat down by Nadia. "I am nervous. There, now you know. I am nervous."

"But you can tell me, you know. I get it."

"I *am* telling you. And I don't know if you get it, but okay, never mind. *Yalla yalla*, Nadia, I need your help."

"Of course, of course."

"No, I mean about something specific. How many times you have been on an airplane?"

"I don't know, three or four times. Why?"

"When they carry bombs, where does the bomb go?"

Nadia burst out laughing; Manal's expression didn't change. "What? Bombs?"

"I am drawing an airplane with bombs and really, it is silly, but I do not know where the bombs go."

"And what am I, the stewardess?"

"You are Leila Khaled."

"*Who?*"

"The Palestinian terrorist. You don't know her?"

"Oh my Christ," Nadia said, standing up. "This I gotta see."

Manal hurried back to the canvas, beating her to it, and covered it. Later, later, later, she promised.

On the first Friday of March, two barefoot men painted the gallery a new coat of white. They brought their prayer mats, faced Mecca three times in the long day, stained their ears and necks with paint in absolution along with water. Manal and Nadia turned on the fans the next morning and began the long work of hanging the art. Brigitte had changed some of the arrangements, scribbling on their layout plan with a turquoise fountain pen. But it didn't always work: Fathi Mourani's painting was half the size he had indicated, and Hannan Fouad's sculpture piece was so delicate they were afraid to post it on even the largest plinth.

Tewfiq lifted Manal's painting up with a shrug. "Where?" She had left it out of the layout plan, fearful perhaps of Brigitte's turquoise pen. A mixture of oil pastel and oil paint, the 24 x 36 canvas was a bold and borderline-shocking green and orange confrontation between a thick nude body, Islamic motifs, and tanks. There was nothing else like it. Tewfiq went around the gallery's two large rooms, lifting it here, setting it there, Manal following behind saying no every time. Finally, he ended up at the back near the desk, the alcove, the framing room.

"Here," Manal said.

"It's practically hidden," Nadia protested. "Maybe because this is not the painting you showed Brigitte?"

"Really?" Manal asked mischievously.

Then there were Imad Hassan's canvases. Two of them were wider than the alcoves, while the third was just dumbfounding. Manal was terse. "I don't care what he or Brigitte says, I am only hanging one."

"*Moscow Nights*," Nadia read from the paper in her hand. "Which one is that?"

Tewfiq pointed to a canvas completely covered in thick smears of white.

"I want to rename it," Manal said. "How about *White Is Cheap*. Or *This Is What I Do When I Have No Talent*."

Tewfiq giggled. "*Titanium Stupid*," he said.

It didn't roll off the tongue, but it was descriptive; clearly several jars of titanium white had given their lives for the painting. It was such a treat to hear him speak English, let alone tell a joke, that both Manal and Nadia gave him high fives. *Titanium Stupid,* they repeated, *Titanium Stupid. Titanium Stupid!*

Tewfiq carried it to the entrance and held it up on the wall facing the door, over the table on which the guestbook would be left open. He impishly raised his eyebrows.

"No one will notice it," he said. "When they enter, their eyes will search beyond to the rest of the room for the art. And as they leave, they will just sign the book and be watching their feet to go down the stairs. It will be a blank wall, nothing more. Just white, just titanium, just stupid." Manal screeched and clapped her hands.

They finished hanging the rest of the paintings, secured the sculptures, tacked the title cards to the wall, prepared the guestbook, picked up the food, bought the napkins and plates, made last-minute calls to the journalists, and went through their list to remind key invitees with quick phone calls.

The afternoon before opening, Brigitte arrived with four cases of French wine and several fresh rondelles of cheese flown in from Paris. She was tanned and in an exuberant mood, resplendent in a white linen pantsuit that flared and billowed with every step. *Khaymat il Malaka*, the Queen's tent, she explained with a laugh marinated in modesty. Her heels echoed dramatically as she toured the space in one last vigil. "*C'est parfait, Manal,*" she said several times. When she stood in front of Imad's *Moscow Winter* she almost entirely blended in.

Before anyone took their next breath, the gallery was filled with glitter, sequins, tie clips, gold thread, shiny polyester, pointy shoes, toupées, wigs, cigarette smoke and vats of cologne. Men stood open-faced and smiling in that particular Egyptian posture where the body formed not so much an S as a question mark, shoulders scooping down, knees slightly bent, hips leaning forward. A body in constant supplication. Women, seeking each other out like Geiger counters drawn to jewelry, shared laughs so high-pitched Nadia wanted to cover her ears. Bodies crushed closer and closer together until one leaned into her, its hand snaking around her with a plastic cup of wine. Smiling, Manal motioned her to follow, held on to Nadia's arm softly, gratefully. "Let me introduce you."

She led her from group to group and presented her to

artists, always with an information-laden preamble: *This is Khaled, he studied medicine at Cairo University but a brush is a much better scalpel than a scalpel, isn't that right, Khaled? This is Ahmed Siwi, he shows at the Galerie at least once a year whether we like it or not. Allow me to present Lamia Mikhail, a German-Egyptian artist who threatens to leave Cairo on a daily basis but is too afraid to never eat a tamaaya again. It's true, Lamia, it's true.* Nadia, in turn, was given an equally informative presentation: "This is my Palestinian-Canadian friend, Nadia Eid. She is in Cairo to learn how to be Egyptian. I am teaching her everything I know, poor her! *Mish kidda walla eh?*"

They reached the end of the crowded gallery. It was a dance, the two of them in a private pas de deux. Nadia felt only the hot hand in hers, heard only Manal's voice over the din. At the door they spun in laughter like a couple ready to tango back across the floor. Manal paused.

"Do you remember?" she whispered.

"What?"

"This is where we met. This is how we met. This is a sacred gallery now." Her lips were inches away, breathing into Nadia's ear with vowels and promises.

The way back was blocked by Imad. He was the only one in his entourage not smiling into a middle distance. He pointed to the white wall against which his painting was invisible, unheralded, unnoticed.

"What is this?"

"Hello, Imad, are you having a nice time? Ah, I see you brought your mother. And your sisters, and your little brother, and all of your friends."

Manal took her time. She shook hands with each and every one, particularly congratulating his mother on her son's fine work and place in the Egyptian art firmament. But his mother, not having quite embraced the conceptual leaps of abstract art, discreetly rolled her eyes at Manal and mouthed a little prayer. Nadia chuckled.

Imad lowered his voice to an angry hiss. "Why is my painting in this spot?"

Manal paced in front of it. "Is this not the best place, *ya Imad*? It greets people as they come and salutes them as they leave. Where else would you put it? Next to Farhat's papyrus collage? Or the cubist triptych Rouha brought back from New York? Really? No, *Titanium Stu—Moscow Winter* stands alone. Its white is shocking. Its size is overwhelming. It is like a wall. The wall in our hearts, Imad? What were you thinking when you painted this wall?"

"This wall?"

"This painting," she said, an honest recovery.

His mother admonished him for being ungrateful. This is not how she raised him, maybe his father, but not her, she said, nodding to all around. She liked Manal and her Canadian friend. She never met a Canadian before. "Speak English?" She smiled impishly and moved in closer to Nadia until they touched shoulders, elbows, and hands.

"Your son is an artist," Nadia said in Arabic, enjoying everything about this moment.

"*Wa fanaana inti?*" Imad's mother asked Nadia if she, too, were an artist, mock bracing herself for the answer. She gestured dismissively towards her son's canvas.

"*Abyad, bes. Abyad. Eh da?*"

"Yes, lots of white!" Nadia grinned so hard her cheeks ached.

"*Yalla!*" Imad signaled. He wanted to lead the way out of there, Moses against the suffocating tide. But murmurs of dissent blocked his exit: still so much food left, here comes another tray of wine, I haven't even had a tour of the room, aren't you going to introduce us to Brigitte, what's the matter, why so grumpy, let's just have a good time, wait I want to practice my English, why is your painting so weird, *yanni?*

Tewfiq tapped Nadia's shoulder. "Someone is looking for you," he said. Behind him her father came into focus.

"*Baba,*" Nadia said in her best Egyptian accent. "I wasn't sure if you would come."

"Of course I come! I only got messages, sorry for not phoning you back."

"*Mafeesh mushkilla!* No problem. Here," she took his arm. "Let me show you around."

She was conscious of her arm as it rested on his. It had just been on Manal's and now it was her father who accompanied her across the room. She wondered if the disparate ends of her life could one day be tied together. She knew what to say about the paintings and could barely modulate her grin as he listened, nodded and asked questions, eyebrows dancing upwards at every Arabic word or phrase she employed.

"You should have come to Cairo much sooner," he said, wagging his head and rubbing his chin. "It suits you to be here, *ya Nadia*. I should have brought you sooner."

"Really?"

"*Tabaan*."

Tabaan. Of course. It goes without saying. Self-evident. Only a fool would think otherwise. An entire life spent waiting and yearning could have just as easily been realized and fulfilled and taken in another direction, given another meaning and more depth and real roots. With nothing more than a snap of the fingers, clearly. Your mother's fears and my inaction and our combined obstructions, all that was just wasted energy masked as concern, or negligence justified by distractions. I left you behind but oh what an oversight. Another life was a plane ticket away after all. Had there been other seat sales? Should have asked the travel agent.

She unthreaded her arm. She needed a moment, just one second of quiet to reorient herself. Some machinery is like that, she thought, it needs a slap on the side to bring it back to life, like their old television. She asked him what wine he liked and made her way through the crowd to the back room. Tewfiq, filling the glasses, saw her go behind the curtain. He poked his head in. "*Eh da, ya Nadia?*"

She smiled and sniffed, looked around for a tissue. "It's okay, Tewfiq. Sorry to bother you."

"No bother." He took a handkerchief out of his pocket. It was worn and yellowed but impeccably clean and ironed.

She managed a laugh. "Not many people carry handkerchiefs anymore."

"*Malesh.*" When she was done he took it back from her, folded it again, returned it to his pocket.

"Thank you, Tewfiq."

He tsked at her then said in English: "Friends never need say thank you. *Khallas.*"

"Never?"

"Not necessary. *Of course* I help. *Of course* I give."

Nadia knew it to be true. There was a deeply reassuring quality of unconditional generosity and acceptance in Egypt, perhaps the Middle East in general. Sometimes she caught sight of it, a lifting of the burden of individuality and aloneness. In its place was an almost maternal warmth and sharing. Sometimes she wondered if Egyptians possessed a sensitivity and a sight that people in the West did not use, able to feel things, the way some animals see ultraviolet or hear higher pitches. Increasingly, as she walked the busy streets she could feel a connectedness, a common humanity, the veins and branches of the tree of life. Everybody was located somewhere on a stretched fabric, inches from the next. Individual movements—*individuals*—shook the fabric with every breath. There was no individual without their impact on the whole. One danced, they all danced. It had to be the secret behind the incredibly low rates of crime and violence. A city of sixteen million and yet she'd never felt safer. More harassed, yes, but safer too. And, strangely, seen.

"*Shukran,*" she said.

She went back out to join her father and spotted him talking animatedly to another man, maybe the father of a Shebab artist. He looked so at ease, so at home. She looked around for Manal's mother, even Uncle Nasser, excited at the thought of them all meeting. If they only knew, she smiled to herself. But it occurred to her that she didn't recall Manal talking about the show to her mother, and now she wondered if she had even invited her. There was something hurting and sad about that. She could understand Uncle Nasser not being wanted here, but Om Malek? By then she had wandered over to within view of Manal, who was staring intently at something. Nadia followed her gaze. A man had paused at Imad's painting, one of the few people to notice it. She recognized him as someone Manal had pointed out at a prior show as one of two Saudi businessmen who had begun attending their vernissages. He was leaning in to read the title card.

"It is a snowstorm." Manal, always where she needed to be, had crossed the room to stand behind him.

I'm so sorry, I don't speak Arabic. Nadia smiled at the memory. A sacred gallery, yes.

"Have you ever been in one?"

"Never." He sounded astonished.

"It is worse than a sandstorm. Sand gets in your clothes but winter gets in your bones. Someone told me that."

"Do you like this painting?"

"It is very ambitious." Shrewd words on which he could hang anything he wanted.

He didn't blink. "How much is it?"

She doubled the price on the spot.

The Saudi bowed, something he had picked up in

Japan and liked very much, he told her. "I do not know if I am ambitious, but I very much wish to be." He smiled, changing entirely his demeanor, a smile that seemed to gather up the entire room, Manal included. Nadia couldn't tell if it was his generosity that was doing that, or his cunning.

He turned back to the painting, at which point Manal's mouth dropped and Nadia let out an audible gasp. Tewfiq was staring at them both with a dark seriousness. In the brief second that their eyes had left the canvas, he had brought Manal's painting from its secluded spot at the back and leaned it against the wall beside Imad's painting. With the white of the wall behind it, the white of the painting, the white of the table, and the blankness of expectation, it exploded with even more violent energy.

"What?" The Saudi sounded shocked. Manal didn't move. "This is, this is, what is this?"

"Nothing, I am sorry. It shouldn't be here." Embarrassed, Manal went to grab it.

"No, no. Let me see it. Let me have a look. It is, it is…"

He stared at it, moved in close, then back out again. Nadia wondered if he was finding it obscene or politically contentious, or simply garish and obvious. It certainly did not have the nuance, if one were so inclined to call it that, of *Moscow Winter*. He consulted his list of paintings but did not find it there. Manal explained that it had been a last-minute addition.

"Who is the artist?" he asked, looking around the room.

"They couldn't come."

He said something very soft, almost intimate, that Nadia couldn't hear. He stepped back again and repeated it. "I want it. It is simply extraordinary."

Heels clacked behind them. "*C'est quoi ça?*"

Manal sputtered and could not look at Brigitte, who in turn was looking equally astonished at Manal's painting. "*C'est quoi ça?*"

The Saudi businessman spoke first. "This is a fantastic painting, very brave, Brigitte," he said. "I must have it."

Brigitte jaw literally dropped. "*Bon,*" she said, still not sure which pieces were fitting where in this scenario.

Imad, behind them and inching forward, was red and wide-eyed. He hissed something to Brigitte who, in turn, turned her attention to the Saudi. With unctuous care and diplomacy, she reminded the businessman, Sofian his name turned out to be, that *Moscow Winter* was an excellent choice. No, an excellent *investment*. The artist was making a name for himself both here and abroad, she said. He needed the encouragement and patronage of not only the Egyptian people, but of discerning international businessmen such as himself. In fact, she had an idea he was sure to find brilliant. Were he to purchase *Moscow Winter* she would also include this painting which is called, which is called—she turned to Manal—which is called, it appears, *Tanks and Arms*, yes, a surprising name to be sure, to be sure.

"Fine, fine," the businessman muttered. He shook Imad's hand somewhat reluctantly. "I must meet the artist of this painting," he said, scanning the room.

Avoiding Brigitte's gaze, Manal introduced herself. But Brigitte, talking louder, sent her to the back room for two glasses of wine. *Non, trois. Bon, quatre.* The fourth glass was for Manal. Sofian, missing the drama, still insisted that Brigitte reveal the name of the artist.

"It is Manal Fahmi."

Tewfiq, still as a sentry by the painting, spoke up. Manal returned with the glasses on a tray. There was a flurry of congratulations. When all had settled, the Saudi businessman said he was impressed by Manal's talent and Brigitte's discernment. *Bien sûr, bien sûr.* With superhuman effort, Brigitte refrained from rolling her eyes.

"Art is everywhere," he said, smiling at Manal. "But intelligence is too rare a quality." He insisted that they all join him for a celebration. He was going to take them to the Ramses Hotel for a cocktail. It was a night to remember, he kept saying. A night to remember.

Brigitte looked at her watch then nodded to Tewfiq. "*Tu fermes?* You close, alright? In an hour, no more." Manal followed Brigitte, Sofian and Imad down the stairs. She looked at Nadia before disappearing, lifting her arms in a helpless shrug.

Nadia was stunned at the speed with which it had all happened, but by then the room was almost empty. Her father was helping Tewfiq fill garbage bags with the detritus of the evening: empty plastic glasses, paper plates, scraps of paper, bits of food, cigarette butts extinguished carelessly on the floor. The ensuing quiet was a relief.

She and Bishara waited at the top of the stairs as Tewfiq went around the room switching off the lights. They shook hands on the sidewalk. Before leaving, Tewfiq addressed Nadia. "You should have gone with her. I should have made you go," he said, as if it had been on his mind.

"Why?"

But he looked away and shook his head. "*Malesh. Ma'a salama,*" he said, and headed for the buses.

"What was that about?" Bishara asked in his wake. Nadia did not have an answer. He insisted on sharing Nadia's taxi in spite of the fact that they were going in opposite directions. "That was a good show, Nadia. Thank you for inviting me. I do not know about art but…" He held up one finger and they said in unison: "I know what I like!"

"Your friends are right," he added.

"What about?"

"I should have spoke to you in Arabic, made sure you knew the language. Not just *shukran wa min fadlak.*"

"Or *beda,*" Nadia added. Eggs.

He laughed. They settled into a shared memory of Saturday morning breakfasts. *Shhhhh,* he always said as he fried up a pound, sometimes two, of bacon then dropped the eggs in the grease with green tomatoes.

"Can you still eat bacon?"

"*Abadan!*" he said in mock indignation. "Not in Cairo, anyways. Not with Noor."

"She's Muslim, eh Baba? Isn't that a problem?"

He shrugged. "Her family is in Germany. Is okay, no problem except for her grandfather, and guess what?"

"What?"

"He is in Germany," he laughed.

"Baba," she began. "I've been thinking. I think I want to stay in Egypt."

"Stay in Egypt? For how long?"

"Well, I'm already here much longer than I thought. I don't know, another month. Or two. Or until the summer. Who knows, *yanni*. Longer."

"Ya-aaaaa," he exhaled. "But Nadia, your life in Montreal. Did you talk to Clare? And your friend?"

"Manal?"

"Daniel. You told me you live with him." He shifted in the seat, sat up straighter. The leaning and lounging had only been for dreaming. "It is big things you are saying, big changes," he said with some concern. "You want to make changes?"

She exhaled. "Yes, Baba, I do. I like being here, I like seeing you, I even like having a sister. I mean, it was a shock, but I'm getting used to it now. She's a riot."

"Thank you. She loves you too. But your job, remember? Daniel? Your mother?"

The taxi stopped and idled in front of her building. Manal's building. Manal.

Her father leaned over and looked up. "Here?"

"Yes."

"She is a good friend? Can you stay here, is okay?"

"Yes, it's no problem." And she's more than a friend, she wanted to say. She ached for him to ask even one question, remove just one stone from the loose dam that was holding everything back.

He nodded slowly, as if thinking it through. "I will help you if you want to stay. Do you need money? Do you want a job?"

"Maybe a job would be good. Do you need a full-time babysitter?"

He threw his head back and laughed. "I say nothing! Noor would not be happy for me to replace her. Can you come once a week? But that is not a job. Let me think, *ya bint*. Let me think. *Yalla bint il asal,* bye-bye."

Before she got out of the car he kissed her three times on the cheeks then once on the forehead. "For good luck."

8

she who spoke again and again

Nadia woke up when Manal came home later, but didn't stir. There was something in the air, a cologne perhaps, a dusty smell of confectioner's sugar and cardamom, warm pastries, warm drinks, cigarettes. She pressed against the wall as Manal got into the other bed and listened intently to her breathing, then its quick descent into sleep. Nadia lay awake until the tiny twinge of fear in her chest gave up its grip and let her go. Hours later, a bird punctured her dream, a low screech bored into her head and let in light and noise and the arid air. She opened her eyes: it was morning. Manal, sitting up and fully dressed, was staring at her.

Last night had given no hint of this morning's beauty, but here it was, in front of her, all around her, in the air above, in the streets below. And sitting on the bed opposite. She was profoundly happy to see Manal. It felt like their lives were deepening and rooting and taking on texture and meaning. It was a feeling she'd never even had an inkling of with Daniel. She thought of Montreal's grid-like streets, their comforting predictability, how they were the perfect landscape for her relationship with

Daniel. He always knew where to go, what was right. She had believed that life came easy to Daniel because he had figured out its magic. But it was the opposite, wasn't it? He had no magic, just advantage. He didn't have to struggle for a single thing, there wasn't one lock whose combination he had to learn to pick at risk of being discovered. Maybe it was the same for her, too. But all was changing. She was living in Cairo and would get a job. Manal had sold a painting and would be an artist. She felt grateful to her, deeply, deeply grateful. She wanted to run headlong into Manal's courage and Cairo's cacophony and her own future's unknowability. "Guess what?" she asked, stretching the bliss throughout her body.

"What?"

"You sold a painting!"

Manal managed a small smile.

"Aren't you excited?"

"Maybe. Yes, I am. Thank you for reminding me."

Nadia opened her arms.

"Tewfiq is at work," Manal said in answer to an unknown question. "Brigitte said I could take today off. It will be quiet today. The day after a vernissage is the time to take a break. Tomorrow will be busy again."

"Come." She made room for her in the narrow bed, her entire body exploding with desire.

"Nadia. Nadia."

"Yes?"

"I am going to take you to the most beautiful place in Cairo."

Manal rushed her through a breakfast of leftover *fûl* and bread, then brought her down the street where they hailed a minibus to the centrale and waited for another. This one was smaller and more crowded, they had to squeeze in with a young girl on a seat for two. The journey away from the *wist il balad* was marked by the increasing appearance of animals. Goats picking through garbage, donkeys pulling carts, water buffaloes lurking in alleys, and carcass after carcass of red-painted sides of beef hanging in butcher shops, trembling with flies.

"Here we are."

They got off at a limestone wall that ran the length of the street. Behind it rose a dome and a minaret, all of it a soft golden brick and stone. At the gate two children sat on their haunches and eyed them imploringly if not aggressively. Manal fished a bill out of her purse and handed it to the older child. He kissed it and blessed her with a short prayer.

"This is the mosque of Ibn Tulun," Manal said. "It is my favourite place." She pulled a white scarf out of her pocket and tied it loosely around Nadia's head, did the same for herself.

"There," she said, stepping back. "Now we are sisters."

The vast courtyard was empty save for a small group of tourists and two men praying. Paths of white limestone radiated from a stone structure in the middle. Rampart walls of arches and passageways formed the perimeter but at a distance, while the sky overhead, cut off from the tangled landscape of the city, was uncharacteristically blue. Other than the incongruous sound of German echoing against the mosaic, the effect of calmness and meditation was powerful. A bird perched on a pillar and called its mate.

"This is where you wash yourself before praying," Manal said when they reached the middle. "It used to be a fountain."

"It's so quiet in here. You can't even hear the city."

They continued walking, Nadia's arm in Manal's, hands wrapped around hands, their steps slow and ponderous. Manal's eyes sometimes fluttered and her mouth moved in soft quivers. They stopped under an arch. Manal turned to Nadia. Her lips hovered just beside her cheek, her eyes softly liquefying.

"For how long are you in Egypt, *ya Nadia*?"

"I don't know, Manal." Nadia hesitated. Any answer would define an ending. "I'm flexible."

"And if I get the scholarship to Paris? In September?"

"*Et alors?* I will follow you to Paris."

"You say that…"

"I mean it."

"I feel so many possibilities, *ya Nadia*. It is all because of you."

"You have so much talent."

"*Yanni*, and a bird has so much wings. But who is going to open the cage for her?"

Nadia adjusted Manal's slipping scarf. With an urge that was painful to resist, she wanted to touch her face, climb her fingers over the cheekbones, nestle in her neck beneath the white rayon, join with her at the hips and fall to the stone floor like candle wax.

"What did you do last night?" she heard herself asking. Manal looked at her then looked quickly away.

But another voice grumbled. A scruffy man in a brown *galabiyya* shuffled towards them speaking in a thick, impenetrable accent.

"He will give us a tour, if you like," Manal said, jumping a little too quickly on the distraction. "Would you like to take a tour of the mosque, my Canadian friend?"

He led them around the inner perimeter, speaking quickly and gesturing here and there almost dismissively. Manal translated, her lips and breath pouring teasingly into Nadia's ear, their bodies rippling against the other as they walked. *It's the oldest mosque in Egypt. Oh, and the biggest too. It is the only one to have that staircase around the minaret. Do you see it? Look up, dear, sweet Nadia, look up. It spirals around like a snake. No, like a vine. I have seen pictures of vines. Do they have vines in Paris? Look at those windows, look at the designs and patterns. They are beautiful, are they not? How beautiful, how beautiful. Oh listen, it was used as a military hospital by Ibrahim Pasha. And then as a warehouse for salt. Only sacred if you are a chef! Wait, and a prison too. History is full of surprises, ya Nadia. And full of mystery and compromise. Ibn Tulun was a Turkish slave who rose to great heights. Aren't we all slaves, ya Nadia. This whole area is twenty-six thousand square metres. Ya allah ya allah. Touch this, ya bint il helwa. This is stucco, the first time used in Cairo. We can stay and pray here now, ya okhti. In this corner. Take off your shoes. We need to give him money. No, a bit more.*

Manal clasped her hands, bent forward at the knees, then sunk to the floor. Nadia, not sure if following the movements was respectful or not, made an attempt or two before deciding that standing as still as possible with a lowered head was the best she could offer. Manal remained down for a long time, whispering a prayer whose familiar beginning Nadia had heard all her life but never knew held any meaning. *B'ism allah il rahman il raheem…*

The day Manal had planned to ask Brigitte for the letter of support, she announced she was leaving for a week to Hurghada on the Red Sea. *Tu prends charge, je te fais confiance,* Brigitte said over her shoulder, then she and her camel leather bag were gone.

"Send the application in anyways," Nadia offered. "You can just put *lettre à venir* or *à fournir* or whatever. It's standard practice to have these things follow. People do it all the time. In any case, didn't you say Brigitte knows them? I am sure if she tells them to accept the letter later they will, especially if it's her fault it's late. I am sure she will support you."

"*Yanni…*" Tewfiq said. He sounded doubtful, as they all felt.

Manal stuffed everything back in the envelope. "You're right. Better I show them my determination than my fear." She clapped her hands and disappeared into the backroom. The fridge opened and closed and she emerged with a bottle of opened wine, enough for three small glasses. "Let's celebrate!"

Tewfiq demurred, Nadia too. It wasn't even lunch-time. Manal started to pour then changed her mind, took a swig right from the bottle. "*Ya allah,* that really is the best way. Just like in the films."

When Brigitte returned from the Red Sea she was tanned and in a buoyant mood. Until Manal brought up the let-ter. "I didn't even know you were applying to this schol-arship. You know it is a special scholarship for emerg-ing Egyptian artists." She looked squarely at Manal. "*Mashrabiya* artists, Manal."

Manal didn't move. Not while Brigitte ground out her cigarette, rummaged through her bag for another, changed her mind, threw her long scarf back around her neck, announced she had an appointment, and left.

Behind the curtain, Nadia and Tewfiq stared at each other and didn't move either.

When they were locking up Nadia had to tell Manal that she wouldn't be going directly back to the flat with her.

"Babysitting? Again?"

"I kept forgetting to tell you. They have a last-minute meeting or something."

Manal looked lost, immobilized. She stopped in the middle of the sidewalk, people moved around them like a rushing river around stones. She reached out for balance, held on to Nadia. "Can I come?"

Nora, occupied with her toys, did not notice the door click that signaled the departure of her parents. Nadia got down on the ground with her and helped her with the blocks that were supposed to be a house. *Beit*, Nora said. "House!" *Beit*. "House!" *Beit*. *Howse*.

"Manal! Did you hear her? She said house! I think that's her first English word!" She picked her up and held her high and kissed her on both cheeks. They went around the apartment as Nadia pointed things out. Nora told her what they were in Arabic while Nadia said the word in English. "We're both learning," she called out to Manal, excited and proud of them both.

As they wandered from room to room there were things in the apartment that she recognized about her father. He liked clocks and shishas and lots of little carpets overlapping on top of each other instead of one big one. Her mother wanted wall-to-wall and was forever tripping over the worn little rugs he'd had shipped from Egypt. "Take off your shoes, you won't trip," he'd tell her over and over. "See? Bare feet never fail you." And it was true, Nadia now saw. Bare feet never fail you. In the kitchen Nadia opened the fridge and the child leaned out of her arms and grabbed a little container. They sat down on the floor and snacked on bananas and labneh.

"Come watch *Sons and Daughters* with me," Manal called from the living room after Nadia put her sister to bed. It was an Australian soap opera that was syndicated in Egypt and subtitled in Arabic. It was about a brother and sister, twins separated at birth, who were now in love and unaware of their origins.

"I can't believe this is proper fare for Egypt," Nadia said. "It's kind of scandalous, no?"

"Wait till Ramadan, the Egyptian serials are worse! Murders, adultery, pregnancy, we do it better than anyone. I think this one copies us, to be honest."

Nadia joined her on the couch.

"I never babysat," Manal said. "Do you do it a lot? Here we send the kids to the family somewhere, an aunt, a grandma. There is always family."

"I guess I'm family then. Anyways, I grew up babysitting for neighbours all the time."

"They pay you money?"

"For sure. It was a job. Boys delivered papers and girls babysat."

"American capitalism," Manal laughed. "My father always said beware, it will eat you and spit you."

"The Canadian version is not so bad. We share the earnings."

"The Egyptian way is we get *koshery* or *liblib* as payment but we're so nice that we give half of it back."

"My father used to make *koshery* all the time. I love it. And *liblib*, wow. He used to buy two-kilo bags from this Lebanese store. He'd eat them in a day. My mother would freak out at the mess."

Manal laughed. "Egyptians never notice any mess. Did your mother cook Canadian food or did she learn Egyptian and Palestinian dishes?"

"Definitely Canadian, whatever that is. I never really

thought about it before, but since I've been here I've been thinking that she didn't really like Arab things. Maybe at first, when it was new and exciting, but I think it mostly just annoyed her."

"That's why he needed an Egyptian wife. Good for him."

Nadia rolled her eyes and got up from the couch. "It's a little more complicated than that. Nothing wrong with Canada. Do you even know anything about Canada?"

Manal pretended to be cold. "*Brrrrr.*"

"No, I'm serious. Everyone's always evil empire this, the bad West that. But they don't really know anything. All they know is Ronald Reagan. First of all, we all think he's an idiot, especially Canadians. Second, I'm not American, I'm Canadian. Do you know we have free healthcare and cheap universities and we ride buses and there's low crime and everyone shares? Oh, and that it gets hot in the summer? Do you know that Montreal is poor and that apartments are rundown and that there are probably a million artists in the city? And that there are so many immigrants that everybody, and I mean everybody, is from somewhere else. And that most of us also speak French. *Tu savais-tu?* Eh?"

"Okay *ya hagga.* Okay." Manal went over to where she was standing by the television.

"And I hate television. Daniel and I don't even own one."

"Daniel…" Manal pondered the name, lowered it to the ground like a heavy brick.

Nadia turned away.

"Never mind," Manal said softly. She reached for Nadia's fingers then ran her own up her arm. She kissed her, once, twice, softer, softer still. Moved her mouth to Nadia's ear, whispered and whispered and whispered.

"What's that?" Nadia asked, dissolving into the syntax of her hands.

"Poetry."

"Tell me about those petting affairs," Nadia asked with a smile. "Did you have many?"

"Many? No." Manal kissed her neck then her collarbone. "Only one. She was an artist. Maybe you'll meet her, she comes to the gallery."

"That would be weird."

"Not really."

"Is she married?"

"Of course."

"How did it happen?"

"How did it happen?" Manal pulled back and tilted her head. "Do you really want to know? It happened because she was desperate and I was curious. It happened because she was lonely and I was ambitious. It happened because her husband was at a conference and her children were at their grandmother's. It happened because I needed to know and be prepared."

"Be prepared for what?"

"For this."

She led Nadia back to the couch, laid her down, squeezed in lengthwise beside her. She made soft sounds, aural accompaniments to the ascending and descending of her limbs. Thick with desire, Nadia had never felt like this with anyone, not even Daniel. Maybe especially not Daniel, where all she could think of to describe their lovemaking were scientific terms: cause and effect, equal and opposite reactions, rest and motion. Daniel had once described Newton's three laws of motion in sexual terms. At the time she found it playful and endearing, evidence of his lighthearted take on the world, something she had been craving. But over time she came to understand that he could sexualize a grocery list, that he and his friends were perpetually sexualizing everything. Sex was reduced to an objective, a prize, a punchline. Manal took both Nadia's hands and stretched them back up over her head so that her entire body was a taut line of longing. How ironic that it took travelling to Egypt to discover touch and breath and the exquisite momentum of another woman's body over hers.

The door clicked. In an instant Manal peeled herself off Nadia and they both sat up, coming face to face with the bewildered expressions of Bishara and Noor.

"We were sleeping," Nadia said quickly, unnecessarily, as they shot to their feet.

"You startled us!" Manal nodded vigorously, her red cheeks doing double duty as sleepy.

Bishara, looking down at his shoes as he removed them, mumbled an apology for being late while Noor disappeared to the baby's room to have a look. "She is sleeping with smile," she said when she returned.

"Thank you, Nadia, you helped us, it was last minute," Bishara said. Nadia didn't know what was more disturbing, that she couldn't read him or that he might have seen something.

"It was very lucky for us you were here," he said again. "Do you need help to find taxi?"

"Nah, we're fine," Nadia forced a laugh.

Noor had been shuffling in her purse, now she held out a twenty-pound note.

"No, it's okay," Nadia said, embarrassed in front of Manal.

"You take. You young, you take. It is good," Noor insisted, touching her heart.

"May I ask you a question?" Manal turned to Bishara as he pushed the button for the elevator. "Will Palestine ever be solved?"

Nadia made an attempt to shush her and rolled her eyes at her father. But he welcomed the question.

"First you must define 'solved' and that is the problem," he said. "There are too many definitions, too many layers, too many histories."

"Too many histories?"

"What can a poor village man with no education? What can a student with no school? What can a government that is not even a government? We cannot compete against a two-thousand-year-old legend. Old story, Nadia, like religion." He laughed. "It *is* religion. Old tribe who lost their land one day a long time ago and—*ouf and poof!*—now they think they found it. But not finished, the story has twist. It has a massacre, a holocaust, most cruel most cruel. Most cruel. *Ya wayli*. What can we do? We lose. We try to compete.Sometimes we come close, but really we cannot. We can only survive."

"How do you survive without hope and without opportunity?"

"*Manal…*"

"*Malesh*, Nadia. Hope is there when your history is there. The Jews know that! And opportunity? You make that every day. Start over, make it again. Look at the Occupied Territories. They are on fire with the bursting hearts of the people. For every drop of blood a flower will grow. The Israelis, what do they see? They see only weeds and want to rip out them all. But we know they are flowers, we know their beauty. The world will see."

"Your father is a poet," Manal said in the taxi.

"You think so? He probably thinks so."

"Why you don't know more? How come you don't talk like that?"

"What?" But it stung.

"You don't have his same passion. You don't talk of Palestine or the Intifada or anything. It is funny."

She couldn't bear to be criticized by Manal, to be seen as less than and not up to snuff. Yet it was true. There was an answer to this; she had to find it.

"He only saw me as Canadian," she said, the thoughts forming as the words did. "I was a foreigner to him, a Canadian daughter. I mean, he told me stuff and said I was Palestinian, but it always seemed like he snuck it in there when my mom wasn't looking. And then he started going to Cairo and we saw him less and less and less. Am I Canadian? Am I Arab? I don't even speak Arabic." Her voice wavered. "Manal, do you know how painful that is? That I don't speak Arabic?"

"Now I know."

"Sounds silly all this, doesn't it."

"No."

"I have spent my whole life wanting part of myself, then pushing it away, then wanting it, then pushing it away. I don't know how else to explain it. He doesn't talk politics to me anymore."

They drove in silence the rest of the way. The *bowab* in Manal's lobby nodded at them then went back to sleep. As they walked slowly up the four flights of stairs, Nadia paused.

"That was close, Manal. Earlier, I mean."

"Everything is close."

They resumed climbing.

The skies were unusually dark on the last Thursday before the end of the show. It was already midday so they opted for a taxi in the unfounded belief that it would get them there faster than a bus or *taxi service*.

Manal stopped before getting in the car and looked up. "I wonder," she said.

"I wonder what?"

"I wonder if the *khamseen* are coming. It is a bit early."

Once settled in the backseat, she explained.

"Sometimes if you are on the edge of the city you can see it coming. It blows through Cairo like there is a broom and all the dust is pushed and pushed and pushed. No matter even if you are indoors, *ya Nadia*, you will find sand in your panties at the end of the day."

"That's amazing."

"And then it is gone. One day, two days, and it leaves us. Goes on to Libya or the Sinai or the Sudan or Saudi, *mish arifa*, I don't know. And we go back to pretending that nature is our friend."

The taxi driver spoke up, exchanged some words with Manal.

"What is he saying?"

"He says *khudi balik*—take care—it is coming soon."

9

horus the falcon-headed man

"Let me see your passport, *ya hagga*." Manal held out her hand, a playful look on her face, and flipped through the pages. "You see? You only have a few days left. I knew, I knew. Why you do not keep track? They could expel you if you are not careful."

"What are you talking about?" Nadia held it this way and that trying to decipher the stamp. "I can't read it. And look here, it's smudged."

"*Tssk*." Manal sounded disgusted, but her smile remained. "I take you. You want to see the worst of Cairo? Are you curious? We go to the Mogamma. Today, *yanni*."

When it was built, shortly after World War II, the Mogamma government building was considered modern. Hulking and brutal, its concave walls embraced the hub of a new downtown in the new cosmopolitan city in an ambitious post-British-occupied Egypt. But it was all moving so fast. King Farouk had barely renamed the streets when Nasser's handsome army claimed the country for themselves and Tahrir Square was born. The illiterate *fellaheen*, once kept busy in kitchens and fields, could now graduate with degrees in accounting or dentistry or education. General Nasser guaranteed them a job for life, if not in the hoped-for economy then in the growing public service. This explained why, on the day that Manal brought Nadia to officially extend her stay in Egypt, upwards of 10,000 people were stationed at their desks throughout the monolith's fourteen floors.

"Bring enough money." Manal did a quick calculation: thirty LE, Egyptian pounds, for the visa, ten LE for copies, five LE for the photograph, and another twenty just in case. "You never know what kind of day they are having," Manal explained.

Set back from the road only a few hundred metres from the Nile Hilton, the front of the building was silhouetted by a tableau of thin men perched on cloth-covered crates banging away at typewriters, interspersed with other men, just as thin, waiting by tripoded box cameras whose black curtains hung limp in the breezeless air. Dotted between them, children, thinnest-of-all, sold envelopes from cloth sacks that dangled only inches off the ground.

"*Yalla*, this way." Taking Nadia by the elbow, Manal pushed them up three flights of stairs; *this way* through a dozen offices where men and women sat lifeless, dusty manila envelopes piled in front of them; *this way,* into a crowded room where grey clods of people careened against a counter, waving passbooks and money; *this way,* through to another room, empty but for a handful of blond people. "*Law samahti, taht umri, min fadlak,*" Manal sang a string of honorifics and platitudes as she placed Nadia's papers into the hands of a large and blinking woman who licked a stamp and placed it on a new set of papers and handed them back.

"Well, that wasn't so bad," Nadia said.

"Not yet."

Manal dragged her back outside and positioned her in front of one of the cameras. They fanned themselves with Nadia's documents as the photographer bent over a chemical bath that was as toxic as it was efficient. Back upstairs, the picture was stamped and stapled to a new sheet of papers by a chain-smoking man who swore with every gesture. The swearing was contagious and Manal took it up as they waited for a clerk to type up a new document.

Nadia lost track. She followed Manal from room to room, signed when told to sign, nodded when questioned, held in her need to pee until it made her ache. When they finally exited, the sky was as lifeless as Manal's mood. But the stamp was bright and legible and gave Nadia another six months in Cairo. "At least," they both said.

They were hungry, so when Manal went into the gallery Nadia headed for the two small shops up the street. She waited while the *taamiyyas* sizzled in the large round metal dish then were stuffed in an open pita and dressed with tahini and strips of lettuce. Next door she smiled at Basel—they were on a first name basis now—as he smashed peeled mangoes and added strawberries. Such an English name, she'd said, and asked if he was in fact British, a left-over from TE Lawrence's army perhaps? He had no idea what she was saying. *Ismi Basel*, he repeated. It's an Egyptian name, silly girl, Manal told her later. It means brave. Nadia returned to the gallery, dribbles of juice decorating her shirt. She stopped when she heard voices coming from behind the curtain.

"But there is a week empty at the end of the month. Remember that scheduling problem? It's still there." There was something in Manal's voice that Nadia hadn't heard before. She sounded pleading, fearful.

"*Oui, Manal.*"

"I don't even need a whole week. Just four days."

"*C'est compliqué, ma chère.* How many more paintings do you have?" Brigitte's words were more clipped than usual, if that were possible.

"Many. Plus drawings. Even more drawings. Some drawings are here, I can show you."

Brigitte seemed to want to avoid this. "Manal, I am still not happy about the vernissage. I told you. What you did was, how you say, *hors norme*. Yes, yes, even though you managed to sell it."

"He bought two."

"And he needs to come back and buy more. How can we make that happen, Manal? How can we make sure our clients can trust us? We need to be completely transparent and clean. *Tu comprends qu'est-ce que je veux dire?* Hmm?"

"I won't do it again."

Nadia heard Manal haul her huge black portfolio up

onto the table and open it. For a few minutes, nothing filled the silence but the sound of thick paper landing on thick paper.

"*Bon*," Brigitte finally said. "If you can sell him another painting—not one of yours—I can let you show at the gallery. I have to believe that you are here for more than your own sales job."

"How can you think...I don't understand. You know I am an artist. Why is it so..." Manal struggled with her words and, Nadia could tell, her temper.

"I can't have you working at cross purposes."

"Cross purposes? What purposes and what cross? Would you rather hire somebody who only knows about shoes? Or *shwarmas*? Or Pyramids? Or when the last Pharaoh was alive? Or somebody to give directions to Khan el Khalile?"

"*Khallas*. Enough." Minutes later, accompanied only by the ruffling sound of drawings being laid upon drawings, Brigitte broke the tense silence. "Are all the drawings like this?"

"They are figurative mostly, yes."

"Are they all nudes." It was a statement, not a question. "What about *these*? Again police? Soldiers? And what is this here?"

"That's the Palestinian flag."

"*Mon dieu*. The Palestinian flag is illegal, Manal."

"Only in Israel and the Occupied Territories, not here."

"*Oh là là*. Manal, these drawings are very, how shall I

say it, sensitive. Nudes...police. And *haram*. A dead body? *Ya allah*. It was bad enough you put your tank in *Shebab ya Shebab*. You know I have to be careful of controversy."

"I am not the first to paint nudes. Khaled Hama's show had nudes. Same with Al Ghazza. And soldiers are everywhere on the streets." Then she mumbled something that Nadia strained to make out. It sounded like: "There are all kinds of controversies."

Brigitte continued to turn pages. "I do not see soldiers on the streets of Cairo."

"Then you are not looking," Manal mumbled.

More sounds of shuffling pages. "They are all of *her*."

"You don't always see her face. Look—"

"*Bon, khallas*." Brigitte's voice rose. She was tired, fed up, finished with being challenged.

Someone closed the portfolio, returned the drawings to their sheath and the canvases to the floor against the wall. "This is tricky, Manal. This would be your first show. You do not have a reputation yet. Are you sure you want to create one like, like *this*? Do not tell me that you want to have an *exposition* of police and naked women. People will talk. If they aren't already."

"How can I ignore what is going on in the world?" Manal's voice raised slightly in pitch as a shadow of anger entered it. "I thought you would support me. I thought you would understand. They are of her because she is the only one who will pose for me. There are so many because I have been preparing for a show. And I have been preparing for a show so I can complete my application for the scholarship and maybe have a chance of getting it."

Brigitte abandoned English altogether at this point, and began switching rapidly back and forth between French and Arabic, which Manal was able to match word for word, protestation with protestation. By now, sauce from the sandwiches and condensation from the drinks were all over Nadia's lap.

Somebody clapped their hands together, must have been Brigitte. "I do, Manal, of course I do. *On verra*, okay. *Tiens, tiens*, let me see what I can do." She strode purposefully out of the storeroom, glancing twice over at Nadia, the second time as if to confirm what she had seen. She left the Galerie without a word. Nadia waited patiently for Manal to emerge. But five long minutes later she stormed out, following Brigitte, minus the glance, and slammed the street door even louder.

Nadia ate both sandwiches and drank both drinks. They were delicious. At the end of the day Manal returned looking like she had wandered over half the city. Her hair, in a neat ponytail that morning, was sticking out in bunches. Her shirt was untucked and everything was weighed down by a fine layer of dust.

"Are you okay?"

"I brought you something." She held out a pastry box from a well-known café frequented by expats, the intelligentsia, and everyone else who wanted to be either.

"You went to Groppi's?" Manal had told her about the old café, promised to take her there and point out the lovers and the poets.

She dismissed the question with a shake of her head. "Did anyone call? Any news?" She took off her little cotton jacket.

"No, nothing. Very quiet. Oh wait, one person did come, an AUC student. They wanted information on the artists. I gave them some flyers."

"*Shukran.*"

"Manal, do you want to talk about what Brigitte said?"

"Nadia, I have another favour to ask you." Manal took her time unwrapping the scarf from around her neck, a mesmerizing uncircling and uncircling and uncircling of fabric. "Can you go home alone tonight? I have a meeting. I will be home later. Late."

"A meeting? Did you just visit another gallery? Is that what you were doing?" Nadia laughed. "Do you have a plan B? How brilliant."

"No, dear Nadia. I have a meeting. I need to fix things. You heard her."

"So what does that mean?"

"I need to sell him another painting."

"Who?"

"Sofian."

Nadia heard something in the way she spoke his name, how she omitted his last name, how it seemed to have too many syllables, how she looked away at the beginning of the name and didn't return her gaze. "You're going to meet him? Tonight? Manal, this is really, I don't know. It doesn't feel right. Do you want me to come with you?"

"No, no. I know what I am doing. It is already

177

arranged."

"Already arranged? When did you arrange this? What am I missing?"

Manal looked away and sighed. "He already wanted to meet me."

Nadia felt the blood instantly drain out of her face. Her breathing stopped then resumed, stopped then resumed. It was like breathing, quite like breathing.

"*Ya asal*. It is nothing. He likes art. Everything is complicated, I told you already. I am an Egyptian girl and you are a lucky Canadian."

Nadia looked at her watch. She had found it at a kiosk one day while strolling with Manal. Its hours were written in Arabic numerals, something she had never seen. But it stopped working only a few days after she bought it, though she kept wearing it anyways. It told her nothing.

Manal forced a smile. "I will close up," she said. "You know which bus? No, take a taxi. Here. Take ten pounds. I know how you love to tip. You pay too much, you know. You are too good."

Nadia grabbed her bag hanging on the chair. "I have money. I'm fine." She stopped at the door. "You look a mess, you know."

"It's okay, I am going to change. I brought clothes," Manal said, then immediately looked like she regretted saying it. It was too much information.

Not wanting to give Manal the satisfaction of seeing that

she'd waited for her, Nadia willed herself to sleep. But she awoke to the air pushing ahead of a slick-running car somewhere nearby in the strobing darkness. Then a car door closing, the scampering of feet up the building's front steps, the long climb, foot after foot, steady and strong, the key in the front door, the thick groan of it closing, the running of water in the bathroom, the flushing back out of the building, down to the river. Another click, another pushing of air, this time a cloud infused with jasmine and incense, cigarette smoke and alcohol. Manal moved quietly in the room, took off her clothes, put on her nightdress, crawled into her bed, lay there not breathing. Then she got up and joined Nadia, curled her body around hers, held it tight. Nadia couldn't restrain herself from sighing audibly when Manal's chamois face settled into the back of her neck. Their breathing slowed until their bodies gave way to the forgiving embrace of the mattress.

Manal was already in the kitchen when Nadia got up. She looked at her over a plate of feta cheese and tomato slices. "Your father called."

"When?"

"Are you hungry?" Manal cleared the rest of the table for her. "Sit."

Nadia's insides felt like crushed stone in the moments before it sets into cement. She tore a strip of bread and used it to pick up a piece of cheese and a slice of tomato. She was having a hard time looking directly at Manal.

"He wants to bring you to the hospital today."

"I'm not sick."

"No, silly girl. He wants to invite you to see his job. And they have a reception tonight. He invites you. You will go, no? Tomorrow is Friday, gallery will be closed. You are free to go."

But she didn't want to be free to go. She wanted to be imprisoned in this room, this apartment, this moment. No, not this moment, not today but yesterday. Yesterday, in another moment, just prior to saying, "Are you hungry? Would you like a *taamiyya* sandwich?" That moment forever. What did Manal say once? Kidnapped. Held without ransom.

"You'll come too?"

"*La, shukran, ya Nadia*. Your father invited me but I will stay home today with my mother." She smiled. "She has been forgetting what I look like."

The Palestine Hospital was not all that far from Manal's apartment, in Heliopolis, but it may as well have been across town. Nadia walked to the end of the street and called out to passing *taxi service*. Like black beetles, the shared cabs darted in and out between curb and median, looking to pick up passengers going in their direction. When she and Manal were too weary to wait for the bus they'd stand on the corner and shout *wist il balad*. She took a deep breath and hollered: *Mustashfa Philistine!* She had the accent, the tilt of the body, the raised arm and flickering hand, and the perfect expression of inevitability.

A van stopped, the driver tilted his head and signaled for her to climb in. The four people inside rearranged themselves to make disembarking easiest for the next person which, given where she was told to sit, wasn't going to be her. A man beside the driver reached back and took her money. All windows open to the hot breeze, they drove in silence, everyone angled to receive as much passing air as possible. In their disinterested quiet, she realized that no one suspected she was a foreigner.

The hospital was an eight-storey white cement and stucco building facing a large boulevard, with *Palestine Hospital* written across it in large red letters. Nadia slid open the van door and, stepping over yielding knees and feet, tumbled out. Inside the lobby, a dozen men, women, and children sat in chairs by a window, while another dozen rested on the floor. They looked at her with only minimal curiosity. Unlike the two women at the reception desk, who did not notice Nadia even as she stood in front of them for several minutes. *Excuse me*, she finally said, in English as she wasn't yet ready to navigate answers she might not understand. "I am here to see Bishara Eid."

One of them opened a large ledger and, finger poised, was ready to go down the names, turn the pages, find more names. "He is patient?"

"No, he works here."

The two women glanced at each other, a brief half-second, as if a foreigner wanting to see an employee was a phenomenon they had yet to encounter.

"He is my father," Nadia said stubbornly.

"He is doctor?"

"No," Nadia sighed. "He's a—an administrator. I think. He is new."

They conferred. One of them had an idea. She led Nadia through a labyrinth of hallways, out another door, across a courtyard, and into another building. She spoke to a man behind a desk and then, without a word or nod to Nadia, left. The room was a drab collection of old furniture and overloaded bookshelves. Stacks of papers slid over each other on a round table. Almost invisible against the melamine and vinyl upholstery, a teenager sat on the couch and stared off into the middle distance, a cigarette smoldering between his unmoving fingers. The man gave Nadia a brief nod then left, closing a door behind him. Fifteen minutes later, the door opened again and in strode her father, all smiles and open eyes. "Hello! *Ahlan, ahlan!*"

He could have been someone else. He held himself erect, arms sweeping the room, sweeping her up. He wore dress slacks and a white shirt with a tie, like Tewfiq, but not a fray or yellow stain in sight. Even his glasses, which she had always thought made him seem unfashionable, now gave him a patrician air, a look of intelligence and ownership. Ownership, but of what? The room? The hospital? Nadia? No, she decided, it was of himself. For the first time since arriving in Cairo, she greeted him unabashedly.

"You found us! Have you had lunch? You are not too hot?" His questions, with an arm around her shoulder, another arm leading the way, also took ownership.

He led her down a hallway, opening doors along the way and introducing her to everyone they came across. *Ahlan, ahlan*, they said one after the other, taking her hand in both of theirs, bowing slightly. At the end of the corridor she turned to him.

"Who are you?" Then corrected herself: "I mean, what is your job?"

He beamed. "I am liaison officer."

She nodded, waited for more.

"I am liaison between the healthcare on the ground and the hospital."

"On the ground?" She imagined him farming or sweeping streets or picking bandages up off the floor.

"Yes, they need much help, their clinics and hospitals are overrun. It is chaos."

"On the ground, like the street…?"

He shook his head a couple of times, brought his eyebrows together, wrinkled his forehead, studied her with one eye. "Nadia *habbibiti*, the Intifada."

"Oh." The reproach, as mild as it was, hurt. "Yes, of course. Sorry. I was just picturing the ground. Forget it."

He led her out a door, across a courtyard and back into the hospital proper. It was surprisingly clean, quiet, and orderly. They wandered down hallways, looked into offices, chatted with staff at nursing stations, climbed stairs to the next floor and did it all again. "I bring you on a tour. There is much to teach you. We have Intifada patients here. *Ya Nadia*, you must learn about your country."

Her country. She had a country, it was Canada.

She had a passport, it was Canadian. She had a Canadian mother, a Canadian upbringing, spoke both official Canadian languages. Yet maybe she could indeed have another country, a second country, a place called Palestine, a place she'd never been but that could hold the key to everything. Then there was the third country, Egypt. Manal's country.

"This is my daughter." It was his second time saying it. "This is Dr. Zuhair."

"*Tisharafna*," the doctor said. You honour us. "Your father will be doing important work for us in the Territories, *insha'allah*."

She looked to Bishara for an explanation but he had already moved on.

"This hospital serves all of Cairo," he said at the door to the fourth floor. "Unfortunately in a country like Egypt either you can afford the excellent private care like the hospital in Maadi, or you go to the public hospital, like the Mustashfa Il Qahira, and get treated like an animal. No, worse than an animal. Palestine Hospital is top care, top top care, excellent and clean—*mish kidda, Nadia*? And it is free to anyone who walks in." He paused, nodded to a passing doctor. "And now we are on the fourth floor," he said somberly. "Look over there, what do you see?" Three men stood idly at the end of the hallway, glanced at them briefly, resumed talking and smoking. They wore rifles slung casually on straps over their shoulders.

"Soldiers?"

"Yes. Guards. We have begun taking in Intifada

patients. We must guard them. First we will go this way and we get permission from Dr. Fareed to visit the patients."

"Baba what did he mean about you going to the Territories, to be on the ground? Isn't that dangerous?"

"Come, come." He hurried ahead then stopped, rapped on a door, opened it. A woman sat at a desk, a large book open before her. She took off her reading glasses and waved them in.

"Nadia, this is Dr. Mai Fareed, doctor of mental health. She is from Ramallah. She was in prison last year—last year? She has come to Palestine Hospital and will stay with us hopefully one month, maybe longer." He quickly got the introduction out of the way then continued in Arabic. Nadia could make sense of individual words and understood that he was asking that they visit an Intifada patient. But the doctor was not receptive. Bishara motioned several times to his daughter, as if underscoring the importance of a complete tour.

The doctor addressed Nadia. "I am very sorry but today is not a good day to visit. We are understaffed because of the reception tonight. Please, can you come back another day." It was not a question.

Nadia, mortified, hurried to explain that it was fine, that she had no interest in seeing a patient, well she had interest of course, who wouldn't? Naturally she was very concerned, after all, but she didn't want to barge in like this and of course she understood that they were all busy. Finally, giving up on sounding coherent, she looked to her father for help but he was half out the door talking to somebody.

"I am sorry. Nadia, you stay here? I will be right back."

Before either of them could object, he was gone.

"I'm really sorry. It's okay, I will leave you alone, you must be very busy."

For the first time since meeting, the doctor cracked a smile. She shook her head and chuckled. "It is a very busy hospital. Your father is, well, he is new here. He is trying very hard." She returned to her chair behind the desk. Then, in a surprising gesture, motioned to Nadia to sit. "You are not Egyptian," she said by way of a question.

"No. I was born and raised in Montreal, Canada. I am here to visit my father, he's Palestinian. He lives in Cairo now." It was the clearest, most concise answer she had given anyone, ever.

The doctor smiled. "We lose people to the four corners of the world. It is rare, and nice, when they come back."

The office was drab and small. Against one wall, half-size bookshelves were filled with books and binders, while against the other wall were a row of chairs and free-standing ashtrays. The doctor leaned back as if waiting. Nadia wanted for once to meet expectations, to rise to the gravitas around her. In any case, if she was going to waste the good doctor's time, she wanted to at least be minimally engaging.

"My father said you were arrested?"

"I was detained for a few days. They questioned me

about my work, of course, but could only keep me for a few days. Unlike most Palestinians, I had a lawyer."

"What were you charged with?"

"I was not charged with anything," she said. "My work was interrupted. I was harassed and intimidated. It is typical. Find me a Palestinian who has not been detained and I will find you the future."

"You had a lawyer, I guess that helped."

"Yes, she is an Israeli lawyer. A wonderful woman. Very brave to do what she does. Plus, I have British passport. They really cannot touch me."

"What is the prison like?"

"*Ya rob.*" The doctor leaned forward over her desk. "You cannot know everything just by asking other people. You must find out for yourself. How old are you?"

"Twenty-five."

"You seem younger."

"I think that's a Canadian thing," she sighed. Gravitas was not coming easy to her. She felt like a dilettante, a philistine. How was it the Palestinian people were saddled with that word? Was there anything worse than being a philistine *and* a filistine? She tried to make up for lost impressions. "How come you have patients here from the Intifada, from Palestine? I thought travel was difficult."

"We find a way. There is always a way. They are mostly young men, a few young women, mostly children. They have been hit by rubber bullets, lost their eyes or a limb, or had their bones broken by Israeli soldiers. The ones who have not been hit are suffering from depression."

"Is that because of the Intifada?"

"Is that because of the Intifada," the doctor repeated, not unkindly. "It is because of the conditions of their lives, from morning to the next morning, from evening to the next evening. A child under military occupation has little access to books, to toys, to regular school. They live in a room, sometimes two, with their six brothers and sisters, their parents, their grandparents, their aunts and their uncles. They eat rice and bread and eggs and candy. They drink Coke and Fanta. When they get sick it takes them twice as long to get better and then when they get better, they get sick again. Their father and their older brothers get up at 5 am to wait on a corner for an Israeli to hire them to build his settler house, a mansion compared to his hovel, and then they pave the road that they are barred from driving on. When they come home at night, they have only a few shekels in their pockets, a few hours of electricity, and a few litres of water for the entire family. The children have no pencils, no paints, no paper. No music. No toys." She stopped, as if out of breath, or out of fortitude. She shook her head and regained her resolve. "So yes, we have observed depression in children."

"What do you think can be done?"

"The occupation must stop."

"And until then?"

"We work to end the occupation."

"What if the occupation doesn't end?"

"Why are you pessimistic? Do you not see the stones being thrown? The occupation *will* end. That is what we are all fighting for. It cannot go on forever. We are not dogs."

"No. I just worry—"

"About what?"

"It's getting so violent. It must feel hopeless sometimes."

"Ah." The doctor leaned back into her chair. "Then you must come to Palestine. You must see the spirit in the people's eyes. Those children, so destitute, so pitiful. Do you know something? They smile and they smile and they smile and they are filled with love. It is humbling. A people who can do that will not lose. God will not abandon them."

Nadia noticed the soft grey around the doctor's hairline, olive skin sitting plumply on her face, the fine cut of her blouse, the long fingers and the wedding ring.

"Have you been there? Did your father take you?"

"No."

"You will go one day. Now is not a good time, too dangerous. But you will go and there will be peace and prosperity, *insha'allah*."

A noise behind Nadia started her. It was Bishara poking his head in the door. He apologized profusely to the doctor.

In her response the doctor addressed Nadia. "No, no imposition. I am very happy to talk to your lovely daughter. She is the next generation. It will be people like her who will take the message of Palestine to the world."

As they made their way back down the hall, Nadia was struck by the possibility of her father returning to Palestine. He had mourned his exile deeply, going so far once as to compare the jettisoned Palestinians to Adam and Eve expelled from the Garden of Eden. "We will return," he always said. "Israel's Law of Return does not include the Palestinians. But God's law of return does, *b'ismallah*. We will return, Nadia, you will see. And I will bring you!" Clare scoffed, the years passed, Nadia waited. What would she do in Palestine now, she wondered. She considered the question for the first time as if it were indeed a possibility. Palestine felt so close, just an overnight bus ride away. Manal was right, everything was close. Everything.

The seventh floor of the hospital was the *dour el hafalat*, the party floor. With its white stucco walls and upholstered benches, it was reserved for parties, receptions and special visits. Artifacts and artwork adorned the walls— picturesque watercolours of the desert and olive trees, ceramic plates and tiles from Jerusalem, framed embroidered dresses from the countryside. People were already mingling about in the large space, at one end of which two musicians played tabla and oud. Bishara kept looking at Nadia. "Beautiful," he said, his eyebrows going up each time, inviting her to agree. "Beautiful. Beautiful."

It was a farewell reception for two Norwegian doctors who had come to the hospital to share their orthopedic surgery expertise.

"Broken bones, crushed bones, splintered bones,"

explained Bishara. "They are the experts."

The surgeons, a man and a woman, stood in the middle of a group of Palestinians, each of them vying for a handshake, a laugh, a word. Nadia had to look away. How is it you come here to serve Palestine when I am already here and can do no more than avoid it? What do you understand that I can't begin to comprehend? Why is this so easy for you? What makes you so smart? That last one was simply gratuitous.

"Ah, here he is!" Bishara towed her to the next group of people. "*Ahlan wa sahlan, Dr. Fathi*. Please let me introduce Nadia, my daughter. She is visiting me from Canada."

A small, weathered man in his sixties reached out with both hands and clasped Nadia's in a hot and pillowy embrace. With his protruding lips and eyes he resembled somebody Nadia couldn't quite place.

"Ahh," he said in a deep baritone, "welcome to our hospital. Welcome to Cairo. You honour us. Come, sit with me and we talk." He pulled her down to a bench just behind them, waved away those with whom he had been speaking. They obeyed immediately, including her father. He drew a curtain around her with his body and asked how she liked Egypt, if she was proud of her father, and when was she going to join them at the PRCS? Nodding obtusely at her responses, his grey eyes never ceased scanning the room. Limned with broken vessels and cushioned by generous amounts of swollen skin, his watery gaze took in everything and yet registered nothing. He put his hand on Nadia's knee. Just then a man approached and whispered into his ear, a cigarette hovering inches from her face. She coughed. Dr. Fathi stood up and retrieved Nadia's hands again.

"You must come visit me at my office," he said. Leaning his round flesh on the younger man's arm, he turned and was led away.

Her father was suddenly at her side as if summoned. "Nadia," he whispered, "what do you think?"

"Ugh," she said involuntarily. "Of what?"

"Of Dr. Arafat."

Was his hand on her knee an innocent gesture? She wanted to give the old man the benefit of the doubt, but also wanted her father to know that his country, his people, his culture was reaching out and putting its fat hand on her knee. "I don't know," she said. "Another dirty old man."

"Nadia, *haram!*"

"Wait, Dr. *Arafat*? Was that Yasser Arafat?"

"No! He is his brother, Fathi. He is the head of the PRCS—the Palestine Red Crescent Society. And a pediatrician."

"Do they ever look alike. I thought he looked familiar."

"Be good," he whispered in her ear. "Just be good. And if you can't be good…" He paused, waited for her to join him. They said in unison: "Be polite."

Someone clapped their hands for attention and an expectant hush ran through the hall. The musicians, now many of them, began playing a rhythmic prelude. From

the far end of the room five men and five women in tra-
ditional costume emerged and took over the centre floor
as people rolled back to give them space. Bishara grabbed
Nadia and joined the circle forming around the dancers.
"They are all nurses and orderlies at the hospital," he said
over the noise.

The dancers stomped their feet and raised their hands,
following, leading, twirling. Hands in the air, then hands
at their sides. Nadia remembered seeing her father dance
with his friends when she was ten. She had been embarrassed by his lack of inhibition, by the way the men held
hands and gave each other sloppy kisses on the cheek.
A young woman, wearing low-cut jeans and a sash, had
pulled Nadia into their circle. But she resisted and spun
out just as quickly, mortified that any of them might
think she belonged there.

And now, here she was, fifteen years later, dancers'
scarves nipping at her hips, locking their arms together,
stomping around in spirals. They separated into two cir-
cles, one male and one female, and spun so quickly and
banged their boots so resolutely, that an unexpected cry
burst up from her belly. She caught her breath while tears
multiplied the dancers tenfold. Discretely wiping her
cheeks, she accepted a Kleenex from an unknown hand.

She slipped out of the room while the clapping was
still thunderous. She needed fresh air, the night sky, to escape. It didn't even occur to her that her father might look
for her. The empty shell of a building under construction
next door glowed with a flickering warmth. She paused

on the sidewalk. A man wrapped in a cloak stood over a steel drum and poked at the fire with a stick. Behind him a woman and children squatted on their haunches, eating from bowls and plates on the floor. Steel bars poked out of the half-built cement walls like rough savannah grass. He was a construction nomad, moving his family from site to site as the job took him. A taxi slowed down in front of her, the driver twisting his hand quizzically. Did she want a lift? She hesitated then climbed inside, told him Manal's street.

They drove in silence for a few blocks. The Palestinians don't need me. The workers are happy. Even Manal. Even Manal. The thought of her was almost panic-inducing. She was desperate for meaning, helpless that there was none.

"*Filistiniya*?" asked the driver.

"*Aiwa.*" Yes, she admitted, she was Palestinian. Whatever. He must have assumed that because he picked her up in front of the hospital, because she looked from here yet not, because her foreignness was not unintelligible and her accent not unfamiliar.

The driver rummaged in the seat beside him and slid a cassette into the stereo. The sound was scratchy and much of the treble failed to make it to the speaker behind Nadia's ear, but the voice was unmistakable.

"Fairuz," he said.

A singer of extraordinary prowess and popular appeal, the Lebanese singer early on threw her lot in with the Palestinians and sang rousing songs both feverishly political and folkloric. Her voice stinging and radiant, the emotion raw and stoic. The driver sang along softly. Nadia tipped him generously when they arrived. He took her hand in his and held it. The gesture awoke her; she wasn't sure if she should be alarmed.

"I am Palestinian too," he said in Arabic. Nadia didn't want to say much because he had obviously assumed she was like him: dispossessed, troubled, a refugee, a native speaker.

"From where?" she asked him, pronouncing it with a Palestinian accent instead of an Egyptian one.

"Khalil," he answered, using the Palestinian name for Hebron. "And you?"

She hesitated a moment, then told him, "Ramallah." She explained in more detail the roundabout trajectory of her life—Ramallah, Canada, Baba, Cairo. They were worlds apart, she and the young chauffeur. Through a quirk in history and longing, she had found herself in a wealthy country that would educate and employ her. He was driving a taxi in Egypt.

His hands were large and shapeless, thick skin and calluses indistinguishable from each other. Nadia wished him good night and Allah's protection. He kissed his fingers that had touched hers and turned back to the wheel.

She had made it into the building's lobby when she heard a horn. He was running towards her, the car door still swinging, his movements fluid in spite of his bulk. In his outstretched hand he held the worn cassette.

"Fairuz," he said, "Listen and remember us."

Unexpectedly, tears began to blur her vision. He pulled out a tissue from the small packet in his shirt pocket.

"*La, la*. Don't cry, it is a beautiful night." He walked back to his cab and called out the window as he spun around and drove off. "Palestinians don't cry. Not yet!"

The next evening, Uncle Nasser scraped his chair and got up from the table. He mumbled something, perhaps a thank you, belched loudly as he left the room. Om Malek had already gone to her room, as the muffled television testified. Nadia ran the hot water and squeezed some soap into the sink.

"Nadia," Manal said quietly behind her, almost a whisper. "I have an idea."

Nadia turned around.

"I want to go to Alex with you."

"Alex?"

"Alexandria. I used to go with my parents in the summer. They had an apartment on the beach they shared with my father's colleagues. We went every summer, I even had friends there," she smiled. "It is so beautiful, *ya qalbi*. It is clean, there is blue sky, blue water, blue waves. I want to go."

It was not what Nadia was expecting. *Ya qalbi,* my heart. "Yes," she said.

10

how cruel is the turquoise sea?

The train station felt like a tidal pool teeming with life and Nadia had to hold her breath against the liquid odours of people and animals. Humanity, generations thick, pressed against a wall of ticket windows, bodies pushed against each other as if by a current. Disembodied voices called back and forth, argued, spoke loudly, prayed, swore, laughed. Every now and then a rooster or a goat punctuated the din. Nadia was vaguely aware that Manal was interacting with the woman behind the wicket, giving her money, taking tickets in exchange. She leaned against her as if for shelter. Then they were moving again, out and through, snaking, swimming, tunnelling. Nadia gave herself over to the animalistic momentum. She gave herself over to Manal's direction, Manal's footsteps, Manal's breathing, the astonishing sensuousness of moving through the crowd like a warm knife through butter. *Itneen*, Manal held up two fingers, handing over some money in exchange for two containers of food. *Koshery for the trip*, she told Nadia. Then they were somewhere else, the air had changed and was now wet with diesel fuel and the hard steaming pumps of hydraulic brakes. They walked the length of the platform, passing foreigners, middle-class Egyptians, students, businessmen, families in clean clothes. Not this car, not this car, not this car. They got in the last one. The whistle blew loud and long and the train lurched out of the station just as their feet left the ground. Manal found their seats, a wooden bench with an upright wooden back. A young girl was sprawled across it. Her parents, in the facing bench, nodded politely and scooped her up onto their laps.

Down the aisle, Nadia could see that someone had placed a crate on the floor. In it four chickens fought noisily for space, their squawks competing with a kettle of water that was already whistling on top of a small propane burner. Closer, two young boys were watching her with great interest as they ate *taamiyyas* from waxed-paper envelopes. Nadia looked away, but not before a gesture caught her eye. She looked back, ready to be admonished—don't stare, don't be rude—but one of the boys was holding out his hand. Want one? his gesture asked. He grinned, raised his chin, and brought his fingers to his lips, indicating how delicious it would be if only she would accept. A child with impeccable manners and profound generosity, would she ever see such a thing in Montreal? She put her hand on her heart and mouthed *shukran. La, shukran.* He may have been disappointed, but the brilliance of his smile stayed with them both.

They passed through the Nile Delta, where the large African river splintered generously and fanned out towards the Mediterranean Sea. The lush greenery was an astonishing contrast to Cairo's limestone dryness. Green with fields and villages, it hardly felt like Egypt anymore. She leaned against Manal's shoulder and half dozed as they passed a never-ending herd of water buffalo.

The thin, fresh air of Alexandria greeted them the moment they stepped onto the platform. Nadia threw open her arms and took in a breath. "Wait, inhaling," she said, preventing Manal from pushing them into the first car they saw. "Ok," she finally said. "That was amazing. Let's go." They took a taxi to the Crillon, a hotel Manal knew. On the Corniche, she promised. You can see all the way to Greece. She signed them into a corner room whose full-length shuttered windows and white cotton curtains blowing inward created a timeless and lulling effect. Nadia threw herself on the bed and begged for a nap. Manal pulled a sketchbook and a chair out to the balcony and waited until she couldn't wait any longer. Finally, she crawled into bed next to her. When they awoke it was dark.

"Some tourists we are," Nadia said.

"We're not tourists."

"We only have a few days, I don't want to sleep the whole time."

"We won't. And what if we did? Dreaming in Alexandria is not the same as dreaming in Cairo." Manal pulled out a map and got her bearings. "Just like I remembered. The Al Samaka is really close."

"The what?"

"The best fish restaurant in Alexandria."

"The best? Can we afford it? I didn't even bring any good clothes."

"Don't worry," Manal said.

It was hardly a restaurant. A long table made up of a wobbly plywood board, around which chairs were pulled in or out as customers ate, finished eating, left, were replaced. Deeper inside, two harsh light bulbs pulsating with moths overlooked an iced trough loaded with fish. They pointed. It was cooked in front of them, laid on newspaper, covered with fries.

"Oh my god," Nadia said, chewing and swooning.

"*Mish kidda? Mish kidda?*"

A thousand seagulls squawked over the rooftops, swooped down to the shore then rocketed back up again. Manal wasn't in bed but on the balcony. "I'm drawing those boats down there, see them?" Rows of wooden fishing boats, each a different colour, leaned on each other up and down the beach. "Are you hungry?"

"Not too much. Maybe."

"There is a small market on the street behind us. Why don't you go get us something and we can eat on the balcony?"

"Me? Alone?"

Manal laughed. She held up her sketchbook. "So many boats."

Nadia spotted the flaps of canvas that were tethered between houses and buildings, sheltering vegetable, fruit, and fish sellers.

"*Tomatim?*" An old woman held out a small red tomato in one hand and a paring knife in the other. Her mouth curved upwards and her eyes, watery and grey, beckoned.

"*Bi kam?*" Nadia asked. How much?

"For you, nothing," the woman said in Arabic. "Give me what you like." She touched her breast with her hand then kissed her fingers, narrowly missing her eye with the tip of the blade.

"*Shukran*," Nadia smiled, delighted that she understood perfectly, and ordered two kilos.

The woman gingerly placed the tomatoes in the bag, one after the other, all the time stealing glances at Nadia and smiling. "Where from?" she finally asked. "*Israëli? Inti yehudiyya? Shalom!*"

Nadia laughed nervously. She had forgotten about being Jewish. Growing up, child of a Palestinian in a Montreal suburb where tiny unpronounceable countries were the butt of ceaseless jokes, she decided at an early age that it was safer to just be Jewish, like many of her friends up and down the street. Jewish by association, Jewish by assumption. The mere act of remaining silent during conversations about Passover or bubbas or synagogues led all to believe that she was partaking, that she was *one of us*. So when they talked about the sabre-rattling Arabs who tried to push the Jews to the sea in 1948, the scourge that threatened Israel in 1967, the hordes that humiliated Zion in 1973, or how the savages snatched the Sinai in 1982, she kept silent, tightened her lips, and hardly breathed at all.

"*Malesh*," said the old woman soothingly. "Welcome

to Egypt!"

"*Shukran*," Nadia said with some reluctance.

"Arabic good!"

"*Shweya-shweya*." Now she was embarrassed to reveal her Palestinian heritage and confess the paucity of her Arabic in the same breath.

"Ah," the woman said, folding her thick hands on her belly. "Me only English. No *Hebrayar*. Sorry. *Shalom Shalom!*"

They ate on the balcony. Sliced tomatoes, olives, feta cheese, and fresh *aish baladi* to gather it together. Manal finished her coffee with a quick draw then returned it upside down on the table with a rough bang. A minute later she picked up the cup and stared inside it.

"What does it say?"

"*Everything will be perfect*," Manal said. "Isn't that what you want to hear?"

"Why not?" she asked, bristling slightly. "Maybe it's true. Oh come on, don't roll your eyes. It's a beautiful day, a beautiful breakfast, a beautiful woman drinking a *laziza* coffee. Let's have a nice time without feeling bad that we're having a nice time."

Manal took another look at the smudges of grain and put the cup down. "So let's not care then."

"I'm tired of caring. Let's go to the beach!"

"*Ya salam* you will ruin me. I am not ready to go to the beach, anyways it is still cold. We walk around. Shall we visit *Iskandraya?*" Nadia laughed at Manal's idea of cold, but she was happy to go along.

Unlike Cairo, Alexandria was a city of colour. Blue sky, blue awnings, white stone walls, brass fixtures that blinded in the sun, trees whose leaves retained their hue, the dust never settling in the steadfast breeze. Speaking in far-off languages of brick and stucco, each building retained the Greek, Italian, and Spanish accents of its settlers, visitors, and converts. As they walked past them, shops and kiosks slid their metal doors up with a bang. On one corner a man in a blue *galabiyya* and a long scarf beginning on his head and ending around his neck stacked dozens of slippers on a low wooden bench. He pulled up his robe and sat gingerly on the end of the bench, not moving a single muscle as they passed by. Farther along, on another street, a steel grate rolled up to reveal stacks of books behind a dusty window on which was engraved "Mumtaza Books - *Livres Mumtaza*." They slowed their walking and, no communication needed, entered. Lingering over various titles they separated to opposite ends of the shop, Manal looking at art books and Nadia in the history section. Behind the counter, a thin man in a neatly pressed white shirt was using a penknife to pick at his fingernails.

"Excuse me," Nadia asked. "Do you have any books on Palestine?"

He pointed to one end of the stacks and shelves then slid off the stool and swayed awkwardly on two polio-ravaged legs. Like so many Egyptians he was lame, limping, crawling, half-blind. The ubiquity of disease and disfigurement had achieved for the disabled what they so craved in the West: complete integration.

His hand waved over a shelf. "They are all written in Arabic." He pulled one out from the middle of a stack, blew on it so the dust sprinkled into a shaft of light. The old paperback was white and bare save for the title and author. He held it out for her but then pulled it back. "It is French." *Les croisades vues par les Arabes - Amin Malouf.*

"I can read French," Nadia said quickly, the speed of her response a result of equal parts veracity and pride. Just because she had never read a book in French didn't mean she couldn't. She followed him to the front desk.

"What is your name?" he asked as he set up his cash box.

"Nadia."

"Where from?"

"Canada."

"My uncle is in Canada. A big city. Edimonton," he said, adding a little space between the *d* and the *m*. Arabic did not tolerate three consonants without a vowel between them. In this way, for example, Marlboro cigarettes wasn't a new brand, just a brand new way of saying it. *Edmonton* posed a challenge and he erred on the side of the intervening vowel, just in case.

"Tourist?"

The questions were as tedious as they were expected. She had learnt to answer them bloodlessly. "My father is Palestinian and he lives in Cairo, I came to stay with him."

"Yaa-aaaa! Inti filistiniya?" He lifted himself up and

held out his hand. "Welcome to Egypt. I am Palestinian too. From where you are from?"

"Montreal," she said, then understood what he was really asking. "My father is from Ramallah."

His cheeks lifted till they stood up like meringue, gleaming peaks against the brown soil of his teeth. "*Laa!* I am from Ramallah, too. You would like tea?" In a quick movement she would have thought him incapable of, he hopped to the door and called out down the street. A few short seconds later, a man came in, out of breath and wide-eyed, filling out his brown *galabiyya* with an enormous girth. His left arm held up a silver tray with four glasses of hot tea.

"What have you done now?" Manal asked her.

"Please, sit down." The bookseller opened three folded chairs, motioning to them while he returned to his stool. Nadia took the hot glass and held it with the tips of her fingers.

"Ramallah," repeated the bookseller to the fat man.

"What is his name?" Both men leaned forward.

"Who?"

"*Baba.*"

"Bishara Eid."

The bookseller frowned, sat up straight, frowned some more, consulted with the fat man. "I knew a Bishara from Ramallah who lives in Alexandria. But it's a big family, Eid," he said, still thinking. "A big family. You have uncle Abdallah?"

Nadia thought hard. "I don't think so."

"His father Wassim?"

Nadia worked to recall her grandfather's name. "No, not Wassim. Nabil."

"Nabil, Wassim," the bookseller said. It sounded familiar to Nadia, but all Arab names now sounded familiar. Nabil Wassim. Wassim Nabil. It could be anybody anywhere, it had so little to do with her. The bookseller turned to Manal to facilitate the exchange. *Is your father a teacher,* she obliged, asking Nadia. *What was his street? What village was his father from? How many arpents? How many Palestinians in Canada? Can she help them with immigration?* Manal smirked at her impatience and discomfort. *How many airplanes has he hijacked?*

"Ha ha, very funny. They did not ask that."

"*Is he best friends with Yasser Arafat?*" Manal continued. "*Can he teach me to make a bomb?*"

"Stop. They mean well."

Manal lowered her voice and eyelids. "I am ready to go to the beach now."

Suddenly the fat man slapped his forehead and ran out of the store. The bookseller laughed. "He forgot all about his customers."

Manal tugged on Nadia's sleeve till they were both standing. "*Shukran kitir.* We should be going."

"Palestine has no one, no friends," the bookseller said in English, reluctant to release them. "Boys are against soldiers in the street. David against Goliath. But boys should not be playing a man's game. We have no one."

"David beat Goliath, didn't he?"

"We are Goliath, the ugly ones," he said. "That is how they see us. We are like ghosts in our own homes. But what is funny, what is very funny is it was the Jews who chased the German ghost all the way to our houses! And now they beat on our doors and beat on our heads." He laughed though his eyes remained serious. "Did you know that the Palestinian farmer is allowed less water than an Israeli in a flat in Tel Abib?" The Arabic language did not have the letter "v" and this was the first time in a long time that Nadia heard the name of that city pronounced by an Arab. "Did you know he pays more taxes?" His voice rose to a thin pitch of disbelief. "We can't own land. We can't plant trees. We can't trade. We can't work. We can't travel."

His sadness inundated the room. It was just another sad story, the story of the Palestinians, there were millions of sad stories. Nadia had never thought about it that way, never felt it. She was transfixed.

"I am sorry." He stacked the empty tea glasses and returned the displaced books to their original spots on the shelves, marked out with clearings in the dust. He let them go.

Manal had pulled her half way down the street when Nadia suddenly stopped. "The book, I forgot the book."

"Doesn't matter," Manal urged.

"But I paid for it!"

"Consider it a donation to the cause. *Yalla*, I am hot, I am hungry, I am very, very restless. I love that word.

Restless. Rest-less. Rest. Less."

Alexandria's beaches spanned the country's north coast, stretching 200 kilometres west as far as the azure Marsah Matruh. But within the city limits the band of sand from the Citadel to the promontory of Abu Qir in the east was where the average non-monied, non-mobile Egyptian tended to congregate. These beaches were accessible, public, and not half as crowded at the end of March as they would be a couple of months later. In any season, they were not, as Manal pointed out, friendly to women who were not completely covered.

"What do you mean not completely covered? What about bathing suits?"

"*Haram!* You will get chased off the beach if you wear a bathing suit. Anyways, it's too cold."

Weather and bikinis notwithstanding, Nadia was determined to swim. "It's the Mediterranean, I have to go!" As they walked along the Corniche, passing beach after beach, her spirits sank. While the beaches were dotted with an assortment of families and single men, they didn't see one bathing-suit-clad woman. Each and every adult woman they saw was moving slowly under layers and layers of wet, blowsy fabric, wading up to her knees in jeans, dresses, anything that was the opposite of a bathing suit. Tired of tromping along the concrete, Nadia suggested they at least take their shoes off and make their way along the shoreline. More Egyptian that way. Hand in hand, they splashed through the cool water until they reached a low concrete wall that blocked their way. Manal read the sign: *Montaza Palace*.

"What's that?"

"An exclusive hotel with a private beach for foreigners." At the last three words they giggled.

Nadia paid the entrance fee, a whopping twenty pounds each, and they entered the grounds of the palace built by King Farouk, Egypt's deposed monarch. Milling about on their way to the changing huts on the shore, they heard snatches of German, Japanese, and American English. On the flower-lined path from the hotel to the water a tall man in a crisp white Saudi *galabiyya* and headscarf was counting a wad of money inches thick. He held it out from him, in view of everyone. A thin, barefoot man held a parasol over his head.

"Saudis," Manal whispered in uncontrollable disgust.

"He looks like Tewfiq," Nadia said.

"Who?"

"Parasol man." Surprised, she added, "You don't like Saudis? Since when?"

Manal arched her eyebrows at the question and, wisely, chose not to answer it. They walked in silence until they reached a pair of lounge chairs underneath a palm. Nadia immediately stripped down to her bikini.

"Nadia, what are you doing? You cannot go in the water, it is freezing! What? Come back, *ya homar!* Come back!" In seconds Nadia was jumping about in the water up to her hips.

"It's not so cold," she yelled out. "Come on!"

Manal swore and cursed, but then went in the changing hut. When she emerged, mortified and still swearing, she ran quickly towards the water, plunging in more out of modesty than anything else.

"I kill you for this!" She splashed Nadia and tumbled into her arms. They spun around in the water, jumped up with every wave, hands reaching for each other like seaweed. Manal wrapped her legs around Nadia's hips and floated up towards her face, giving her tiny fish-like kisses. In the water, the waves, the splashes, they were impermeable.

The building's exterior stone walls bulged out slightly with age and neglect. The *bowab* stood up from his mat and eyed them suspiciously until Manal told them where they were going. *Josephine, Josephine*, the old man repeated. He slid open the elevator gate and reached in to push the button to the second floor. Nadia hesitated outside the dark mahogany door, the piece of paper in her hands now wet with sweat and humidity. "I should have called." She rang the doorbell.

"She doesn't know we're coming? *Ya Nadia*, that is not, it is not...Ouf, that is not good. We are like an ambush now."

"I tried but she never answered."

"Old people never answer their phones. Did you let it ring fifty times *yanni*? A hundred times? Did you call in the morning? In the night?"

The door suddenly opened and a small woman looked

at them, a stretched smile revealing the few teeth she had left. Nadia stammered slightly, held out her hand. *Tanta Josephine*, she began. But Manal slapped it down and introduced themselves. They were ushered in.

"That's her maid," Manal hissed in her ear.

"*Aiwa?*" The voice was deep and sonorous, musical almost. It came from deeper in the apartment. An old woman emerged, dressed in clothes for lounging, not cleaning.

"Aunt Josephine? It's Nadia. From Canada."

"*Eh da!* Nadia? Nadia Eid? Bishara's Nadia?"

"Yes," Nadia smiled. "I'm in Cairo and I wanted to visit you. I tried calling, many times. I'm so sorry we just came like this."

"*Tsk tsk*, I hate the telephone. Come here my dear, let me look at you more closely. You look just like your father. You look even like his cousin, what is her name, Mounira. You have grown, that much is true. You have grown. How old are you? Wonderful, wonderful. Sit, sit. *Ahlan, ahlan wa sahlan*. Saida will get us some tea. And your friend?"

They exchanged pleasantries as Saida busied herself noisily in the nearby kitchen. It didn't take long for Nadia to realize that Josephine did not know that Bishara was living in Cairo permanently or that he had effectively left her mother. Like Manal's place, Josephine's apartment was dark and shuttered. She had been in this room before, eaten in the kitchen down the hall, slept in another room further along. Saida brought them glasses of mint tea and a plate of Egyptian cookies that Nadia was thrilled to recognize. *Ghorayeba*, made with clarified butter, were the shortbread that the Scots wished they could make, while *kahk*, coated in a powdered sugar almost lighter than air, made her swoon with its hint of rosewater and pistachio. Saida whispered and laughed, her hands flitting over Nadia's shoulders, arms, cheeks. She stood back and took in the full measure of the girl and recited prayers of thanks and astonishment. She was there too, Nadia suddenly remembered, shocked. Only a few years older than Nadia, Saida was "the little Muslim girl" that had been waiting on her aunt since she was a child. Plucked from a little village in the Delta, Saida had been cooking and cleaning for Josephine her entire life. Today, she was toothless and most certainly still illiterate. She looked ancient, set in amber, almost petrified, with hard skin on her face and heavy pendulous hands like a labourer. Hands that do everything, absolutely everything. *Ahlan, ahlan*, Saida said, and other things Nadia could not make out. Clare had been mortified; that shame now invaded Nadia, she could feel her cheeks flush. Clare and Josephine fought daily—*The girl can eat with us. She most certainly will not! Do not hit her, I forbid you to hit her. Your opinion is neither wanted nor relevant, I must do as I must, she is a peasant. So, she is still a human being! Bob, I will call the police, I swear it. Clare, khallas, please. The police will laugh at you.* Josephine coughed, Saida returned to the kitchen.

"How is your mother?" Josephine asked, as if unable herself to resist the shame.

"She's good, thanks."

"Why she is not with you today?"

"Oh, she didn't come to Egypt. She's still in Montreal."

That was enough for Josephine. She was satisfied and a little less uneasy. The wall behind them was busy with old photographs in ornate frames. Manal got up to look and Josephine quickly followed, maybe to stop her. *Where was this taken? And this one? And who is this?* Josephine, peering over Manal's shoulder, narrated their history. *The port of Haifa. The beaches of Tiberias where we visited friends. Nadia's grandfather's tile shop in Ramallah. Olive trees, olive trees, beautiful olive trees.* Nadia stayed in her chair, content to watch them. She remembered the photographs alive with stories as her father picked through them to narrate his seemingly magic life. They never had enough time to look at them all, she remembered. He was always tucking some away, putting them on the table behind him, or on the ledge too high for her to reach. *Another day*, he'd say, *another day. But who is that*, she wanted to know, *who is that?*

"And who is that?" Manal had taken a picture off its hook and was looking at it closely.

"Let's put that back, shall we?" Josephine swiftly put it upside down on the table.

But Manal picked it up. "But who is it?"

Two boys, no more than eight, maybe ten, stood with their arms around each other. Behind, an older woman that Nadia recognized as Bishara's mother, her grandmother who she had never met. She had been caught out by the photographer and was smiling, one hand up over her eyes, shielding them from the sun.

"Nadia's grandmother, Warda," Josephine said.

"And the boys?"

"Bishara, obviously."

"And the other boy? There are other pictures here of him as well. Look, this one. And this one."

"That is enough. Saida. Saida, tea."

"It's okay, Auntie," Nadia said. "She already brought the tea."

Josephine sat down but Manal remained at the wall, walking back and forth, her nose inches from the photographs. Josephine looked uncomfortable and impatient. Finally, in exasperation, she turned to Nadia. "So how do you like Cairo?"

"Nadia," Manal said. "I didn't know you have an uncle. This is her father's brother, right? I mean it must be. He's in every photograph."

"*Ya lahwi, khallas ba-a!*" Josephine stood up.

"He is?" Nadia was faster than her aunt, and she followed Manal's fingers as she pointed to photographs she had never seen. In almost every single one, a boy stood next to her father, no more than a year or two older. Slightly taller, more serious. Where her father concentrated playfully on whatever view they were standing in front of, the other boy's dark eyes peered thoughtfully at the photographer every time. The question was in the air, she didn't need to ask it. She and Manal turned around at the same time to look at Josephine. Her aunt broke eye contact, sighed loudly, and sat down.

"Wael was two years older than Bishara. He was his

214

protector. A very smart boy, very special, very loved. Your father too, of course, *tabaan*. But Wael was special. Everyone could see that. So you know about the ship from Alexandria to Haifa. Yes? Yes? Wael was sick. There was diphtheria on the ship." She paused. "He and his mother were very ill. They kept the ship in the Haifa harbour for too long, a week, maybe two, I don't remember. The Israeli Army would not let them off to see a doctor, and they would not let a doctor board. For two weeks the ship was not allowed to move until finally they sent it back to Egypt. Your grandmother got better, *il hamd'il allah*. Wael, no."

"So what you're saying is my father's brother died? Before he could come back to Egypt?"

"That is what I am saying. Warda and Abdallah came with only one child. They left their first-born son, their life, their land, their homes, their hearts in Palestine. Warda was never well again, never. *Yanni*, no one was. Eventually Bishara left. Who could blame him?"

After a long pause, it was Manal who spoke first. "I understand now."

"Understand what?" Nadia asked.

"A boy loses his brother and his country at once. I understand why he must return."

It was as if the room collapsed after that. As if the walls, made soft and weak by the release of secrets, buckled inward. The plaster ceiling crumbled all at once and rained a layer of dust over them, into their teacups, forcing them to blink. Nadia felt like she couldn't breathe. Saida cleared the table, Josephine said it was time for her siesta, and Manal, awake-alive-pulsating Manal, pulled Nadia out of the apartment before it completely imploded.

On the train back to Cairo, Nadia must have been dozing, but woke up to a whispering. "Here, this is for you." Manal put a photograph in her hands. It was her father and Wael, their arms around each other, the sea behind them. A distracted boy and a serious boy.

"You shouldn't have taken this, Manal. She'll notice."

"You look like Wael."

"I do?"

"Yes, more than your father. See? Look at his mouth." She touched Nadia's mouth. "Look how serious it is. Look how kissable."

"*Manal*."

"Life is so short, don't you think?" She leaned into Nadia, pressed her against the coolness of the window, and kissed her. Softly, then urgently, then softly again, her lips, her tongue, her lips again. Nadia could only moan.

They crept quietly through the dark apartment. To the right, a shaft of light from under Uncle Nasser's door skidded sharply along the tile floor, hitting their feet. Nadia shuddered, grateful she never had any reason to turn right. They tiptoed left instead, prancing like children, heels never touching the ground. The dampened soundtrack from a soap opera in Om Malek's room surprisingly kept time. Shutting the bedroom door behind them, they tumbled over each other with abandon, bodies still warm and salty. The trip through the delta, the train interminably rolling and bouncing, lulling and teasing, had left them craving more touch than they could steal on the journey. They knew each other's bodies now, and were able to anticipate reactions, teasing pleasure out of the delicate interplay of time and distance. Manal, particularly, withheld and tantalized. This time it was her lips that she kept from Nadia's mouth. Kiss me now, kiss me now, Nadia's whole body repeated in arches, in swerves, in rising to meet her lover's. But Manal kept up a playful smile and she held herself only inches away, even less, just millimetres, no, microns, moments. *Damn you*, Nadia whispered through gritted teeth, hips raising then bucking as Manal filled her, teased her, then filled her again. *Now you.* Her voice was hoarse and breathless, just a grating sound in the dark, but it was enough. Manal was under her, first facing then away, then over her, then under again, the heat and the sweating turning them into oiled seals, clapping clapping clapping their chests together. Manal, always much quieter than Nadia, this time let out a sound that was either musical or animal—Nadia couldn't decide which. *Shhhhh*, Manal said to herself afterwards. They laughed, lying on their backs, on each other's outstretched arms, until tingling and numbing forced them to stir.

The singsong voices of children in a schoolyard rang up through the apartment. The school, a simple two-storey cement block surrounded by an enclosed yard, abutted their building. Now, Nadia had a clear vantage point from the balcony and wondered why she hadn't noticed it before. In their uniforms of dark blue smocks, the children bounced in and around each other energetically, whooping and trilling and hollering as teachers stood by in poses of half-hearted seriousness. Even the call from the muezzin could not eclipse the lively din, certainly not with its charmless pre-recorded sputtering. But it must be late, Nadia thought, if the *zuhr* call to prayer was already underway. Earlier, Manal had whispered in her ear, "Don't get up, don't get up." She dozed to the lovely rustling sound as she got dressed in the quiet room. "Come later, come whenever, don't come." Soft words grazing her cheek like a ribbon, sending her back to sleep. But now, halfway through the day, Nadia wondered if the *don't come* part was the real message.

Once she and Daniel had decided they were a couple—two lunch dates and a kiss into their relationship—the wondering was over. He was there when she needed him to be there, he was there when he promised, he was there with advice and to-do lists. Their relationship quickly solidified, like a house on solid bedrock, the expansive and trustworthy Canadian Shield. She assumed that was how relationships worked, that was how affection, if not love, thrived and deepened and established itself, hopeful as pine trees gripping the scraggy rock. She didn't know that it could also be the exact opposite. There was nothing solid about her feelings for Manal. Rather, what she felt was wind-like, storm-like, flood-like. It was porous and frightening and thrilling, keeping her insides in constant flux as if from earthquakes. She had been wrong, in fact: *solid* was precisely the wrong thing to look for. Maybe what you wanted was to be hanging onto cliffs, one hand wedged in the only crag within view. Or to be crossing shifting sands that erased your footprints even as you made them. She stood on the balcony and almost swayed with the pulsating heat. Maybe she wanted to be a cliff diver watching the waters below, waiting and waiting, timing the waves as they hit the rocks, then hit them again, then pulling out and coming back and hitting them again and again and again, until she *knew*. She'd find that convergence of time and height and distance that was just right. And then she'd jump.

She hunted down the envelope of applications and threw its contents onto the bed. Art schools from all over Canada, beginning with the Concordia University Faculty of Fine Arts in Montreal. After that one, she moved on to the other universities in the envelope. It took her the day to complete them, including writing the artist statement over and over and over till her hand cramped.

But when Manal came home she didn't want to look at any of it. "I waited for you," she said sullenly, pausing at the bedroom door as if she had lost some claim to the space. "Did you even leave this room?"

"No. Yes. Well, I went to the kitchen and the bathroom. Just take a look, come on. I did it for you."

"I waited all day. Even Tewfiq wasn't there until the afternoon. He's always late now, I don't know why."

"You need to read the artist statement and make sure I got it right."

"I'm sure you got it right." She sat down on the bed and gave the papers a cursory look. "You always get it right. Put it in an envelope and send it."

"We need to include slides of your work."

"So we send slides."

"We need to make them first," Nadia said.

"*Tayyib, tayyib,*" Manal growled, but it came out truncated and abrupt: *tub, tub.* Okay, okay, fine, fine. She pulled Nadia down and climbed over her astonished, yielding body.

By the end of the week the applications had been completed, packaged, and sent. Manal had borrowed Brigitte's Nikon and taken pictures of her work, which they processed into slides at the camera shop on Kasr el Nil street. They had fat envelopes for not only every art school in Canada, but also schools in New York, Chicago, Toronto, Boston, London. Nadia could imagine herself in all of those places.

"I can't believe I am doing this," Manal said as they walked back from the post office. "I always wanted to be an artist, now I am an artist. I always wanted to study abroad, now I am applying." She took Nadia's arm and tucked it under her own. "It is because of you."

"Nah, I'm just the secretary," Nadia said. But she had been waiting for the acknowledgment. She wanted to be useful, even needed. She had never quite felt *needed* before.

"No really, *habibiti*. Before I was just someone with talent, but because of you I can see art in me, really art. Not even Brigitte let me see this. Especially not even Brigitte."

"How about Sofian?" Nadia dared.

But Manal tsked and looked away.

"Does he like your art? He must, he bought it."

"He is an art buyer." She stopped and touched Nadia's cheek. "You are an art lover."

"Manal?"

"More questions."

"Why are none of your paintings hanging at your apartment? Not one. Wouldn't your mother be proud of you?"

Manal stopped again. "She is proud of me, and they are. You didn't look very hard."

Nadia thought for a minute. "Not the landscapes? That's just, I don't know, they're not even of Egypt. They look Swiss, for crying out loud. Snow?"

"That's the art my mother likes. These are paintings she can enjoy."

"And you?"

"And me? I do what I must."

The road was bordered by apartment buildings baked white in the heat then smudged black by the pollution. They were mid-block; no other streets veered off in any direction. In front of them, in some incalculable middle distance, the heat melted the architecture behind curtains of vapour. A quietness had descended upon them. For a minute there was no one else, no cars sliced the street with noise and dust, no other footsteps crowded around them, no dogs barked in alleys and under bridges, no men argued, no women trilled.

Manal stopped. "Shhhh, listen."

They looked at each other and listened to the lull. Just a lull and all the more precious for it. Nadia had never felt such steely love before, as if her heart had been broken open and left to the elements. She cupped Manal's face in a gesture that felt to her protective and nurturing, even priestly, as if performing a sacred ritual. She had never imagined herself capable of such a gesture.

"I will stay," she said. "I will stay the summer, I will stay as long as it takes, I will stay."

Manal chewed on an errant thumbnail, looking both disbelieving and guarded. "As long as it takes what?"

"To get you to school. And then I will come with you."

"Nadia, Nadia, you say so much. It is a lot. You don't know."

"Listen to me," Nadia said. "It is not too much and I do know. I know I love you and I want you to be an artist and I want to follow you to whatever school gets the brilliant idea to accept you. We just have to wait."

The cars returned. A man exited a storefront yelling at an invisible thief. A dog defecated in a doorway.

"*Yalla Nora.*" Nadia smiled as the girl leaned away from her mother and into her arms. "You go, we'll be fine."

They stood at the window and looked down onto the

street below. "*Feen Baba?*" When Bishara and Noor exited the building, the child squealed. "Oh look! There they are," Nadia said. They ducked into a taxi and drove off. "Bye-bye," they waved. "Bye-bye."

There were no pictures in the apartment of her or of his life in Montreal, as if it hadn't existed or was just an interruption. She found herself hunting in every closet, searching in every drawer, peering into every corner. She made a game of it with Nora. She hid a little toy in an obvious spot, and while the girl bobbed around looking, Nadia concentrated on more ambitious sleuthing—for what, she had no idea. His passport was in an upper drawer, along with a bundle of letters written in Arabic in an elastic, and an envelope of black and white photographs, old ones, two boys in shorts and white shirts with the sun in their eyes. It was a Canadian passport, stamped with visas from Egypt and Germany.

As she tucked the girl into bed, Nadia calculated that she would be fifty when Nora reached the age she was now. Is that how parents think, she wondered, counting off the years ahead into a diminishing half-life? She didn't know if she felt like Nora and she were sisters—what was that supposed to feel like? They didn't even look alike. The child was darker, with rounder features and curlier hair. Not only was her first language Arabic, but her culture and all her references would originate from the Middle East. Nadia, on the other hand, had inherited many of her mother's Scottish attributes. Too many, she increasingly thought.

She wasn't sleeping when they walked in, but lying down and reading on the sofa. Still, in the shadow of the incident with Manal, she rubbed her eyes and pretended to be waking. She hoped that these new informational vignettes would at one point negate and overwrite the memory of her and Manal lying in each other's arms. Just sleeping, one of them will eventually say to themselves, they were just sleeping.

Noor tucked twenty pounds into her hands with a little squeeze. Noor's hand over hers, the little shake, the smile, mahogany eyes that searched for connection. At first it felt odd, almost fearful, but Nadia was starting to feel the warmth in it. She was also starting to need the extra cash. The money she had saved up and brought with her was running out, and she could make cash advances on her MasterCard only so many times before she'd bankrupt herself.

"*Shukran*," Nadia said, meeting her gaze.

"Nora is learning English. Thanks to you," Noor smiled.

"We have fun," Nadia said. "What words does she know?"

Her father was pressing on the elevator button. *Ding, ding, ding.*

"*Hidinseek.* What is that?"

Nadia blinked. "Oh, ha! It's a game we play. Hide and seek."

"Sound like fun. She open everything and say *hidin-seek*," she smiled. "*Hidinseek!*"

Ding, ding, ding. Nadia hurried out to the hallway just as the doors opened. Bishara lit up a cigarette on the sidewalk. A taxi drove by, slowed down. Nadia called out *Heliopolis*, but her father waved it off.

"*Yalla*," he said to her. "Let's sit. Shall we talk? Have a conversation?" He led her up the street to a bench. "Ahh." He exhaled loudly as he sat down. "I love the night. It is full of life in Cairo. Do you feel it?"

"Yes, I guess so. I guess when the sun goes down people take advantage of the coolness."

"That sounds Canadian." He chuckled and stared off into some neon lights in the middle distance. "Really."

"Well, that's what I am, Baba. I am Canadian. What am I supposed to do about that?"

"Nadia, you are Palestinian."

"How can I be Palestinian? You're not even Palestinian. I mean, you're Egyptian and you're Canadian. Palestine is just, it's just… It doesn't even exist anymore." She had blasphemed, she might as well have said *fuck*. It was as sacrilegious—and as meaningless.

He held out his arm and slapped the inside of it. "*Dammi filistini*." Palestinian blood. It used to thrill her when he did that, especially when he did that to her. Like they belonged to something compelling and mythic. It was so much bigger than being Canadian, a bland country that didn't seem to be able to lay claim to a single abiding feature. But now, watching him do that, like beating a drum, it just looked jingoistic and desperate.

"I have something to tell you." He ground out his

cigarette and turned to face her more squarely. "Noor and I, and Nora of course, are going to Palestine, to Ramallah."

"When?"

"We will live there, Nadia."

It took a minute for it to soak in, the way a dry sponge resists water. She played the words over again until they fit together and created meaning.

"I don't get it. How can you? I mean, I thought you were not allowed to return? You always said that you could never go home. What about your job?"

He nodded. He was prepared. "I can travel as Canadian, not as Palestinian. You are right, I am Canadian," he smiled for a moment. "Much has happened this few weeks, *yanni*. Noor is psychologist, Palestinian but with German passport. Very lucky combination. She can work in mental health in Palestine. They need her."

"I just got here, Baba. Now what? It doesn't make sense. Once again, nothing is making sense. I keep trying to jump through your hoops and you keep moving them. Over here. No here. I don't want to go back to Montreal, but how am I supposed to stay if you're not here?"

"Nadia, *malesh. Malesh ya bint.* Maybe you can stay a bit longer anyways. It's up to you, *yanni*."

She leaned over with her elbows on her knees, feeling heavy with fear and anticipated grief. "When do you leave?"

He inhaled deeply. "In two month, maybe three. *Yanni*, maybe one."

The night sky was black, starless, maybe lifeless. Where were the stars in Cairo, she wondered? They felt a million miles farther away than in Montreal.

"How can you bring Nora to the Occupied Territories? If it's so difficult, if things are so awful, how can you take her there? You're putting her in danger."

"No, no, it is not dangerous for us. We will be safe. But we need to serve the people, *yanni*. We need to be available and dedicated. *Fahimtik?* You have heard about Hanan Ashrawi? Haidar Abdel-Shafi? He is a doctor, *ya Nadia*, Moustafa Barghouti also. The Intifada has uncovered our rage, yes, but also our leadership. We thought we needed the PLO, but all those years in exile have made them, how you say, fat and lazy. And maybe not so honest." He looked around and whispered half-conspiratorially. "Say this to no one! Hanan is a poet, Nadia, do you believe that? We can have a leadership of poets and doctors. How can I not go? I beg of you to understand."

"Fine, I get it, I get it. The people need you. Intifada and all that, right? Arrests, clashes, confrontations, curfews, rubber bullets, broken bones, eyes getting shot out, fires, bombings, raids, checkpoints. Lots of fun for Nora."

"*Khallas, khallas*. I never said bombings."

"Oh, good. I feel much better."

"Nora will be fine," he said.

"How do you know that? You'll both be working. Do you want to abandon another daughter? Is that it? One's not enough?"

He *tsked*, shook his head, began to plead with her. But

then he changed his mind, maybe lost the fight. His body slumped with the shift. He stared at the still-burning cigarette between his fingers. "Is that what it feels like?"

"Yes."

"Then you must forgive me."

Arabic had always seemed a little too rhetorical. As if there were twice as many words as were needed, or that half of what was said was only there to provide lift, to reflect well on the speaker, to formulate a projection of intentions rather than actual actions. Nadia wondered if in asking for her forgiveness her father was simply nudging the conversation on to its next step, closure. Would he check his watch, were his eyes glazing over, was he hoping that Noor wasn't going to be angry that he took so long? Did he just want to shake Nadia off like a dog does fleas? Wasn't that what *Intifada* meant?

He waited. He didn't check his watch or stare into the distance or lose his train of thought.

"There is much to think about," he said finally.

"You can say that again."

"There is much to think about." He smiled. Then he wrapped his arm around her shoulders and they watched the dark clouds dissipate from the dark sky, bringing forth the stars.

That night she dreamt of a boy she had seen on the road a few days earlier. The winds had picked up and red sand, like an invasion of locusts, filled the air. They were in a taxi when a young camel, part of a small herd of a dozen being led to the Imbaba market, broke free of his ropes and crashed out against the traffic. Cars screeched over the median and onto the sidewalks while pedestrians ran for cover. The animal's panicked squeals were matched only by the boy who, armed with a stick, was chasing it. It darted past the taxi, the driver cursing while Manal paid no attention. The boy stopped and leaned against the hood in a moment's bewilderment, breathing hard with fear and helplessness. His body slumped down the length of his arm; so young, yet already the labour of sinews and muscles showed themselves through his shabby *galabiyya*. Tears cut rivulets in his face. His mouth opened and closed in an attempt to holler, but he coughed in the dry air instead. The taxi driver honked his horn again and again and yelled at him to get away from the car.

In her dream, she opened the passenger door and wrapped him up in her scarf, took him home and lay with him in a hot bath strewn with rosemary. He slept in her arms as she took care to keep his face above the water, always above the water, the rocking of her breathing lulling him deeper and deeper into sleep.

But the young camel had continued to run and the boy resumed his chase, the sound of his desperate cries fading behind the noxious throttle of the taxi's engine.

11

the gazelle waits for the hunter to arrive

After the cold nights, rains, and floods in the Muqattam hills, springtime in Cairo burst forth like a noisy crowd streaming out of a mosque. The scent of jasmine and lilies perfumed the air as the great spring festival of *Sham el Nessim* got under way. Families and bicycles, donkeys and cars, chickens and goats—every ribbon and bell and flower in place—invaded the parks. Mountains of food were laid out on blankets while countless songs competed loudly from countless cassette players, each of them tinnier than the next.

Nadia joined Manal, her mother, and her uncle at the Azbekia Gardens near Ataba, a neighbourhood whose market was the poor cousin to the tourist-thronged Khan el Khalile. They arrived early and staked a claim but still ended up sharing their blanket with other families: strangers' feet on the bread, elbows on the cheese. They played badminton, tossed a volleyball, cracked open a new deck of cards and dealt out an Egyptian version of rummy. Between shuffles they gorged on olives and feta and tahini and lamb and rice and *fûl* and, best of all, cold, cold *karkaday*. The afternoon was long and restless. Uncle Nasser soon wandered off, recognizing old friends, searching for new ones.

"See, there's one." Manal, lying on her stomach next to Nadia, pointed discreetly.

"Where? How do you tell?"

"Look at her eyes. Look."

A woman lingered at the edge of the park, near enough to a falafel stand that the men waiting for their sandwiches could not avoid seeing—or staring. A loose headscarf landed airily over her shoulders. Her long skirt was hitched up at the sides and tucked into the elastic of her underwear, revealing thin ankles and plastic sandals. Nadia had trouble estimating her age. She could be twenty-five but look forty, or the reverse. She could have already lived a life of hardship and hunger, or it could be just beginning. There was hardly any difference in how it bore out on her face, future lines already casting their shadows.

Every now and then a man would take a long, hard look, like drinking whisky straight up, grimacing and sucking in his lips. Unlike other women, she did not lower her eyes, did not raise the scarf to her lips, did not turn away. She matched the stare with an equal hardness, lifted her chin to an equal height. Two pairs of dark eyes competed for contempt.

"Keep looking," Manal whispered.

Out of the group of moustached and shirt-sleeved men emerged a rotund and balding one, pushing the last of his sandwich into his mouth, where it formed a rock of bread that made him squint in one eye. He flicked his fingers together and on his pants. He caught the woman's gaze. She nodded in a long, slow arc. He spat on the ground and walked to the edge of the park, his stride purposeful, pelvis jutting forward, hands jingling coins and keys in his pockets. She turned and followed a few feet behind. The man and the prostitute entered a shoe store on the corner of the street.

"What are they doing?" Nadia asked, unwilling to jump to the obvious conclusion.

"Shhhh," ordered Manal.

Within minutes the man emerged—"So fast!"—in his hands a bag with a pair of shoes sticking out.

"He'll give the shoes to his wife or his child. The store is always busy, of course. Everyone gets a profit."

The woman emerged shortly after, concentrating on walking straight, the way a drunk does. As she made her way toward the park her body regained control. She looked neither down nor straight ahead but focused somewhere in the middle distance, feet seeming to carry her almost against her will. More than anything else, she reminded Nadia of a soldier.

"What kind of woman does that?" she whispered.

"A poor woman. She has a husband and children for sure. The *sharmoutas* are almost always mothers."

She returned to the falafel stand and found her spot on the periphery, impervious to the music and children that swirled around her. Out of the crowd of men another one stepped forward as if a bell had rung, locking eyes with her as before, swallowing his sandwich as before, flicking his fingers into the non-breeze. This time it was Uncle Nasser.

"Oh my god."

"I see him every time." Manal turned on her back and stopped watching. "He is a dog."

Ten minutes later Nasser returned to their picnic. He laid a new pair of sandals at Manal's mother's feet and walked away. Om Malek did not look at them or put them on.

Later, Nadia and Manal walked arm in arm around the park, dodging balls and badminton birdies as the sun turned the clouds pink. For a moment the sky cracked and Nadia saw the storm behind it, or the machine, or the blood.

"Do people know what's going on around them?"

"Of course," Manal said, spitting a seed shell. "There are no secrets in Egypt. Just lots of big rooms where no one talks."

Two young girls chased after a ball their brother had snatched away. They tackled and tickled him, threw grass in his mouth. Ball in hand, the girls ran away and the boy gave chase.

Nadia wanted to tell Manal about her father leaving for Ramallah, but she didn't have any answers yet to whatever questions it might raise. Part of her feared Manal's judgment. Was she still a child, her actions tied to the decisions of her parents? Was she a coward, unwilling to stake a claim on her own future? Sometimes it felt like her aimlessness was in inverse proportion to Manal's determination, and it shamed her.

"Manal," she began.

She went unheard. "I have a letter," Manal said, rummaging in her bag. "I wanted to read it with you but you were always so busy."

Nadia bristled at the hint of reproach. But she looked at the envelope. It was from the Paris scholarship.

Manal hid it against her chest. They continued walking, but faster now, until they reached the iron fence that rimmed the park. A large tree had interrupted its bars and forced them open with generations of effort. They sat under it. Nadia tore the envelope open gently, careful not to rip anything, read it quickly.

"Okay. It's just a confirmation letter, Manal. They just wrote to tell you they received your submission. Wait. They've ticked off some things they still want. Your letter of reference. And you did not provide them with an indication of any exhibits you'd had. I can't tell if you *must* have an exhibit, but you have until June 1st to provide the necessary information." She looked at Manal, who was looking away. "I think that's pretty good. They got your application; you are missing one thing; you have two months to get it. I think that's really good, Manal."

Manal took the letter and looked it over herself. "Brigitte," she said. "Brigitte Brigitte Brigitte."

"Manal, if Brigitte says no or if it can't be done in time, aren't there other galleries? Can't you go somewhere else? Couldn't somebody else help you?"

Manal squinted at her. "I see you still know nothing about Cairo, Canadian girl." She stood up. An errant soccer ball came flying in her direction. She could have kicked it back but instead stepped to the side and let it go over the wall. A group of kids yelled and swore. She swore right back.

Manal told Nadia she didn't have to bother coming to the gallery for a few days. It wasn't busy enough, and anyways she had Tewfiq to help her.

"But I like coming, I can just hang out with you," she said.

"Why don't you do something a little more exciting than spending your days in a boring gallery?"

"I don't find it boring."

"*Yalla*," Manal said sharply. "I need to be alone in the gallery this week."

Nadia must have looked hurt, because she added: "Brigitte is back and I need to talk to her and there will be no chance if you are there."

On the second day, when she came home to find that Nadia still hadn't left the house, Manal gave her a list.

"Pyramids? Without you?"

"It is a shame that you haven't gone yet. Really."

"Let's go together."

"Yes, we should go together. Okay, cross it off the list. What's next?" She looked over Nadia's shoulder. "Egyptian Museum."

"Boring."

"Go."

"Boring boring boring."

"Go go go." Manal kissed her on top of her head, blew through her hair. "Imagine I am honey dripping down your scalp," she said. "Go to the Egyptian Museum."

"No."

The telephone rang less than a minute after Manal left for work, followed by footsteps in the hallway. Expecting to inform Om Malek that her daughter had already left, Nadia was surprised when Uncle Nasser opened the door.

"Telephone," he said, pronouncing it with a heavy Arabic accent. *Tellefonne. Tdellivon. Dillivone.* Dull, lifeless, invasive.

"Manal just left. Should I run after her?" She hoped the answer would be yes.

He stepped inside, took the room in with his sweeping eyes. "It is for you."

He stayed in the room, a foot in the threshold. The only way to the phone was to squeeze past him, which she did as quickly as possible. He didn't budge. She felt his eyes on her as she picked up the receiver.

"Hello?"

It was her father inviting her to spend the day at the hospital with him. "Are you busy? Is bad time?"

"No, it's perfect. Now?"

"Sure, sure." He hung up.

Nasser was still in the doorway. "Do you need

something?" Nadia asked, trying to sound dismissive, intimidating, and polite all at the same time.

His body tilted slightly away from her, as if the words electrocuted him slightly—only slightly. "You stay here with Manal." Was that a question, Nadia wondered, or an observation, or even some sort of conundrum? "She didn't ask me," he said.

"Oh. Sorry about that. I'm just here for a little while. Um, just a short visit." She held up her thumb and forefinger, collapsed the space between them. "*Saghayar*." She still had trouble with the throated *gh* sound and cursed herself for this enforced deference. "Is Om Malek here?" Nadia hoped the reminder of his sister-in-law would force some propriety and distance into this increasingly uncomfortable excuse for a conversation.

"Asleep."

He looked for a second like he wanted to say something else, as if a long-held grievance was about to emerge. But he only shook his head and mumbled. Then he shut the door.

Nadia exhaled loudly. She didn't care if he heard. "*Fuuuuuck*."

Bishara's office was empty. She continued down the hall until she spotted him and three other people in another office. They were huddled over a phone and a speaker box. He motioned for her to wait outside, then changed his mind and swept his hand quickly back and forth, *yalla yalla*, indicating that she should come in the office and sit down on an empty chair by the wall. The conversation was loud and hurried, with lots of overlap and little listening. Her father and the others exchanged frequent glances, sighed often, wiped their brows, put out cigarettes, lit up more. The thickening atmosphere made Nadia nauseous. She opened the window wider. The call ended abruptly and the office quickly emptied, no one taking notice of her. Bishara caught his breath, then left the room. Nadia half ran to keep up.

"What was that?" Nadia asked.

He abruptly turned around and returned to his office, rifling through the drawers of his small desk, pulling out folders, business cards, notepads in the hunt for something he didn't seem to find.

"Very bad incident," he said. "I thought it was going to be a quiet day, sorry."

"What happened?"

"Abu Jihad was killed. Assassinated."

"Yasser Arafat?" She knew he had a nickname that began with Abu.

"What? *Ya salam*. No. I said Abu Jihad. Is like his right-hand man."

"Who killed him?"

He waggled his head back and forth as if it were obvious. "Who else?" He continued to look at her as he built a little pile of books and papers on the desk. "Hm?"

"I don't know, the United States?"

"Yes, you are right. Israel."

Nadia frowned. "Huh?"

His day derailed, he was either in meetings or on the phone trying to manage the hospital's response to the demonstrations in the West Bank and Gaza that had turned into violent clashes. Already there were fatalities—mostly children—creating shockwaves of both action and rhetoric. Nadia kept to the background, fetching files from adjacent offices, following him from meeting to meeting, and picking up his papers when he turned a corner too fast and they flew across the floor. He looked back briefly, reassured that she was gathering them, and hurried on. The hospital vibrated all around them, nudging them wherever they went. Every now and then a passing doctor or orderly stepped in and, in silent greeting, grabbed her father's hand and squeezed it. In the urgency there were no words, just touches. Wherever they went she was *Bint Bishara* and he was *Abu Nadia*. She dared let the words take shape inside herself.

"I should be there already, I should be doing my job on the ground," he said to her during a brief break in the mayhem. He was looking at her, his regard both harsh and worried. "They need help, my help."

"Why you?" she asked, the petulance in her voice not fully disguised. It struck her that maybe she had been summoned solely so he could show her how important his work was to him, and how critical he was to his work. "You've been on the phone all day, in meetings. Anyone can do that."

He threw a notepad on his desk with more force than he intended. "I am on the phone and in meetings precisely

239

because I am here. *Fahimti?* Do you understand me?"

"I know what *fahimti* means," she mumbled.

"I must go there," he said. "I need you to understand."
As if it hadn't already been decided, Nadia realized. As if
he had left a place in his plans for her reaction or her blessing. It softened her heart.

"I'm trying to understand."

"*Lakin,*" he said. But. "Maybe you come too."

Her first thought was Clare's voice in her head:
"You're taking her where?" It made her want to go. He
went into detail.

Had she known Manal would be napping she would have
opened the door more slowly, barged through it less
roughly, and banged around the room less noisily.

Manal sat up with a growl. "*Eh da.*"

"Oh, sorry! I didn't see you." Nadia flopped on the bed
beside her. "Scoot over. I need a shower. I'm drenched."

"If that means stinky, yes, I agree."

"Tell me about your day," Nadia asked.

"Why? It was fine, like every day, and just as boring."

"Did you sell any paintings?"

"No."

"Did Tewfiq tell any dumb jokes?"

"No," Manal frowned. "But today he left early again.
I don't like it."

"Was Brigitte there? Oh wait, right." Nadia remembered Manal's mission that morning, remembered Manal's disappointment, remembered Manal.

"Was Brigitte there?"

"Why are you so happy?"

"Nothing, sorry."

Om Malek called from the kitchen. "*Manal.*"

"I'm going to help my mother make dinner."

"Great." Nadia was hungry.

"No." Manal stopped her before she could stand up. "It's okay, you don't need to come."

Nadia remained motionless on the bed, stunned, as Manal's footsteps faded on the cracked tile. She strained to listen to the voices in the small kitchen. Then they were quiet and suddenly, as if she had not left, Manal was standing in front of her again, an expression of contrition on her face. "Nadia, *ana asfa,* I'm sorry. I am how you say, grumpy. Come, we make *waraq einab.* My mother—no, *we*—could use your help."

"I'm sorry too, Manal."

Manal thrust up her chin and clucked her tongue. It was over. She held out her hand and folded Nadia's into hers, dropped it only when they got to the kitchen and her mother looked up. Om Malek wrapped an apron around Nadia and, with the same large hands as her daughter, sat her down in a chair. In front of them were the fixings for *waraq einab*: several piles of grape leaves rinsed in water and a large bowl of freshly mixed rice and meat stuffing. Om Malek and Manal took turns demonstrating to Nadia how to hold the leaf, exactly how much to fill it with, a spoonful. "Or more if you are adventurous," Manal winked. How to roll without tearing, how to roll like you're going down a hill.

"Are you awake?" Manal whispered in the dark. She was opening the shutters, flooding the room with streetlight and moonlight.

"Now I am."

"I want to draw you."

"Now? Are you serious?"

A thick pencil was already in her hands, a large spiral sketchbook opened to the first page.

"You're serious."

"Shhhhh."

"Do I just lie here? No poses?"

"Shhhh."

Nadia settled into a comfortable position. "I don't know why you even woke me."

"I woke you because I wanted company in this sacred moment."

"Sacred? *La allah il allah wa Mohammed rasoul il llah,*" she said, intoning a prayer.

"*Eib, eib.*" She gave Nadia a stern look and began again. "Sacred art, sacred love, sacred line, sacred curve, sacred body, sacred heart, sacred hoping, sacred wanting, sacred waiting, sacred smudge, sacred sheet right here on this shoulder there like that, sacred lips, sacred light, sacred moon..."

The rhythmic incantation and the scratching on the thick paper lulled Nadia back to sleep.

12

we who trusted fortune and figs

Was it the heat that was pushing them down, the heat that was now persisting past sunset, the heat that took Nadia by surprise even though it shouldn't have? She'd been to Cairo in the summer, the only time it made sense for them to travel. She remembered Clare waking at night, pacing the room, angry at Bishara for not taking them to a better hotel. And so he brought them the next day to the Nile Hilton, where they had air conditioning and a television and little fridges stocked with ice and chocolate. Nadia's memories were stored like postcards—perfect pictures, friendly smiles, colours faded to pastel shades. But between the lines were curses and sharp looks and disappointment over dinner. Punishment lunches, her mother used to call them. They were being punished because the market seller took advantage of them; because the taxi got lost and with all four windows down Clare's hair was ruined; because no one told Clare not to go around bare-shouldered and thus spare her the constant attentions and gropings of hordes—hordes!—of men; because Bob should have known it was Ramadan and therefore a terrible time to be in Cairo and expect any kind of service at all. Everyone's napping! Patient, yielding, trying to please, he was able to remain calm until—*Not Bob*, he hissed. His voice was thin and sharp. *Not Bob. Not here, not again, not ever.* It was on that visit that he began insisting she call him by his real name, Bishara. Not Bob.

This year Ramadan was in April. It was due to start in a few days, with the sound of a canon and the setting of the sun to mark its commencement. Manal shrugged. She assured Nadia that it was more about the eating than the fasting, that people weren't dropping their heads on their desks because they were starving but because they were saving their energy for a night of feasting. And that the women would be especially depleted because they spent all day cooking and preparing the food that would be inhaled the minute the muezzin rang his dinner bell.

"For every exhausted man, imagine five women fainting in the kitchen. Religion is always about something different than what it pretends to be, don't you think?"

"I guess so," Nadia replied.

"A Muslim's relationship with Allah is private and precious, *ya Nadia*. You can never take it away. But some people find a way to make it less private and less precious." She continued in a lower voice. "Have you noticed Nasser's *zebaiba*?"

Nadia giggled. "His what? His *zibab*?" Penis! The word just appeared, she was ten years old and still giggling.

"Nooooo!" Manal snorted. "*Zebaiba*. His forehead! It has a dark spot, a bruise. Have you seen it? There is a race between all the men in Cairo. They compete to see whose forehead can be the most bruised and the most dented by the end of Ramadan. *Yalla*, down they go on the prayer mat—*bang, bang, bang*." Manal mimed the gesture, folding her knees and bowing on the floor until her forehead hit it. She looked around theatrically as if to ensure her piety was noted, then bent forward again, hitting her head even harder. "*Bang, bang, bang!*" She stood up and clapped, whether as part of the prayer routine or from the dust Nadia couldn't tell.

"You will see, *ya Nadia*, you will see. The most pious men in Egypt will suddenly be visible from far, like lighthouses. And if you can't see them, they will send you a storm!"

"*Haram, ya Manal.*" Tewfiq stood before them, his light voice carrying much weight. They hadn't heard him come out from the back room.

"We're just joking, Tewfiq," Manal said, waving it off as good-naturedly as she could. "Right, Nadia? Besides, you don't know Uncle Nasser."

He wanted to say something else but seemed stuck for words. A natural shyness prevented him from further admonishing Manal.

"*Malesh, ya Tewfiq.*"

"*Malesh, Manal.*"

Each asking forgiveness, understanding, tolerance, and a little leeway.

"There's something going on with him," Manal said after Tewfiq left, early again.

"Maybe he has a girlfriend."

Manal nodded. "He found love, yes. A girl, no."

"He's gay?"

"*Eh da? Haram aleiki, ya Nadia.*"

"What *haram*? Why *haram*? What about us?"

"I don't know what you are talking about."

"I don't know what *you* are talking about."

"I think Tewfiq is being influenced."

"Influenced by what?"

"*Il ikhwan al muslimeen.* The Muslim Brotherhood. They are in his neighbourhood. *Il Islam huwwa al hal*, the posters are everywhere. 'Islam is the solution.' Remember we saw them?"

"Vaguely," Nadia said, thinking back. They had been underneath a flyover near the Ramses train station. The most vivid part of the drive was the stench of urine as the car idled in the congestion by a cement column. Children weaved in and out of the traffic selling socks and chewing gum. Pasted all over one arch and in the process of being ripped and washed off by soldiers were about a dozen posters with Arabic writing: *Il Islam huwwa al hal.* Both Manal and the driver were beside themselves. Not here, not again, they said over and over. Not here, not again. "Is it that bad?"

"Bad? It is worse than bad. It is stupid."

"*Haram, Manal.*" Tewfiq was there again. Nadia marvelled at how silently he could move, as if the space had a different relationship to him, as if molecules and atoms could be generous and he in turn could reward them.

246

He said something to Manal, slightly harsh but also indulgent and, even, disappointed. He gestured to Nadia several times.

"He wants you to understand," Manal said. She began translating as he spoke. "It's different for him than it is for us. He's from a poor area, his circumstances are not like mine. Compared to him I am wealthy and have every opportunity. As do you. Especially you."

"But what does religion have to do with any of that?" Nadia asked, genuinely curious.

Manal took in his answer. "Everything. Everything," she said. "He wants to ask you, when did Israel take Palestine, when did they take the West Bank and Gaza?"

"I don't know, 1948 and then 1967."

"Of course you know," Manal smirked. "Yes, 1948, 1967. When did the Intifada start?"

"Last December."

"*Bizupt*," she nodded, exactly, agreeing with Tewfiq, throwing her lot in with his, adding to the tale. "It took a generation, then another. Things take time. People have to not only believe the injustice, they have to live it and then die in it. Then, it will be their children throwing stones at it. Time, time, time. Nasser promised change, Sadat promised prosperity, Mubarak promises stability. Only Islam is promising justice. You wait, Nadia. You wait."

"Wait for what?"

Manal spoke ahead of Tewfiq, throwing him a look. "For the police to come and put him in jail."

"*La, la,*" he chided. "Justice."

"But why would the Egyptian government be afraid of that? Justice is so simple. I mean, most people just want to live simple lives, don't they? A job, a meal, school for their kids."

They both laughed at her.

"What?"

"Thank you, *ya Nadia,*" Tewfiq said, a warm smile rippling over his face.

Manal, on the other hand, shook her head reprovingly. "One day you will see that the most simple things in the world are sometimes the most dangerous. One day."

Brigitte came by before the afternoon was over, Imad trailing her like a thirsty puppy, touching the paintings, touching the sculpture, sniffing at Manal. He trotted around the gallery and grinned while Brigitte busied herself in the back room. After a minute she popped out and said she had to run some errands, could Imad wait for her here? You go, you go, he said, his fingers trilling the air as if they were piano keys. He plunked himself next to Manal as the street door shut with an echo.

"*Yanni.*" He raised his eyebrows and waggled his head. Manal ignored him.

"*Yanni...*"

"*Yanni eh?*" she snapped.

"Have you heard?"

Nadia imagined that Manal knew exactly what he was referring to.

"No."

He nodded rhythmically, picked up pens and note cards from the desk, inspected them, put them down again. She sighed loudly, gave in to his game. "Have you?"

His hands went up in the air in mock innocence. "Maybe I will hear today."

Manal got up, crossed the room, straightened a painting. Imad followed. "Let me thank you again for the sale at *Shebab ya Shebab*. It's really great."

"*Il afwan*." You're welcome.

"No, really. It's the best sale I've ever had." He paused then seemed to make an effort to be sincere. "It's really good. It makes me look like a real artist."

"I'm happy," she said, looking directly at him for the first time since he came. "That's my job."

"You are good at it, Manal. How is Sofian, by the way? We were surprised to see you there when we delivered the painting," he said, his eyebrows rising and falling like mares on a carousel.

She said something sharp and cutting and brief. The words reached Nadia but then retreated immediately and pretended never to have existed.

Imad raised his hands. "Just that, just polite. It doesn't mean anything."

"No, it doesn't mean anything," she said. She glanced over at Nadia again. The three of them stood motionless as if turned to stone. Only the sound of the door clicking downstairs broke the spell. Brigitte's sandals clacked purposefully nearer and nearer. She stood on the landing and stuck her head into the gallery. "*Yalla Imad, tu viens?*"

He took a last look at Manal, performed a half-bow and clicked his heels like a Cossack. "Good evening."

Manal held Nadia's eyes for a long time.

They walked to the bus station in Tahrir Square. Micro-buses came and went as both the driver and the people on the street shouted out destinations and waited for a match.

"I change my mind." Manal took Nadia's hand and crossed the street.

Nadia started to talk but Manal shushed her with a single click of the tongue and a raising of her chin. She waved down a taxi and exchanged quick words with the driver. She pushed Nadia in ahead of her then leaned back, looked out her window, was silent. They crossed the river over a bridge Nadia did not know. The sun hovered over the other side of the Nile, its reflection rippling around the rows of wooden boats that lined the shore. Manal's fingers tapped the plastic-covered seat, reached out briefly to touch Nadia's, then retreated to tap the seat again. They rode on in bumpy silence.

All at once it grew dark, as if the sun had fallen out of the shimmering sky. A wall of stone loomed outside the taxi's window and leaned over the car with an ominous weight. Nadia cried out. *Oh my god. A Pyramid.* The taxi driver chuckled. Manal opened her wallet.

"Nadia, do you have five pounds? I need a bit more."

"Sure, sure." Nadia handed back her purse and got out

of the car, never taking her eyes off the massive structures.

They blazed into the sky like upturned knives, long blades with long memories. Each stone was unbelievably immense, many metres high and wide. Stones the size of shipping containers. Vivid images filled her mind, of glistening men hacking at them in far-off quarries, hauling them over the desert, shoving them into place, filing their edges, falling into the mortar with their last breaths. She shuddered involuntarily and could barely speak. Manal threaded her arm through Nadia's as they walked up and towards and around the literal weight of history. They weren't alone; tourists scuttled around them like beetles. Just slightly beyond, the suburb of Giza fanned out in broken walls and patched roofs. From that distance it could very well have been thousands of years old. A thin whiff of sewage rode the knotted air to where they stood.

"When it flooded, the Nile came up to here," Manal said. "They hauled the stones up on barges."

"Thank you, Manal. Thank you."

Manal pulled at her hand again. They circled the larger of the three Pyramids. Nadia didn't know its name and didn't ask. Then Manal pushed her between two large jutting stones, wedged her in with her entire body, looked around, then leaned in and kissed her on the lips. She wouldn't let go, took her bottom lip in her mouth, her breath exiting her body in strips and rags. Their hands reached for each other, Manal's grasp almost desperate. The sound of a motor inserted itself, pried them apart. Manal caught her breath then smiled. "People come here to fuck, you know."

"Manal!"

"Well, it's true."

They approached the Sphinx from behind, like cautious dogs. Smooth and hard like a dead body, he seemed to be inhaling through hidden pores, scanning the distance for his lover to return. But she no longer cared for him or his mausoleums of dust and filth. Maybe her family had forbidden their union. Maybe she had fled the soft banks of the Nile and, following the river, swum to cities of chrome and steel that lay far beyond, leaving him behind to watch his own skin crumble to dust, limbs pillaged stone by stone, face smashed in by marauding armies speaking the languages of other rulers. The flat African nose, the utter beauty of him—why do people not talk about him incessantly, this Nubian king?

"He's a rock star," Nadia said.

"Do you have more money?"

Nadia looked in her wallet, handed it over.

"I have another idea."

They walked towards the edge of the surrounding village, to a line of low buildings that turned out to be horse stables. A stableman gave them each a marvelous creature who pawed at the sand and snorted through cavernous nostrils. "Best horses in the whole Middle East," he boasted. He placed Nadia's left foot in the stirrup and helped her up.

"He's so big!"

"Have you been on a horse before?" Manal asked,

252

already astride a magnificent beast even larger than hers.

"A handful of times. You know, trail rides as a kid. Well, maybe you wouldn't know."

"My father used to bring me here."

The stableman led them out to where the sand began and faced them towards the setting sun. He slapped the animals' rumps.

"To Khartoum!"

They plunged over the stony plain, the horses eager to let loose upon the desert in spite of the heat. Nadia squeezed with her legs as the rest of her muscles hardened with fear. Her body bounced and slid over the saddle in a terrifying tease. Dust and stones flew up, pocked her face and mouth, coating her in a veil of yellow sand. She grabbed the animal's mane and found a position that was more or less secure, if inelegant. Just when she thought they must have galloped all the way to the Sudan, the horses eased up and turned onto a shaded path. They trotted leisurely through a series of fields and orchards, dark canals alongside. Her body relaxed into the animal's warm haunches. Then there it was again, a precious and furtive silence. The only din was the sun hopping off the leaves, the leaves meditating in the heat, insects sawing and sawing. Silence.

Ahead of her, Manal reached out to a squat palm tree and plucked a small banana. Nadia, managing to remain on her horse, did the same. She peeled it and put it whole in her mouth. "Oh my god," she whispered. It tasted nothing like anything she had ever called "banana."

She wanted to yell and holler, to dance and eat ten more. Manal was chewing with her eyes closed. They rode on quietly as the night sky wrapped them in its arms.

When they got home, plates had been left for them on the table, each one covered with a cloth. Om Malek shuffled softly out of her room when she heard them and insisted they sit down to eat.

"You mean you haven't eaten all day?" Nadia asked Manal. "You're fasting? Why didn't you tell me? I didn't even know."

"*Malesh*," Manal said modestly. But when her mother, satisfied they had been taken care of, left the room, Manal let out a little chuckle. "I'm *not* fasting, *ya Nadia*. Remember? The banana? But she will be sad if she knows."

"Does she think I'm fasting, too?"

"I hope so." She laughed some more. "You can't eat a bite of food in her presence for three more weeks. Now you're really Egyptian, *ya Nadia*. Suffering!"

The next morning the phone rang early. Manal jumped up and ran down the hall. When Nadia opened her eyes, Manal was standing over her, squinting strangely.

"It's for you."

Nadia sat up. "My father?"

"No."

"My mother? Does she even know this number?"

"It is Daniel."

They shared a silent cab downtown. Manal could not look at her. They parted on Champollion. Nadia wanted the walk from the gallery to the hotel. She wanted to take her time crossing the broad boulevards, navigating the shifting tides of people and vehicles, dodging the boys who sold papyrus and postcards and the men who whispered and hissed. She wanted the traversing to take long minutes so that when she climbed the steps of the hotel she would be already stained and claimed by the perspiring city. She had put on Manal's clothes that morning, a long-sleeved shirt, a long skirt, flat loafers. She smelled of Manal, walked like Manal. It gave her an advantage over being Nadia.

Even from far away she could see that the Nile Hilton's terrace café was full of tourists consulting maps, diplomats plotting over breakfast, and discreet lovers assuming no one was noticing. And then there was Daniel. He was standing on the top step just outside the hotel's doors. He had been watching her approach from across the Midan. A great film covered him, something impermeable, like the many layers of Vaseline that swimmers put on when they wanted to cross frigid Lake Ontario. They embraced but she could feel herself sliding off.

He looked at her stonily, fearfully. "Let's sit. Are you hungry?"

"No, not really. You?"

"I'm starving and I need a coffee. I need ten coffees. How is the coffee here?"

"Terrible. Have tea."

Neither of them smiled, but nor were there

255

recriminations, though she waited for them. They stole looks at each other. The waiter put a plate of eggs and toast in front of Daniel; olives, feta and tahini for Nadia. Daniel ate quickly, without pause. When he was done he placed his knife and fork across the plate and drank his now-cold coffee in one long drag.

"I couldn't stand it any longer." His voice was ragged. "I had to come. Then I couldn't find you."

Nadia nodded.

"I just assumed the Nile Hilton but you weren't here anymore. I called Clare and she said no, you were at your father's. She gave me the number."

"You called my father?"

"He's never home. No one was home for days."

"Days?"

"Finally, a woman was home. And guess what?"

"What?"

"She doesn't know where you live." He forced a laugh. "I had to wait another day. No, two days."

"Daniel, how long have you been in Cairo?"

"So I talked to him, the famous Bishara. Nice man. Why does your mother call him Bob? He gave me your number. Well, Manal's number."

Did he know anything? Nadia wondered. How could he? Why would he? She's here to connect with her father, that's what this trip is about. It's her trip. *Her* trip. She never wanted him to come.

"Then you called me this morning."

"That was yesterday. *Then* I called you this morning."

There was so much she could do right now, throw herself upon him, kiss him like the long-lost lover that he was. Laugh along with him at his fearful courage. He waited, he waited. As she did nothing she could see him collapse in upon himself. He called the waiter. "*L'addition, s'il vous plaît,*" he said, as if they were in Montreal. He had spent everything he had on waiting for her.

She put her hand over his. "Daniel."

He clutched it, turned it around, looked at her palm, ran his fingers along the thin lines of her future. Tears burst over his eyelids and streamed down his face. He worked frantically to erase them.

His room looked out over the Midan. She could see Champollion Street from the window. She abruptly looked away. He pulled her to the bed, lay alongside her, then on top of her. As he buried his face in her neck great thrusts moved through his body, but they were sobs. She held him as tears and snot poured out, held him until he stopped. They moved away from the wet pillow and re-settled on a dry spot.

"Sorry," he said sheepishly.

"Hush." Nadia was hoping she would not have to speak at all. "Hush."

Was she cruel? she asked herself over and over. Perhaps her courage was in inverse proportion to his. Would she cross the ocean to look for him? No, she had to admit, no. But she would cross the planet ten times over to look for Manal.

"Tell me what is happening, Nadia."

She wondered if she would feel great stores of shame, shame at loving a woman, a shame that would prevent her from telling the truth. She looked for it but did not find it. She had no shame. Rather, she was wondering what Manal was doing at that moment, if Tewfiq would be working on a frame, if there were any customers or tourists wandering through the gallery, if there were any phone calls that needed to be made or errands that needed to be run.

"My father is working at a hospital but then he is going to Ramallah. He might have a job for me at the hospital. And he thinks I should go to Palestine when they go. He could bring me. He's going to Ramallah in a month or two. Or earlier, he's not sure anymore, things are very chaotic over there. I guess you know all about it, the Intifada and all that. It must be on the news. It's terrible."

"Your father hasn't seen you in days."

She blinked. "I have other things going on, Daniel. It's a big city. Sixteen million to be exact."

"*Câlisse de tabarnak!*" He slapped the bed. "Why did you stop writing? Why did you stop calling? Why are you not returning my letters? Ha, you don't even get them, do you? Are they just piling up at the hotel reception? Do you even ask if you've gotten any faxes from me? You know, we can check. I'm going downstairs to check."

He stood up, but his legs gave way. He sat down again.

"First we talk. *Vas-y, explique-toi.* Explain yourself. Who is this Manal?" He tremored slightly as if counting the seconds. "You know, stupid me, I just assumed it's a woman's name. But maybe it's a man's name, eh? Is Manal a man? Are you living with a man? Are you fucking sleeping with another man?"

Nadia couldn't help it, she let out a little laugh. "Oh, come on, Daniel."

"Don't you laugh at me!"

"Manal is a woman. She works at the gallery, we met by chance. When I decided to stay—because of my *father*—she offered to let me stay at her place. She lives with her mother and her uncle and she has a spare bed. A little spare bed." She was amazed at how easily truth could be woven. A coat riven through with holes was still a coat. "I sleep there."

He didn't move for long minutes, as if catching his breath. "Can we go for a walk?" he finally said.

He wanted to hold her hand and she let him. She felt like she was a tourist now, attracting attention even more than when she walked alone. He was an incurable *aventurier*, stopping every third step to exclaim excitedly *look at that, look at this, check ça!* He stared, he pointed, he laughed, he rubbed his chin, he complained about the heat, he wondered about the street food but dared not touch it, he grew thirsty but would only drink bottled water, wouldn't go near the delightfully bountiful juice stands. In spite of everything, he was happy and bright, like new chrome. Even in his sadness he was not sad, Nadia realized. She was supposed to love him for that, wasn't she? Manal, on the other hand, moved in a liquid melancholy.

She wanted to immerse herself in it, to dive, devour, and drink it.

"*Mon dieu,* look at that." He pointed at a huge movie poster that covered the side of a building. It was garish and melodramatic, with large strokes and primary colours. *Yom mor, yom helw*, Nadia read to herself. *Bitter Day, Sweet Day*. It was the latest social realist film by Khairy Beshara, and was being hailed a masterpiece. It starred Faten Hamama, an Egyptian version of Catherine Deneuve. Manal had promised to take her to see it.

"I wonder what Egyptian movies are like," he said. "Do they dance and sing like Indian films? Probably all karate and harems, eh?"

"Like anybody's movies. Why would they be different?" Impatience had taken up residence in her voice. "Some of them are supposed to be good. And I doubt there's karate." She stopped. She didn't want to tell him anything about this film.

"Let's see an Egyptian movie," he said enthusiastically, pointing the way with a gallant arm.

She wanted Manal to take her, to translate it for her, to sit in the dark next to her and grab her arm and cover her neck with kisses. "No."

They passed Groppi's a little later. Nadia slowed her pace, looked inside. It was beautiful and run down. It was a place for lovers, she could see that right away. But she wanted to walk right by it, to save it for later, for Manal.

"Look at this," he said. "I bet it was once a fancy place. It's like a really bad Parisian café."

"It still is a fancy place," she said stubbornly.

His laughter was full of judgment and distance. "*Bon*, shall we go? I would like to try a fancy Egyptian pastry."

"No," she said. She tried to temper her voice this time; she didn't want conflict, she didn't want to explain anything to him, she didn't want to be with him. "Can we just keep walking? Let's just go back to the hotel and have a pastry there."

"*Chrisse*, Nadia."

13

what fate wrote cannot be unwritten

Nadia was frantic with impatience and longing for Manal, and worried at the reception she might get when she did see her. She hadn't phoned her to let her know she would be spending the night at the hotel; it was making her sick with guilt and worry. In the morning, she tried to explain to Daniel why she needed to go to the gallery.

"I don't understand, is this a job? Do they pay you?"

"No, I help out."

"So call them." He picked up the telephone beside the bed. "Just call them."

"No," she said. "They're not, it's not, it's not like that here. I can't just call, I have to go."

"Fine." He gathered his wallet and sunglasses. "Let's go."

"I'm just going to go alone, Daniel. You don't need to come. Can you wait here?"

"Why? It's already late and we can leave from there, go to the Pyramids or something. I'd really love to go to the market, and the Arab quarter."

"The what? It's an Arab city, how can there be an Arab *quarter*?"

"I don't know, Nadia. It's what the guidebook says."

"Fuck the fucking guidebook. You stay here. I'll be back in an hour."

His shock at the swearing gave her a head start. She closed the door then ran to the elevator.

Manal was already looking towards the door when Nadia ascended. Tewfiq was beside her. He gave Nadia a generous smile and continued explaining something to Manal, oblivious of the tremors underground. Nadia smiled back, kept the smile on her face as she sat down in the window bench. She stole a glance at the clock behind the desk: 10:20.

"Are you hungry?" Manal asked a little while later. Nadia knew she was expected to follow. They headed toward the *shwarma* shop but Manal pulled at her arm. "We'll get them on the way back." She kept going until they reached an apartment building. A *bowab*, nibbling at a plate of food, nodded as they entered the lobby. She must have known the building; they sat down on a bench by the elevator.

"Talk."

Unnerved, Nadia composed herself and put as much energy into not reaching out to touch Manal as she did into explaining herself. "Daniel wants me to go back to Montreal with him. He is upset." She waited for a reaction but got none. "I told him I wanted to stay. Of course I want to stay. I just got my visa, after all," she said, making an attempt to laugh. "And you know, I told him about my father going to Ramallah and that maybe I would want to visit him or something. All the reasons why I want to stay here and not go back to Montreal. Then there's the main reason, but I didn't tell him that."

"Many choices," Manal said flatly.

"My choice is to stay here. With you."

"It's difficult to know that," Manal said, "because these days you are at the hotel."

"It's just for now, Manal. He came all this way."

"And he can go all the way back."

"Are you jealous?"

"*La*." Manal looked away, then turned back and punched Nadia's arm.

"Ow! I think you are."

"*La!*"

"It's just for a few days."

"Do you kiss him?"

"Manal."

"Never mind, don't answer. I already know anyway."

"How do you know?"

"I know because you are not good with decisions. *Yalla*, Tewfiq will be hungry."

When they returned to the gallery Tewfiq was wearing a crisp white *galabiyya* over his clothes. "You took so long, I have to go," he said.

"Dressed like that? What is going on? Why now? Tewfiq..."

"I have to go," he said and hurried past them. He stopped at the stairs. "You have food?" Nadia held out the bag. He reached in and retrieved a sandwich. "*Shukran. Yalla, bye.*"

"He looked nice," Nadia said.

"Nice? It's not even Friday. Why is he wearing that?" She settled herself at her desk, began eating. "I am worried about him, Nadia. It is not good. I don't like it."

"I thought you understood him, I thought you were agreeing with him."

"In theory. Of course, in theory. In practice he goes to jail."

Nadia took another bite of her food then jumped up. "Oh my god I can't believe it I have to go too. What time is it? How did this happen? I have to go. I'm really sorry, Manal." She put the last piece of sandwich in her mouth between sentences. "I'm really sorry. I told him I'd only be gone an hour and it's been two at least. Oh my god, four. Come here." She leaned over and nuzzled into Manal's neck, her mouth still busy with the sandwich.

"Come home tonight," Manal said.

Nadia stopped and grinned. "Home?"

Manal cocked her head, shrugged. As if she had said more than she had intended but now that it was out there, she was okay with it.

"So what," she said, repressing a smile. "Home."

Daniel had left a note. *Je suis parti pour les pyramides. Bonne journée.* He was using his language as a wall against her and a protection for himself. Her first instinct was to return to the gallery. But she resisted; the least she could do was wait for him this one time. His suitcase lay open on the floor, a T-shirt and a pair of shorts discarded on top. She knelt down and folded the rumpled clothing, noticing a small pile of souvenirs he had already acquired—three papyrus paintings wrapped in plastic, a black *galabiyya*-style men's shirt, a carton of Cleopatra cigarettes, brass key chains in the shape of camels and pyramids. She continued touching, moving, rummaging, inhaling familiar scents. Lying flat on the bottom of the suitcase was a manila envelope emblazoned with the hotel's logo. It wasn't sealed; inside she found the faxes he had sent her. So he did go to the reception and get them. He had already known that she hadn't been retrieving them, let alone reading them.

The door clicked. Nadia jumped, almost screamed. "Oh my god, you scared me," she said.

He put the key on the table beside the television. "Who else were you expecting?" He was weary and layered in a day's worth of dust and dirt. "What are you doing?"

"Nothing," she said. "How were the Pyramids?"

"Still there. You'd think after all these years they would have found a better place for them, like Paris." He looked at her rolling eyes. "*C't'un joke.*"

He sat heavily on the bed farthest from her and fell backwards on it with his arms outstretched. "*J'en peux plus,*" he groaned. "I've had enough."

"I bet it's hotter here than you expected."

"Unreal. When does summer start?"

"Aren't the Pyramids amazing? I was speechless when I went. So beautiful."

"Well, it was overrun by tourists. A big bus unloaded half of Japan. They were clicking their cameras before they even hit the ground. They didn't even look first. They had their cameras to their faces as they stepped down the stairs, *comme ça*." He sat up and mimicked them, hands in front of his face, feet flailing blindly. "I mean *tabarnak*, don't you want to look first? *Trouver le bon angle, hostie de câlisse*." He stared at her then abruptly fell back on the bed.

"Who did you go with?" he asked from his Jesus-like position.

"Go where?"

"To see the Pyramids. Bishara?"

"Manal."

"Manal."

"Yes."

"I want to meet this Manal."

"Daniel, what is the point of this."

But he sat up. "No, I'm serious. Can I meet your new Egyptian friend? I don't know why, Nadia, *tu me diras*, but I have a feeling she has a brother. Or some friends. She must be a special connection. Does she?"

"Does she what?"

"Does she have a brother?"

"Jesus Christ, Daniel. I'm not even answering that."

He got up abruptly and splashed water on his face in the bathroom. "I want to see the gallery and your friends."

"No Daniel, stop. Not like this. There's no point."

"No point?"

"What is the matter with you? Why are you acting so weird?"

"So weird? I am weird now? I am trying to be social. I am trying to meet my girlfriend's new world. I am trying to figure out why she is staying in this disgusting dirty noisy stupid country! I mean really, look around. It's a garbage pit. I had no idea. Nothing works, nothing looks nice, everyone is disgusting, and the only half-decent activity is to visit some five-thousand-year-old piles of rock. Yet, like magic, my girlfriend has found a bed to sleep in and new friends and a new life. So I ask myself. What is wrong with this picture?"

"Wow. I thought you might be happy for me. You know how important this trip was for me."

"Really? Really? First you leave so quickly, then you don't even tell me you change plans, then you stop calling and stop communicating. And now? Now it's been four months, and you know what?" He looked away, his lower lip was trembling. He swore to himself, regained some composure. "I have been waiting, I have been patient. And I have even told myself once or twice, well, she's on an important trip, don't bother her. But you know what that makes me?"

She was doing this all wrong, she knew now. "What?"

"A fool."

"Oh, Daniel."

"It's now or never, Nadia."

He rummaged through his shoulder bag and took out an EgyptAir ticket. "I'm scheduled to leave the day after tomorrow." He held it out to her. "You are too. I bought you a ticket." He lowered his arm when she didn't take it, the envelope slapped against his leg. "You have a life in Montreal, Nadia. A life with me. I can't believe I even have to remind you. Come home."

Home. Home. Home. Home. Home. She couldn't think, she could barely feel, even the room seemed to lose focus and definition. She got up and she was in one corner, then at the window, then on the bed again, then at the door, not knowing how she was getting from one place to the next. He was talking to her, but it was in slow motion, or coming to her from the far end of a long pipe. A buried transatlantic cable from the previous century. *Home. Apartment. Life. Mother. Family. Future. Together. Please. Please. Please.*

She tried to counter it, balance everything out, legitimize and justify what she knew now was errant and irresponsible and even cruel. *Father. Family. Sister. Palestine. Roots. Now or never.* She ran out of words.

"What?" He said something that made her stop. "What?" she asked again.

"You missed my birthday."

A wave of heat slapped her in the face, leaving a mark on her cheeks. She stepped towards him, but he put his hands up, a dam, and kept her back. "I thought, what could make her forget? What could it be? People travel all the time, they don't forget birthdays. Is she so busy? Is her father keeping her so busy? I was worried, Nadia. Can you believe that? I started to worry about you. Maybe she's sad, I thought, or stuck. So I decided to come. You can imagine my shock when Bob said he sees you once or twice a week, maximum."

"Bishara."

"So what can it be? What is it that keeps her so busy? What can it be? It must be another person with another birthday. That was my conclusion, *en tout cas*."

"Daniel, it's not what you think."

"You won't tell me?"

"Tell you what?"

"Who is your lover?"

"My lover? Two minutes ago you didn't even know if Manal was a man or a woman."

"I never said Manal." He chuckled bitterly. "I should be a detective." He took her hand; his was slippery. "Tell me the truth. Tell me everything." His expression promised redemption; his body language said otherwise.

Nadia removed her hand, held it with the other and returned them both to her belly. She wondered what Manal would do in this situation. What does one do in a country like Egypt, she wondered, with an uncle like Nasser, a gallery like Brigitte's, and an ambition to be an artist. How far does talent or even ambition go in a landscape of moats and quicksand? And then there was the question of their relationship. Nadia didn't want to articulate the word lesbian, she didn't want their relationship to exist outside of the sealed world they had created, and she most certainly didn't want to jeopardize Manal. She needed to protect her. "There is nothing to tell," she said, and meant it.

He seemed more bemused than disappointed. Her duplicity was surprising him no longer. After a moment he went to the bathroom and ran the shower. She didn't move. When he came out, rubbing his head with a towel, the sky had turned dark.

"The sun sets earlier here than in Montreal," he said.

"Yes."

He dressed. "It's getting late. Shall we eat?"

"Alright, Daniel."

He was inexplicably hungry and wanted to try the Oriental Buffet at the Ramses Four Seasons. "It has everything," he assured her, reading from his guidebook. She only picked at the kebabs.

Nadia stayed at the hotel three more days, until the evening of Daniel's departure. They had gone to the Egyptian Museum and Khan el Khalile and the Cairo Tower and toured Coptic Cairo and the Mosque of Al Azhar. They ate at the Ramses, swam at the Marriott, and she took pictures as he rode a camel in Giza. By the end of it she was rotten with rage and helplessness, as if the noxious remains of every meal and experience were piled in her gut and giving off a rancid stink. She couldn't understand how he didn't smell it too. By the end she hated his voice, his touch, his gaze, his enjoyment, him—and herself by association. The second they parted it was as if he had never come. She jumped in a taxi and had it speed to the flat.

"*Yimin*," she told the driver, instructing him to turn right. "*Shimal*." Left. She pushed out the words with equal parts ownership and desperation. She ran up the four flights of stairs. Barely catching her breath, she called out Manal's name as she opened the front door.

"Hungry, *ya Nadia?*" Om Malek was in the kitchen.

"No, *merci, shukran.*" She smiled but walked past, undeterred. The bedroom door was closed. The door handle slipped in her moist palms.

"Manal?"

She walked out to the balcony. "Manal?"

Om Malek called from down the hallway. "She's gone out, *habibiti.* Come eat. Join me. I've been alone all day."

"Where did she go? Didn't she leave work ages ago?"

Manal's mother was putting plates of leftovers on the table, utensils, a plate for Nadia, one for herself, a bottle of cold tap water from the fridge, glasses. Nadia didn't think she'd be able to touch a bite.

"With Sofian," Om Malek said with a conspiratorial grin.

"Sofian?"

She nodded her head with maternal excitement. "He has a full day of activities for her."

Nadia tore off a piece of bread. Om Malek was unusually energized. She spoke at length in a singsong Arabic that Nadia could have understood better had she wanted to. All sorts of words stood out—hope, marriage, wedding, love, children, finally, fate, security—but she refused to string them together. Clare had once woven a necessary melding between her and Daniel; perhaps Om Malek was doing the same. *Bring him for supper,* Clare had said. *When do I meet his parents? He is so polite. He's serious about his future. I like him, Nadia.* After supper she could barely get to the bathroom in time. Her insides spilled down the pipes all the way to the rotting feluccas of the Nile.

It was her turn to wait. A punishment day. It was late when Manal returned. Dark. Even the city had nodded off to sleep. She let out a long, low whistle. Nadia reached for the clock. *Shhh, don't look.* Manal crawled into the small bed with her. *Go back to sleep.* Her long arms threaded themselves around Nadia, constricting her, preventing from sitting up, speaking, thrashing, crying out, saying Sofian's name like a curse over and over.

"*Malesh, malesh.*"

"What were you doing?" Nadia asked through tears.

"I should be asking you that. I am surprised to see you. Sometimes I thought you go back to Canada."

"Don't be stupid. Why do you keep seeing him? Why are you always going out with Sofian? You don't tell me but I know."

"*Ya Nadia*, why do we do anything? Why did Daniel come to Cairo and keep you from me for a week?"

"It wasn't a full week, and you know why. And anyways it's finished, he's gone back."

"*Il hamd'il allah.*" Manal went to kiss her.

"And Sofian? When does he leave? You need to stop this, Manal."

"Like a tree stops birds? Like a road stops cars? Like…"

"Oh my god! Your riddles!"

Manal laughed. "Then I give you my kisses."

14

a house of small rooms is never empty

Bishara said they needed someone who could type English and that it could be a job for Nadia if she wanted. She left early and walked to the hospital. It took over an hour during which the strap of her sandal rubbed one foot raw near the arch, first raising a blister she tried to buffer with a leaf, then finally drawing blood. She made it to the front steps in one piece, which felt like a blessing considering the run-in she'd had. Her father was aghast. "You threw what?"

"A brick. Well, not exactly a brick, a red stone. Big though."

"But why Nadia, why?"

"Because. I told you. They passed me once then twice then they turned around at the corner—screeching—and were going to pass me again. They were screaming and whistling and coming in closer each time. What if they had hit me?"

"They were just playing," he said. "Just stupid boys."

"Well, now the stupid boys have to explain to their daddies why the windshield of the Mercedes is smashed to bits."

"*Ya Allah! Ya salam!*"

"Oh come on," she said. "They deserved it."

"You are…you are," he searched for a word. Found one, discarded it, kept on going for another. He was changing his mind every time. Finally, he put his hands on her shoulders. "You are warrior!"

"How do you say that in Arabic?"

He thought for a moment. "*Inti filistiniya.*" You are Palestinian.

Then there was a knock on the door. A young man stuck in his head.

"Nadia, this is Dr. Abdallah Khoury. He will be submitting a report to UNRWA. We need you to type up some of the medical testimonies."

"But in English though, right?"

"Yes, yes. Abdallah will take you."

He walked with small shuffling steps in flopping sandals, an incongruous look with his crisp, white medical jacket. He didn't say anything as he led her up a flight of stairs and into a series of offices in a wing she hadn't yet visited. A half-dozen young women were around a desk chatting and laughing. One of them pointed to a nearby desk with a typewriter. Ahmed said something to her and she took on the task of explaining and translating his instructions to Nadia. She opened the file and spread out about fifty pages of handwritten copy, half of it scribbled on and annotated. They were medical notes in English that had been taken by foreign doctors.

"You type," she said, smiling. "Look good, English good."

When Abdallah left, Aisha, the only one who spoke English, introduced Nadia to the other girls, their curiosity bubbling and crackling like roasting seeds.

"This is Zakariya, she is from Tulqarm and way too pretty," she said, jabbing her in the arm. "Iman is from Gaza, she has begun studies for nursing. Hannan is from Al Quds and is learning computer."

"How long have you all been in Cairo?" Nadia asked.

"We are born here," Aisha said, not seeming to understand the question. "Except for Iman. They came at night. *Mish kidda, Iman?*" She conferred with her, Iman nodded vigorously. "Iman is born in Khan Younis, in Gaza," Aisha confirmed.

"You're Egyptian now? My father has a similar story."

"We are not Egyptian. We do not have papers. We are from Palestine and that is all." Aisha slapped her hands together as if slapping off dust. "*Kidda.*"

"Are you here legally?" Nadia immediately knew she overstepped by asking that question, but she couldn't help it. She felt like she was getting somewhere finally, getting to an understanding of the liminality of their being.

Aisha laughed. "What is legal?" She and Iman conversed back and forth, then she turned to Nadia again, this time with an edge of seriousness. "You will not get arrested for speaking with us. The crime of being Palestinian is not contagious, don't worry."

"But I *am* Palestinian. My father is Bishara Eid.

Anyways, that's not why I was asking."

"*Ya-aaaaa!*" Aisha did a double take, took Nadia's hand again, hugged her, kissed her three times on her cheeks. She apologized for assuming she was "just an American." Then she put her hand over her mouth and ululated so loudly that heads poked in the office on and off for the next half-hour asking what the celebration was.

Her job was to type up the notes taken in the field by healthcare workers in the Occupied Territories since the December uprising, and which were to be included in a larger report for Al Haq, the Palestinian human rights organization in Ramallah. Scrawled in English by often-overwhelmed doctors, nurses, and paramedics who were volunteering with the Palestinian Red Crescent Society. They were from places like Norway, Japan, Canada, and even the United States. The casual violence they attested to shocked Nadia.

Mahmoud, age twelve. Both hands smashed (soldiers) when he was caught running away from a demonstration. Upset we cut his jacket off. Third and fourth finger, left hand, thumb and fourth finger right hand: multiple compound fractures. He is missing school and when presented had not eaten for two days. He was not taking part in the demonstration but looking for his bicycle.

Suheir, age seventeen. Left eye impacted by rubber bullet, state of vision to be confirmed, possible blindness, ocular hairline fracture. Contusions to left cheek and hairline fracture of bone. Second X-ray recommended as patient was moving (pain). She was crossing checkpoint into Jerusalem when clashes erupted. Unclear whether she took part in clashes or was bystander. Has left school for the winter session. Acetaminophen, double dosage.

Samir, age eight. Witness to execution-style slaying of older brother (Khaled, twenty-one) suspected of collaboration. Has not spoken in four weeks and refuses to leave home. Referred for mental health assessment. Easily startled, does not want to leave mother's side. Observer was unable to engage in conversation.

Wael, age eighteen. Bricklayer. Was working when Israeli tank rammed wall, pinning him. Two broken legs, at tibia, compound fr. Witnesses say patient had refused to remove Palestinian flag from worksite. Recovery potential: excellent but long term disability a certainty.

Tawil, age seventeen. Five broken fingers after altercation with Israeli soldier at checkpoint. Left shoulder had been dislocated. Some swelling.

Elham, age fourteen. Possible permanent deafness after rubber bullet grazed right ear. She had been in backseat of family car. Family unharmed. Nightmares.

Rawi, age eighteen. Right arm broken (two oblique fractures) by soldiers at checkpoint. According to patient he had refused to strip for search and was hit by the butt of rifle. Escaped arrest.

The next day she put on different shoes. Sneakers.

"Already?" Manal asked.

"Already what?"

"Already you are busy with other things?"

"You know I need a job. I can't stay here and not work."

But Manal pouted. "You don't like the food here?"

"Come on, Manal. You're being silly. You haven't even wanted me at the gallery lately. It's okay, we can both work and then we see each other after. I'll see you later, right? Let's go see a movie. *Yom mor, yom helw* is still playing. There was a really good review in *Cairo Today* about it. Let's go on a date, okay?"

"Okay."

But after lunch Bishara asked Nadia if she could babysit. Noor would need to come to the hospital for a lecture by a Scottish doctor on mental health in the West Bank and Gaza. Could she take a taxi to his apartment and watch Nora for them?

Nora was sitting on a blanket in front of the television, a bowl of peanuts keeping her busy. Noor hunted down a spare key for Nadia and showed her where the stroller was. "Go outside," she suggested. "Park is close. At end of street," Noor nodded. "Not far. You go, very nice!"

Nadia joined Nora to watch the familiar *Dumbo* but dubbed into Arabic. They cried when the mother died. "Let's go to the park," she suggested when the movie ended. She tried it in Arabic but didn't know how to say park. "*Shagara, shagara, shagara*," she said, not that there was any guarantee they'd see a tree.

Nasser City had a completely different feeling from downtown Cairo. Dense with apartment buildings, it was also airy and empty, its wide streets and chalk-white sidewalks giving it a ghostly feel. It hardly felt like the same city that harboured a Manal. And, she couldn't help thinking, a Sofian. He was nice-looking, dressing like a wealthy

European and carrying himself with a physical restraint and pride that she didn't see in most Egyptians. It was like watching a male ballet dancer around men who found it a chore to stand up straight. Maybe he saved his white *dishdasha*, narrow attitudes and slouching ways for Riyadh. Did he really like art, she wondered? Or did he just like Manal? A fly landed on her arm and she slapped it away, hard, too hard, jerking the stroller with the movement. Nora sat up and made a noise, then sat up straighter and pointed: "Park!" It was tiny. A small corner of the street, mostly cemented over but with a handful of trees and small bushes. In the middle, a metal swingset and a seesaw.

"Park!" Nadia said. "You said park. Smart girl!"

Nora scrambled to the swings, then the seesaw, then back to the swings. In her excitement, she couldn't choose.

"Well, fuck me!" A voice rang out, distinctive, British. "Well really!" It was coming closer but Nadia couldn't find its source. Until a tall man stood in front of her, amiably leaning forward and holding out his hand. "Remember me? You're, um, give me a minute."

"Nadia. Hi, Wills."

"Nadia! I don't know what it is, but I have a knack for running into people. A city this bloody massive, and I always find my friends. Is this your daughter? Do you live in Nasser City? I was visiting a friend. It's the middle of nowhere, I can't find a taxi! Is that even possible in Cairo?"

Nadia wasn't sure what outburst to respond to. "Nora is my sister, she lives just a street over, with my father." It felt like enough.

"Brilliant." He sat down on a bench while she pushed Nora on the swing. "You're Canadian, right? I've been here going on two years now, haven't even gone back to the UK for a visit. What's the point, really. You can't be in two places at one time. Love the one you're with, and all that."

Nora kept Nadia busy, tumbling from swing to see-saw to swing again. Wills took over pushing duties at one point, which was a surprising relief.

"I never imagined how exhausting it is to push a swing," Nadia said. "I think I have some parents to thank."

"Oh yes, it's the worst. Sit, I've got it. But don't ask me to play Barbies. My little sister used to, it killed me, really did. Death by Barbie."

"Sounds like a movie."

"A German movie: *Death by Barbie*," he said in a German accent.

When Nora ran back to the seesaw they took turns on that too.

"So why have you been in Cairo for two years?"

"I'm doing my doctorate on Islamic architecture, so I came for a year study at the AUC. But then I stayed, and now it's been two years. *Kidda!*"

"Why did you stay?"

"You met Tena, right? Need you ask?"

"Ah, yes." Yes, she needn't have asked. "And why's Tena in Cairo? She's Yugoslavian, if I recall."

"Right. Good question. I don't have an answer to that one, I'm afraid. Some things better left to mystery," he laughed.

Nadia hadn't packed any water or snacks for Nora, who was now teetering on the brink of either explosion or implosion. She corralled the toddler back into the stroller and, with Wills in tow, made the short trek back home.

"So. This is where my father lives. I babysit a couple of times a week."

"Right. Well, I should be heading back downtown. Are there no taxis in Nasser City? Is this even Cairo? I thought there was a law that there needed to be a hundred cabs within view at any given time on any given street in *Misr, om il dunya*." The familiar refrain: Egypt, Mother of the World. It could be said either with pride or with irony—Nadia could guess Wills's intent.

"Not today," Nadia chuckled. "Not on Tuesdays."

"Right, right. Forgot about Tuesdays. Bloody Muslims."

"Hey, why don't you come up and we can wait for my father and Noor to come home and then we can take a taxi back together? They won't be long, it's already dinner time."

"You sure? Brilliant. I won't be a bother."

Nora was whiny by the time they got home. Nadia took her straight to the kitchen for a snack, finding the usual assortment of leftovers in the fridge. It wasn't long before they heard the click of the door. "*Baba!*" Nora ran out to jump into her father's arms. Noor came directly into the kitchen with a bag of something. She stopped short when she saw Wills. As Nadia made quick introductions Bishara appeared, Nora in his arms.

"Hello, hello," Wills said, shaking hands, making eye contact, chuckling deprecatingly, doing all the right things.

"He's a friend from the art gallery," Nadia said. "We ran into each other in the park and he stayed so we can share a taxi home. Nora had fun at the park, didn't you, Nora?"

The girl squealed.

"No, you must both stay," Bishara said, putting away his bag and putting on his slippers. "You must be hungry. Noor will make a delicious supper." His wife smiled and nodded.

"It's fine, Baba," Nadia said. "We're just going to go."

"Why? Where?" He shook his head, threw open his arms and twisted his hands into question marks. "Where?" He waited for an answer.

Nadia looked at Wills, who shrugged affably.

"Okay." She put down her bag.

Nora jumped down from Bishara's arms, ran to the living room and turned on the TV.

"*Nayya, nayya*," she called.

"See?" said her father, pushing Nadia towards the living room. "She wants you."

"Hey, you." Nadia gave her a kiss on the cheek.

"You're Egyptian, then?" Wills asked as they settled into the couch. "Or Canadian? Or both?"

"None of the above. I am Palestinian."

"Oh, really?" His eyes widened. "That's, that's, well,

that's brilliant. It's tough right now, though, isn't it, Intifada and all that? I was just reading about the breaking bones policy. You hear about that? It's an actual policy, one of Rabin's strokes of genius. Catch the buggers throwing the stone and then break their bones. Brutal."

"My father works for the Palestinian Red Crescent." She was proud of her father, proud of being Palestinian. What an odd feeling.

Noor came out with a tray full of plates and dishes. "Wow," Nadia said. "You just made that?"

"*La-a*," Noor laughed. "It was endings."

"Leftovers," Nadia and Bishara corrected in unison. They manoeuvered Nora into her high chair and passed plates around, tore off strips of bread, dipped into tahini and labneh, *waraq einab,* chicken on rice, olives, and pickled turnip. Nadia was hungry and obviously so was Wills. This was the second time she was sharing supper with someone at her father's and it felt good. She wasn't burdened this time by memories or old resentments or questions that clawed at the back of her throat. She didn't regard Nora with jealousy or seethe with anger as her father gave his attention to someone else. There was enough to go around this time.

The taxi from Nasser City took them through downtown, where Wills was to disembark. But he winked at Nadia and leaned forward to give another set of directions to the driver. "The night is young," he said. "Shall we go to Fishawi's? For an '*ahwa turki* or something? You know it, right? And tell me you like Turkish coffee."

284

"Fish what?"

"Good god, girl."

She'd never been to the Khan el Khalile market, another source of concern on Wills's part. It was too full of "tourists and trinkets" according to Manal. And it was, but there was so much else. Although many of the shops and kiosks had closed down for the day, their tables covered and shopfronts rolled over with garage-like metal doors, there were still enough spices, perfumes, linens, toys, jewelry, and soaps to supply a small country. Lamps strung along the stone walls and overhead created a multicoloured canopy of light and shadows. Far-off music rattled away to the rhythmic sound of men and women shuffling in their plastic slippers. Wills led her expertly through the snaking alleys, pausing here and there to look at chess sets or watches or leather bags. At one point a lane opened slightly wider, then wider again. On either side dark mahogany walls emerged, lined with dozens of round wooden tables occupied by hookah-smoking Egyptians and tourists. It was impossible to tell where the café began or even ended, but now they were in it. Wills grabbed a table, ordered two coffees, and paid for a hookah to be filled and lit. "Ahh! Now this is how you want to live."

Nadia looked at her watch.

"What? You have somewhere to go?"

"It's nothing," she said, embarrassed. "It's just that, where I'm staying, I just don't want to stay out too late."

"You're staying with Egyptians? It's a shame, isn't it, we have all the fun."

"There's lots of Egyptians here," Nadia said, looking around.

"All men, did you notice?"

She had. They were like figures in a painting, leaning this way and that over their coffees, over their ashtrays, over their shishas, their hooded eyes tired and bored, animated only by the occasional backgammon game in a corner. But as she looked closer she saw an Egyptian woman at one table, then another farther down, then more. It's not so simplistic and not so simple, she wanted to say to Wills, but she was surprised to see him waving. Tena emerged out of the crowd and planted a big kiss on Wills's lips and herself on a chair. The kiss rippled through the surrounding café-goers like a shock wave, each man seemingly comparing his luck, his experience, his virility, and coming up wanting.

Tena never stopped talking, quieting even Wills. She wanted to kill her boss, find a decent shoe store, take Wills on a quick trip to Sarajevo, scratch that, her family would murder him, so a return to Dahab would have to do. Nadia, have you been to Dahab? The most beautiful beaches and you stay in little huts run by the Bedouins, and spend all day in little restaurants where you eat fresh fish morning noon and night, and everyone is stoned, absolutely everyone. Except the children! Well, who knows, there are tourists from Israel, who knows what the children on kibbutzes are doing these days. So you come with us on our next trip, it's settled. When, Wills, when do we go?

Nadia could see he was smitten, this blond firecracker

stretching up to him as if he were a broad expanse of sky. Her attention was pulled away by something behind Wills and Tena, a movement familiar yet somehow unbelievable, and she refocused her gaze. Two portly *galabiyya*-wearing men in a ceramics shop, just on the outskirts of the café, were bending over a table, snorting some kind of powder up their noses.

"What the heck?" Nadia said softly.

Wills and Tena turned around. "Oh that," Wills said.

"It's everywhere." Tena rolled her eyes. "You'll get in trouble if you let anything shock you in Egypt, dear Nadia."

Nasser was in the kitchen. Nadia hesitated in the hallway when she heard him, the loud breathing giving him away. She was not used to seeing him in the kitchen. Good morning, she said in Arabic. *Sabah il kher*. He responded just as automatically with its pair: *sabah il noor*. Morning of prosperity, morning of light.

"*Qahwa?*" he asked, holding out a cup of coffee for her.

"*Shukran.*"

He put the jar of Sanka back in the cupboard. Its watery taste was a marked contrast from last night's deliciousness. Nasser obviously didn't have the skill or patience for Turkish coffee. He was staring at her. Sipping loudly and staring. She wanted to talk to him, if only to offset the awkwardness of being in the small green kitchen drinking horrible coffee with only each other to look at. She didn't know anything about him, not where he worked, what he did, or what he liked. At this close distance he wasn't looking as old as she had given him. He must be Manal's father's much younger brother, quite a bit younger.

"Canadian passport?" He went first.

"Sorry?"

"You have Canadian passport?"

"Oh, yes. I was born in Montreal."

"Montreal," he repeated. "Canada. But your father is Egyptian." Why did he want to know about her passport? She'd already been warned to keep it safe, that there was a brisk market in lost and stolen passports. Would he go into her bags? Would he sell it? She knew that a relatively empty Canadian passport was the gold standard as far as passports went. Or maybe he thought she was a bad influence for Manal. A foreigner who chose not to be born in Cairo and who came home late at night stinking of smoke and market perfumes.

"My father is Palestinian, and he keeps my passport at his apartment."

"Intifada," he nodded solemnly.

"Yes."

"Bad situation, not good." He finished his coffee and put the mug in the sink. "Wait," he said. He went to his room, opening and shutting the door noisily. He returned with a book, had to shake it a couple of times in front of Nadia until she understood she was to take it. It was entirely in Arabic, swashes of lines unintelligibly crisscrossing the cover.

"Mahmoud Darwish," he said.

"Who?"

"Palestine poetry. Mahmoud Darwish. You read."

He had given her a book of poetry.

The next day Nadia had had enough of the rigours of work and the constrictions of her schedule. She left a little bit early and took a taxi straight to the gallery. Manal was surprised and delighted to see her.

"We are alone," she said, pushing Nadia against the wall and leaning into her heavily. "*Wahishtini wahishtini wahishtini.*" I miss you I miss you I miss you.

The banging street door shocked them and they were on opposite sides of the room when Tewfiq ran in, shouting something. He kept going, into the back room. Manal followed but he shouted something and she stopped. She looked at Nadia. "Don't say anything," she ordered.

"What's going on?"

"*Iscouti,*" Manal hissed, gesturing that she stay put and shut up. She sat down at the desk, pulled the accounting book from the drawer and let her pen hover over a random page. Then, as if thinking further, she retrieved the calculator. She began adding, writing on a pad of paper, adding again.

"What the heck are you doing?"

Again, just as loudly, the street door slammed open and closed. The footsteps on the stairs this time were numerous and heavy. A police officer came into the gallery, two others right behind him, his severe eyes quickly taking in the landscape of the rooms.

"*Salaam aleikum,*" he said to Manal.

"*Aleikum salam.*"

He asked Manal questions, rapidly, one after the other, said the name Tewfiq more than once. Manal in turn balanced it by saying Brigitte as often, as if it were a kind of insurance if not protection. Frustrated, he turned his attention to Nadia. "She's Canadian," Manal said. "A tourist visiting the gallery."

"Canadian? Do you have your passport please?"

"No," Nadia said, a small panic erupting. "I don't usually carry it with me."

"*Malesh,*" he said. She was of no interest to him, but she could see that her presence had taken the edge off the situation. He turned back to Manal, asked her more questions. He paced slightly as she spoke, began leaning this way and that into corners of the rooms. He stared at the black curtain. Manal got up and took them in the opposite direction. She opened the guestbook by the front door and slid her finger down the list of names as she read them off methodically. This was needless information and he grew impatient. A few minutes later, after a lecture of threats and warnings, he and the other officers left.

Nadia exhaled. "What the hell was that?"

"Quiet."

Manal returned to punching at the calculator and recording meaningless numbers. After an hour it was time to leave and close up.

"What about Tewfiq?"

"Hush," Manal said. "We go. We just go. *Yalla.*"

They closed up, turned off the lights, locked the doors behind them. Manal wouldn't say a word as they made their way to the bus centrale. She insisted they take a crowded bus instead of a minivan or taxi service. It took them twice as long to get home and, with their remaining energy spent on keeping erect penises and straying hands away from their bodies, they were twice as exhausted. It wasn't until they shut the bedroom door behind them that Manal let herself relax. She flopped on the bed, a long string of Arabic and French expletives filling the air.

"This is really bad," she finally said. "The police are looking for Tewfiq."

"For what?"

"He has joined the Muslim Brotherhood, *yanni*."

"That's not good, is it."

"Not good? They're illegal."

"But he doesn't have a beard. I thought they all had beards."

"Hmm. Maybe he's in disguise. There must be a reason for it. He's a spy or something."

"Spying on what? Art?"

"I don't know," Manal said wearily. She fell back again on the bed and groaned. A knock on the door startled them. "What is wrong with this day?" she complained under her breath.

"*Tiliphone*," Nasser said from the other side of the door.

"Who was it?" Nadia asked when Manal returned.

"What? Nobody." Manal was distracted, impatient.

"Manal, how old is your uncle?"

Manal stared at her. "What? Why do you care? I don't know, thirty-five, sixty-five."

"Thirty-five? He looks so old, yet I noticed the other day that he's really not so old. Like, he's fat and bald and has the worst posture in the world, but he's just a few years older than us. Isn't that weird? And look what he gave me."

Manal flipped through the pages, read snatches. "You need to learn to read Arabic, Nadia. He gave you this? Look at this." She showed her a signature on an inside page. "My father, this was my father's book. He has no right to give this to you. He's probably never even read it. He's an ogre." She tossed the book on the bed behind them.

15
full moon of the night

It wasn't long before Brigitte heard about the police.

"He's not a criminal," Manal said, shocked at her quick condemnation.

"I will not have the police in my gallery arresting my employees. What is this, Manal? When did this happen? How is it possible we have a, a, *fundamentalist* in our midst?" She said it with such contempt and loathing that Nadia thought Manal would start praying then and there, just to shock her further. But Manal said nothing, there was no point. Tewfiq was, as of this day, not welcome back in the gallery.

"Your art," Brigitte finally said after a long silence.

"My art?"

She just shook her head, as if expecting Manal to understand what she was getting at. "I hope you will understand. It is not a good time."

"What?"

"*Bon.* I will be clearer. It is not a good idea to show your art at the gallery. Not right now. Things are delicate right now. Can you see that? Demonstrations here in support of the Intifada—do you know how many people were arrested, Manal? Dozens. And everywhere *huwwa il hal*, yes, I see it, I see it. There will be crackdowns, there already are crackdowns. I cannot have controversy at my gallery, I have said this before. No tanks, no machine guns, no prisoners, no Palestinian flag, no aggression against the state..."

Manal snorted at *aggression against the state*. Brigitte glared, but they had nothing more to say to each other. Neither sought understanding or even peace, just quiet.

Much later, they crossed each other in the middle of the room. Nadia could feel the air turn electric.

"Did you write that letter of support? For the scholarship, like you said you would?"

"You are mistaken, I never said I would."

"I asked you."

"I told you that Galerie Mashrabiya supports one emerging artist a year."

Manal paused. When she spoke again her voice had lost its courage, replaced only with anger, which she put her entire body into masking. "That artist could be me."

"I don't know what to tell you, Manal. It is not you."

"Why not?"

Brigitte lit up a cigarette.

"Is it because we are not fucking?" Her back was to Nadia, maybe purposefully so, Nadia thought. Manal would rage alone.

"*Qu'est-ce que c'est ça? Mais vraiement, Manal.* You have nerve. You are out of line."

"You don't want controversy? No machine guns, no

soldiers? But everyone knows who you support, who you fuck. It's one and the same, year after year. Everyone knows. It's so obvious. Half the people who buy art here just do it because they want to fuck you. Is Imad as good in bed as he is with a paintbrush?"

"Enough! *Khallas!*" Brigitte threw her cigarette on the floor and grabbed her purse. "You are, are, this is impossible. Enough! You can leave and never come back. That's it, I have had enough." But it was Brigitte who left, who stomped down the stairs and slammed the door.

Manal looked at her, an expression of pain so raw it caught in Nadia's throat. "I'm fired, but it's she who has left and I still have to lock up." Nadia could see she wanted to laugh at the absurdity, but there was just a strained sound that quickly evaporated in a hoarse cough. There would be no laughing, and there would be no crying. Nadia tried to comfort her, but she pushed her away.

"What's this?"

Dozens of bits of paper torn off the telephone notepad were piled on the bedside table, all scribbled with the same name and number. "*Tewfiq called.*"

In the hallway, Manal dialled the number, keeping her voice low and cupping her hand over the mouthpiece. Even so, Nasser came out of his room for long minutes. He had an ear for urgent whisperings. Nadia, now in the doorway, coughed and moved slightly. He shrugged and padded back down the hall, his frayed *galabiyya* trailing on the floor.

"*Tayyib, tayyib, tayyib.*" Manal exhaled loudly and hung up. "*Ya waylie, ya rob.*"

"What?"

A slight creak alerted them that Nasser had opened his door again. They retreated to the bedroom. "This is really bad," Manal said. "More bad."

Tewfiq had been at home in Shubra with a group of men, including his brother, when they were raided by the police. One of the men was Muslim Brotherhood, though Tewfiq insisted that he himself was not. He was not willing to say so about his brother. Now he had lost touch with his brother in the past couple of days and was fearing the worst. He wanted her to know.

"But I don't understand. What did they do exactly? What crime did they commit?"

"Nadia, the *Ikhwan* is growing. It is still in the shadows, still underground, but it is growing. Tewfiq may be stupid to think they are the *hal*, the answer, but then a lot of people are making the same mistake. No matter, it is an honest mistake, *yanni*. It is the only real opposition here."

"Opposition to what?"

"To the government, to Mubarak, to the *mukhabarat*, to this whole pretend life we have here, *ya Nadia*." She gestured to the room, the air, the city around them. "What, did you think it was real? Did you think we knew what we were doing in Egypt? That people were living their lives like they were actually alive? We are not alive here. In Egypt you can be only two things. Either a vulture or a corpse."

"Come on, Manal."

"Yes, yes" she said. "It is true. Either you eat the dead bodies or you are a dead body yourself. I don't like the *Ikhwan* but at least they want to be alive. There is nothing here, nothing. I am not happy he is doing this but I understand."

"Manal, did you tell him he was fired?"

"*La*, of course not. He needs hope and a normal life, *yanni*, somewhere." She rolled her eyes. "I wonder when Brigitte realized that she fired both of us on the same day. I wish I saw her face."

"Well, you'll both have other opportunities and other jobs, Manal. You are still an artist."

"Ha! No one has opportunities, *ya helwa*, they only have *wasta*. Do you know what that means? It means who-do-you-know and how-much-money-can-you-put-in-my-pocket. Without my father, I have no *wasta*. My uncle is no help. I have no one, not even Brigitte. She could help him too, if she wanted. She has influence."

"What will happen to him?"

"He is going to Tanta. Either his brother has been arrested or he has gone back to their village. If he is arrested, the police could take weeks before telling the family. They will need time to torture, of course." Manal nodded in defiance of Nadia's wincing. "Or he has not been caught. Tewfiq will go to Tanta and start the search."

"We passed Tanta on the train," Nadia said, remembering.

"Yes," Manal said. "It was pretty, wasn't it?"

Manal stretched, smiled, yawned loudly, scratched herself, hit Nadia with the pillow, sang, sat up, lay down again, hit Nadia again.

"Oh my god, okay, okay, I'm awake, stop hitting me."

"Nadia, wake up, today is the first day. The first day!"

"The first day what?"

"The first day I have no job! I am free!" But she could only hold her broad smile for so long.

"Come here," Nadia said, and held her.

Nadia considered calling her father at the hospital to cancel but Manal talked her out of it. One of them needed to work, she said. So she reluctantly grabbed a cab and spent the day on the fourth floor typing yet more reports. She did it over and over until a month had passed. She had a job at least as long as the reports kept coming, as long as conflict raged and foreign doctors wrote their notes in English. Did that make her a vulture?

Money had been tactfully left out of the discussion when her position was made official. She assumed, therefore, that at the end of the month she would receive a hundred and fifty pounds as was standard. Not a lot by any stretch, but it would see her through. So when the time came and she joined the noisy crowd at the window till to collect her pay, she was mortified when the cashier, a heavy-set woman of no apparent civility, began loudly counting the notes out of the drawer and into the envelope.

"Twenty pounds, forty, sixty, eighty...two forty, two sixty, two eighty...four hundred, four twenty, four sixty...five eighty, six hundred, six twenty, six forty...seven hundred...seven twenty, seven forty, seven hundred fifty pounds." She stopped, took a deep drag of her cigarette, and looked at Nadia. The whole room looked at Nadia, the only movement being the smoke rising from fingers and ashtrays.

"Why so much?" she asked, mortified.

"Because you foreigner," shrugged the woman. "All foreigners seven hundred and fifty Egyptian pounds. Not enough?"

The room erupted into laughter and Nadia's head spun. She quickly stuffed the money into her purse and fled. As she made her way home she began to expand with excitement and purpose. She had money. She took a detour to the main shopping road in Heliopolis. She looked for something for Manal, choosing finally a silver chain bracelet from a man in a tiny kiosk. Heavy and delicate at the same time, it would suit her perfectly.

Brigitte called countless times to apologize and entreat Manal to return, especially in the first week, even threatening to come by her house to discuss in person. But Manal refused to see her and refused to discuss. Nadia thought Manal had made her point and now it was time to shake hands, let bygones be bygones, and admit that the gallery was a good gig. She was afraid of what this chaos and instability could bring. Beyond holding her and whispering platitudes, she didn't know what Manal needed from her. That scared her more than anything else.

"*Khallas*. I will not work for her anymore. Three years, just a fancy floor sweeper."

"Then paint. Just paint. I am working, I am making money, and you can paint. Soon we'll start hearing back from all those schools. And if none of those work out, it's still not the end of the world." She put her hands on Manal's shoulders, ran them up and down her arms as if bringing her back to life. Her mother used to do that when she came in from the cold. "Life is not a straight line, there are ups and downs. We'll figure this out. I will work and you will paint. It sounds very amazing. Okay? Say yes."

Manal said nothing.

"We can even find other galleries. You can have a show somewhere else."

Manal looked away.

"You will sell, Manal. Your work is amazing. Say you'll paint."

"I'll paint."

"Really?"

Manal wrestled herself away from Nadia's hold. "What do you mean really? I said I will paint."

She escaped to the balcony but Nadia followed. She held her wrist and clasped the chain around it. "Now you have to wear this forever," she whispered in her ear. Manal murmured softly and leaned back into the soft body behind her. "Now paint."

Nadia was surprised when Manal wasn't home after she

returned from work on the first day. By the end of the week, when Manal had been out late every night, a low-grade rumble of fear and disappointment kept a dissonant beat like pebbles on a drum. She managed to tamp it down, the distractions of work and subsequent fatigue rescuing her from worry. On Friday morning Nadia lay in bed, savouring the beginning of the Egyptian weekend. Manal stirred then reached over to the table between them and looked at the alarm clock.

"Get up, you are late."

"It's Friday. I have today and tomorrow off."

"Both days?"

"Yes."

"Egyptians only have one day off, not two. I worked on Saturdays, remember? You forget already."

Nadia felt chastened. But they were both home now at the same time, and Manal was in bed. It was time. "What do you do when I'm at work, Manal?"

She had thought she'd kept her tone neutral, conversational even, but tone was irrelevant. Manal was spitting out more words than she could wade through, most of them in Arabic. Finally, she threw back the sheet and began rummaging through a freshly washed pile of clothes for something to wear.

"Manal, Manal. What is going on? What are you doing?"

"I am busy today, I forgot to tell you."

"Doing what? Can I come? We've barely seen each other all week, I thought we'd do something today, anything. I have so much to tell you, Manal, and so much I want to know."

"So much you want to know about what?" She took off her T-shirt and threw it down like a gauntlet.

It was like a poison had entered Nadia's system and was discovering her veins and stomach and lungs, all at once. "Where are you going?" she asked softly, barely audible. The sound of her voice changed the dynamic in the room. It wasn't true that you needed to yell to be heard; a pained whisper could travel the Nile and be heard by all. Nadia began to shake, then taste her own tears. Manal's hands wiped them away.

"I am meeting with Sofian," she said, her voice just above a whisper.

"Don't go."

"My options have all run out. Please understand."

"That is not true, it's not true. You're not seeing what I am seeing."

"Brigitte gave the empty week to Imad. He is having a solo show, his second. And he got the scholarship."

"What? How do you know all that? I fucking hate his art. This is so unfair."

"I went to the gallery to get my sketchbooks and my paintings."

"It's been a hard few weeks, Manal, we've hardly seen each other. So many changes. Please don't do anything crazy, don't make any decisions. Don't think there is no hope. Honestly, there are so many fucking things left to do."

"I don't like it when you swear."

"Nobody likes it when I fucking swear. *I* like it. Don't go. Okay?"

Manal stood up. "I must, *ya rohi*. Today is—today is a special day. I have to be, I have to go. It is…*malesh*, I cannot say."

"It is what? It is fucking what?"

"It is the day I meet his parents."

Nadia got out of bed, held on to furniture and walls. Her entire body burned then froze then burned again. Manal was on the other side of the room then beside her. It felt like they were moving in two different time zones or parallel universes. In the same room but not. Then she ran to the toilet and threw up.

Manal wet a cloth and wiped her face, kissing the spots she had just cleaned. "Like this I can take care of my mother, Nadia. You have to understand. I can't just go away and leave my mother here alone."

"So none of it was real? The art schools, the universities around the world? The fucking scholarship? None of it was real?"

"It was all real. All, all, all, all real. All out of reach, all real, all torture."

The next morning Nadia found Manal on the balcony, a cigarette in her hand. Manal offered her one, lit it for her. They took light puffs. It was important to smoke. Destruction had to be in the room with them, it had to obscure their faces, pour down their lungs, darken the space with lies and irredeemable mistakes. Something. Might as

303

well be cigarettes.

"I've been meaning to tell you something. They found him, he's been arrested. Tewfiq."

One of Tewfiq's friends had contacted her to tell her the news, Manal explained. They had arranged to meet in an art-supply store off Talat Harb Street, speaking softly as Manal chose paintbrushes she didn't need. They hadn't really done anything, Ahmed told her, just met and prayed, met and prayed. They were moved by poverty, by the despair around them, and desperate to find answers in the beauty of the Quran, he said. Why is that a crime? Are they not all Muslims? Do they not all share the word, the holy, the beauty of the word, the hadiths, the teachings of the prophet, blessed be his name? They were bringing a doctor into Shubra, that is all, to set up a clinic. Someone to visit the families and deal with the bilharzia and the polio and the tuberculosis.

"Why not go to the hospital?" Nadia asked. There were other free hospitals besides the Palestine Hospital.

"Some people cannot even leave their homes," Manal said. "The hospital is free, but not the medicine or the bandages. And they are not treated well. A clinic in their neighbourhood is better."

They wanted to bring in a teacher, too, Ahmed told her. They wanted to raise money for a small mosque. They wanted to teach the children about the glory of the prophet. They wanted their lives to be more than just shaping bricks or serving tea or begging under bridges. And so they prayed, they organized, they prayed some more. There had always been a blind eye to this, Ahmed explained. It allowed the government to get away with not offering services to the poorer neighbourhoods. The Muslim Brotherhood was saving Mubarak millions of pounds. Maybe they got too loose and confident, he mused. They had other ambitions and they let them fly. Tewfiq's brother even wondered if one of them should run for office, to challenge the American-protected tyranny of Mubarak, to insist that the law should be above the whims of politicians and the wealthy. A weakness in the system that comfortable Egyptians were willing to overlook.

"Comfortable like me," Manal added.

They were watched and followed. For too long they thought they were smarter. Some shaved their beards, others didn't even grow them, thinking that this would fool the *mukhabarat*, the secret police. The women continued working and going about their business like ordinary Egyptian ladies.

"How does a Muslim Brotherhood Egyptian lady act?" Nadia asked.

"Like this," Manal said, and covered her entire face with a scarf, up to her eyes.

"It's strange he never discussed any of this with you," Nadia said.

That stumped Manal, she lowered the scarf. "Do you think so?"

"Aren't you friends?"

"I am a dangerous friend," Manal said. "A friend who

does not understand. There are many of those."

They were meeting when the police came, really just praying. The police beat them, mostly around the legs. Ahmed was the only one to run away, he had been in the bathroom and escaped through the window. They were thrown into a small van and taken away. The van killed a goat as it got lost in the neighbourhood. No one has been able to see them since their detention. They were using one of the Muslim Brotherhood's lawyers but he was not being given any access or information. They could only wait—and lose hope.

"How terrible," Nadia finally said. "How unbeliev-able."

"Terrible yes, unbelievable no."

Three hens roamed the long grassy space between their apartment building and the one next door. A goat occasionally made an appearance but then it would be gone after a few weeks, only to return a couple of days later. The sound of scratching and cawing filled the morning air along with a dog barking, a braying donkey, and the usual honking cars.

"*Na-naaaaaaaaaaaaaaaaa-aaaa. Na-naaaaaaaaaaaaaaaaa-aaaa.*"

A man pushed a cart slowly up the street, the *a*'s gurgling in his throat like boiling water, the last few scalding pain-fully. "*Na-naaaaaaaaaaaaa-aaaa. Na-naaaaaaaaaaaaaaaaaaaaaa-aaaaaaa.*"

"Mint," Manal explained. "I go." Nadia watched as

she emerged onto the sidewalk and halted his slow progress. He handed her a large bundle of mint leaves, whacking them first against the wooden wheels of the cart to shake them free of dirt and flies.

In the kitchen, she put the kettle on to boil and made Nadia smell the bread she had picked up from the baker next door. It was almost too hot to touch. "And eggs too, look. Are you hungry?" She put the water on to boil, sliced a dozen red and green tomatoes and dropped them in the buttery pan for a few minutes, cracked four eggs on top, and sprinkled it all with paprika and salt as it slowly cooked and bubbled. She laid olives and cheese and pickles on the table and brewed the mint in with the tea. The bread, wrapped in cloth, went in the middle of the table. At the last minute she retrieved a bowl of labneh from the fridge, indented it with a spoon, and drizzled it with oil.

"Manal, I want to tell you something."

"Is it good news? I can't take any more good news. I hope it is bad, very bad."

"My father is going to Palestine soon, to work. I think you knew that." She looked for confirmation, got blankness. She pushed on. "He's leaving earlier than we thought because things are getting worse there. Nora is a psychologist and she has a German passport and it will be easy for her to cross the border. My father, he has a Canadian passport. So he can go too." Nadia waited, hesitated, stumbled. "They want to move there. For now, anyways."

"*Yanni…?* And?"

"I also have a Canadian passport."

Manal slowly lowered her fork, the egg slid off with a *plop*.

"I've been thinking, especially since yesterday, that maybe I should go. Nora is so little and I can look after her, Manal. I can be with my father, his family. Well, my family. My sister." Manal pushed herself away from the table, went still again. Sat up straighter, went still again.

"It's why I came here, Manal. It's why I came to Egypt in the first place. To find my family."

Suddenly, a plate left the table and hit the wall. "It's not why you stayed. It's not why you stayed."

Nadia was dumbfounded.

"*Yikhrib betak ya Nadia,*" Manal said. "I can't do all this if you're not here. We can still be together. Sofian, marriage, none of it matters. I told you, people do it all the time."

"What?"

"I can't do this if you're not here."

"Oh my god, Manal. What are you saying? You're asking too much. It's too much. I can't just stay in Cairo while you get married and have children and get fat, have an entire other life, and we see each other—what?—every second Tuesday of the month?"

Manal sighed. "I won't get fat."

She loved Manal's humour, her crooked mouth, her artist's hands, her muscular shoulders, her long legs, her hair that hung over her face when they kissed, her breasts that leaned on her own when they lay together, her soft sighs, the arch of her back, the way the hairs on her neck stood up, the cries that they muffled with each other's hands in the night. Tears came uncontrollably. I can't do this anymore, Nadia thought, live this slow-motion eviscerating of my heart. She got up from the table and went to the bedroom, then out the balcony door. She bent at the waist and leaned out over the railing. Dogs roamed slowly in and around the parked cars. Nadia watched them, blocking out as much as she could the movement of Manal's arms as Manal lowered her onto a chair. One of the dogs whimpered softly and kept his tail between his legs as he moved. The other was more sure of himself. Nadia wondered what drama enveloped the lives of dogs. Manal's lips made soft contact with her forehead. A third dog lay panting on the hood of a car. Manal kissed one cheek, then another. Softly, slowly, her lips took long seconds to leave the tensile gravity of Nadia's skin. The more pathetic of the three dogs stiffened. He howled at the dog on the car, paws splaying out to support himself as if the effort of barking tore at his meagre insides. That was when the first dog threw himself at the barking dog, his jaws closing around the neck. Nadia listened to the yelping as Manal cupped her face. She closed her eyes, hearing only screeching and the tearing of flesh. Manal's tongue ran over her lips. Then her face was not above hers but below. Hands pulled firmly at her own till she found herself kneeling on the concrete of the balcony. The dogs, the dogs, Nadia wondered. Manal parted her lips with her thumb, ran her tongue across her teeth, which also parted. The barking receded in the distance, men's voices yelled across the road. The tips of their tongues met like two electric wires teasing with their current. Nadia's head fell back and she felt she would slide under the chair. Manal raised herself up over her, pushed her back, pushed her down, until they were on the floor, bodies matching limb for limb, hidden from the street behind the tangled branches of the lemon tree. Manal's hands sought Nadia's body with ferocity. Plunging into the thin space between pants and flesh, her fingers entered, finding wet and warmth. She pushed with violence and desperation. They both gasped in pain. Their mouths never left each other until they were underwater somewhere off the Alexandrian coast, the undertow swiftly drowning bathers and dogs alike.

"Stop," Nadia managed, but Manal's mouth smothered hers, tongue plunging down in thrusts that matched her hand.

"You don't go," Manal cried softly. "You don't go. I will have nothing." A knee rammed violently against her thigh as they struggled, the weight of each body burying the other.

"Manal, please. Not like this."

"This? This? This?" She slammed again into Nadia's body. Then again.

An unmistakable click forced them up to the surface where, like animals who play dead, their bodies stiffened as if in death. Nadia opened her eyes to see Manal staring back at her. Fingers twitched between legs. They looked through the cluttered bedroom to the door where a figure stood silhouetted in the morning dust.

"*Manal...*"

Manal shot up from the floor, pulled down her top, and ran her hand through her hair. Om Malek stepped inside and inhaled the musk coming from the balcony, wafting inward like incense. "Manal, I thought I heard you." She saw Nadia on the ground and looked quickly back at Manal.

"Get out," Manal growled, pointing to the door. "Get out and leave us alone."

"But, Manal. Are you feeling better?" She continued in Arabic while Manal spoke in English, her voice scraping like nails on a blackboard.

"I said get out. And don't come back."

"But Manal, you need to get ready." Her mother said more, mostly in an apologetic mumble. Nadia understood *store* and *shopping* and *new dress*.

Manal swore again. She spun around, picked up the first thing she could find, a book, and threw it across the room. It fell leaning against the wall. Mahmoud Darwish and his blistering poetry. The door closed with a painful click.

"Why is your mother taking you shopping?"

Manal managed a smile. "Your Arabic has really improved."

Nadia smiled back; even in this moment flattery had its power. It was true, her Arabic was effortless, almost fluid. It had always been in her, hibernating like a Canadian bear waiting for the Egyptian spring. So little happens in a straight line, she thought. Instead, life can sit on the shelf for ages until suddenly, warmed by a ray of light that comes in sideways, it ferments and bubbles over. Then: alcohol! *Al kohl*, an Arabic word for a powder, then a sublimated substance. The Arabs knew how to sublimate, she thought, and the ecstasy of submission and surrender. She felt strangely alive in that moment, almost drunk, so pulled in every direction and outside of her skin.

"Come here," she said, gently, almost maternally. She gathered Manal's long limbs, put her arms under hers and pulled her towards her, walked her into the bedroom. She pulled off her T-shirt, then her skirt, let them fall on the floor. They lay down in the bed, smiling at the predictable creaks. Nadia traced a line from Manal's forehead to her toes, first with her hands then with her lips. "Nothing will change," she said.

"Nothing."

"Funny, isn't it? Time."

"Time is torture."

"I will think of you every day."

"You were right."

"About what?"

"About everything."

"You are a great artist, never forget."

"Shhhh. It will be our secret."

"No, you can still do it. You can still be everything."

"Not true. But being nothing is not so bad. I think it is my destiny."

"I love you."

"You will come back."

"Will I?"

"Yes."

"And I will paint you again. But it will take so much more charcoal *yanni*, because of your wrinkles."

They both awoke, the sound of the fan on high blocking out the street noise. Nadia turned under the light sheet. Manal turned with her. She whispered in Manal's hair. "It was my dream too. It was for the both of us. I was going to go with you."

"It was always a long chance, *ya Nadia*. Did you really think I had a chance? I never exhibited, Brigitte did not support me, I have no real experience, *yanni*, and more and more like that. I did it because you made me think for one minute that maybe it was possible. One minute!" She sighed and kissed Nadia's hands. "It is not everything, I don't lose anything, it was just a dream. Just a dream."

"Don't you care? How can you be so cavalier about this?"

"*Ya helwa*, I care so much that I have stopped caring."

"But Manal."

Manal turned around again, this time to face her. They watched each other fall back to sleep.

16

the girl who caught the dew when it fell

She thought she was going to throw up. The clock in the living room, a tabletop brass piece with a glass bell jar over it, ugly as hell, she thought, ticked loudly. Om Malek fussed with the tea in the kitchen, not able to choose the right tray. She swore, Manal shushed her. It doesn't matter, she heard Manal say. "Everything matters," Om Malek said, talking about the tea and the plates and the linen and the wet cloth to wipe the endless unceasing dust. "Everything matters."

It all mattered. The waiting, the excruciating waiting. It was a torture Nadia knew she deserved so she had acquiesced and agreed to it all. It meant being here, today, in the dark and lacquered living room, waiting for Sofian. She was assisting Manal in her own torture by giving her blessing, sharing her approval, sending her off in a damp mist of well-wishing. Even Uncle Nasser was here. Bored, belching, filling the room with cigarette smoke, but here nonetheless. Nadia laughed out loud when she realized they shared the same godawful expression. The next time he lit one up he held out the pack to her, offering, as if he knew, as if for one solitary minute in one solitary day he could see her and she would allow it. Nadia took the cigarette, let him light it for her. Luckily, she choked on the second drag. She put it out and let the tears fall freely down her cheeks.

The bell rang and from somewhere in the house a scream. Uncle Nasser ambled to the door. They exchanged greetings, shook hands, a quiet pause. Nadia wouldn't look. She'd have to turn around to see him, stand up to greet him. She did neither. Until he was in front of her, blocking the light from the window, she wasn't going to move. Like the Pyramids once upon a time. Monuments, monoliths, destiny pushing deep into the sand. When she could avoid it no longer, she held out her hand, let him shake it, stared at his faintly bearded chin.

Years later, even moments later, Nadia would forget the rest of the afternoon. It was a blur of non-movement and the unsaid. Manal, out of consideration perhaps— she liked to think so—kept the conversation in Arabic. Whenever someone would switch to English, with a nod to their Canadian guest, Manal would haul it back, speak faster, tell jokes, quote songs. Anything and everything to take it away and spin it out into another universe. There could be no intimacy here, nothing shared. It existed on another planet, one they chose to keep hidden in the night sky. Nadia watched everything from the window-sill, even herself. She saw as she blew on a hot glass of tea, sipped it, burned her mouth, nibbled on a sugar-covered cookie, flicked the sugar off her chest, smiled, nodded, said *aiwa* and *shukran* and *malesh*. Everyone caught up in the moment, vibrating too fast for their own thoughts. Only Uncle Nasser, against the current, had slowed down. Nadia had the impression that he was watching her, that he could see her traumatized shadow lean out the window and gauge the distance to the ground below. He plied her with more cigarettes, cooed like a pigeon each time, kept an arm ready should she fall over. At the end, when it was finished, only he and she remained in the living room. Finally, he spoke. "Will you return to Canada?"

She looked at Nasser closely, something she had never bothered doing before. His eyes were hooded, his cheeks too large for his face, his upper lip carrying a mustache that had already begun turning grey. All across his face were arid lines criss-crossing each other, like the canals on Mars that seemed to hold water but which, upon closer inspection, were filled only with loneliness. She looked for the darkened mark on his forehead and could not find it. As always she could not determine his age. Perhaps only the soft skin around his eyes gave away his relative youth.

"Not right away," she said. "I'm going to go to Palestine, to Ramallah. I'll work there and live with my father."

He nodded. He looked away, as if also imagining escape. What exactly did he understand, she wondered? For a brief minute it seemed to be everything. He poured her a glass of *karkaday*. She accepted the gift gratefully.

"Good," he said. "Good."

It was at most a six-hour drive but because of the state of the roads as well as the cars, many drivers included an overnight stop in Al Arish, preferring to take their chances at the Rafah crossing into Gaza early in the morning. Her father had hired the car for them alone but at the last minute they discovered that the driver had been paid by another family as well. They all squeezed in, grumbling, three in the front, four in the back, and one on the floor. Nora, spending equal time on six laps, was the only one to enjoy the trip.

The crossing was uneventful. The mostly harmless brusqueness of the Egyptian soldiers' attempts at bureaucracy only meant that it took interminably long. No one's pride—or life—was harmed in the process. They found a new car on the Gaza side, and the new driver took them to a guest house next to the PRCS clinic in Gaza City. The next day was a blur as Bishara and Noor made arrangements, and Nadia fought off fatigue while taking care of Nora. Noor woke them all up the next morning to be ushered into another car for another trip, this one slightly more hazardous as it took them through Israel to the West Bank.

It was only a fifty kilometre drive, on a road of dust and broken rock and barbed wire, desolate except for Army trucks and taxis. They passed one Israeli town and village after another, keeping as wide a berth as was possible each time. The gleaming concrete homes and lush greenery made them hungry and thirsty all at once. Maybe they did make the desert bloom after all,

Nadia wondered. Her father closed down that conversation with four words: West Bank water table.

Whether out of nervousness or boredom, the car was filled with a flurry of nonstop talking. Mohammed, the Israeli Arab driver who met them on one side of the crossing and who would hand them over at the next, kept up a running commentary on politics, the economy, and the latest Egyptian soap opera. He wanted to know everything and was acutely disappointed when neither her father nor Noor could confirm whether or not Hoda and Hisham had married. They were brother and sister and then they weren't? *Eh da!* Mohammed said in his best Egyptian accent.

The language was shifting all around them. Bishara, after spending a lifetime speaking the matter-of-fact Egyptian dialect, was reverting to the singsong musicality of his childhood. His voice even seemed to pitch higher. He was almost beside himself, talking louder and louder, laughing and gesturing in broader and broader strokes the closer they got to their destination. Strangely, it reminded Nadia of herself. We are always travelling towards something, she thought, and it was more often than not the past. Her own Arabic, newly acquired, would no doubt soon yield to the Palestinian rhythm and swing, the accent she was meant to speak in all along. Then what was Manal's? A detour, she mused, remembering her father's words. She wished the drive could last days, long enough to remember every word Manal had spoken, long enough to encase it in amber—*anbar*—and clasp it around her neck. A heavy melancholy settled upon her like dust. The dust of the road, the dust in the car, dust from the cookies Om Manal had packed.

Their elderly next-door neighbour, Abu Saif, rang the doorbell. Nora wailed when Nadia put down the cards and dolls and went to answer it. The intermittent curfews and accompanying sirens and gunshots had stripped the child of her resilience. Bishara was not worried and Noor pretended not to be. "She will be fine, she will be fine. It is only temporary," they both said, with diminishing confidence.

Abu Saif showed the child a whistle he had carved from olive wood. Nora grabbed it and blew it discordantly and loudly while he gave Nadia a package that had travelled by post from Cairo. She didn't know why he would have it or why he would be charged with its delivery. She didn't care—all she saw was Manal's name in the return address. She thanked him. She should have offered him tea or a chair to sit in, and at least a half-day of conversation. But she was trembling. Knowing he would forgive her foreign uncouthness, she shut the door and immediately turned on the television to a cartoon, and made sure Nora was occupied. She hid the whistle.

The package was battered but still intact. In it was a sketchbook: drawings that Manal had made of Nadia. Portraits and studies of her body, her hands, the nape of her neck, her mouth, her legs, most of them she hadn't seen before, some of them drawn while she slept, each

319

meticulously dated and annotated: "before lunch"; "I love her legs"; "during the sandstorm"; "middle of the night"; "and then we kissed"; "you will wear this forever." She turned the pages.

There was so much to tell her, so much, so much, so much.

ACKNOWLEDGEMENTS

Many thanks to my publisher Linda Leith and the editorial team at LLP. To Elise Moser for her constancy. She told me at the beginning, "Your faith in the story isn't lost; I am holding it for you. It is safe with me." Years later, to both our surprise, she was my editor.

Many thanks to Gail Anderson-Dargatz for workshopping this story and reminding me of its drama. And to Ehab Lotayef for taking a look at the Arabic. If errors remain it is because I was too stubborn to give up my idiosyncrasies. A very grateful nod to my sister Nadia for letting me use her name. She would like everyone to know this story is not about her.

I am indebted to a close circle of friends and family who read early drafts, including Julian Samuel, Louise Davey, Katherine Kasirer, Nicole Périat. Thanks to Diana Bronson for her unflagging enthusiasm, and Kathryn Harvey for nudging me to go deeper. Profound gratitude to Samia and Emma for their robust belief and unconditional love. Anything good I do is always for them. Anything bad, they forgive.

Finally, without the real-life inspiration of friends

and family in Canada, Egypt, Lebanon and Palestine, this work of fiction would have never been written.